CONSCIENCE

Chris Jackson

Martin Sisters Publishing

For Jessie

Chapter One

"Forgive me, father, for I have sinned." He had a flat, emotionless voice.

"How long has it been since your last confession?"

"I was here this morning."

"And you needed another dose of forgiveness?" There was a hint of mirth in the priest's voice, just enough to open the door for a good-natured chuckle but not enough to be offensive in case the sin in question was not a laughing matter.

Apparently it wasn't.

"I'm not here about my sins from this morning."

"So you did something else this afternoon?"

"No, father but I'm about to."

The priest's skin crawled at the words and he struggled to find an appropriate response. His job was to provide a safe place where the darkest sins of humanity could find absolution but what was he supposed to do if the sin hadn't been committed yet?

"I don't understand," the priest stuttered.

"I won't be able to come back here afterwards so I wanted to confess my sin in advance. Will you let me do that?"

"Of course." The priest found that his mouth was dry and the words came out hoarse and strained. "What are you going to do?"

"I am going to murder the father."

Did he say *the* father? Sweat popped out on the priest's forehead and his collar suddenly grew itchy and tight. The confessional was stuffy and he was beginning to feel a bit dizzy.

"You're going to murder the father? Which father?"

The silhouette on the other side of the shaded screen recoiled slightly. Priests weren't supposed to ask for details; they were supposed to grant unbiased absolutions and then assign the appropriate penance. Something didn't feel right. He turned to go.

"No, wait!" The priest whispered urgently. "Please continue."

The young man (he sounded like a young man) paused briefly and began to talk again and while he did so, the priest inched his cell phone out from under his robe and found the keypad in the dark. He punched 9-1-1 hoping the muted confessional walls would conceal the phone's beeping.

"What are you doing?" The man asked sharply. "Who are you calling?"

Then he was gone, bounding out of the confessional booth and sprinting through the sanctuary and down the aisle toward the lobby.

"Wait!" The priest shouted, trying to follow him to the exit but getting tangled up in his robes. By the time he emerged from the confessional booth, all he could see was a shadowy backside slipping through the lobby and slamming itself into the massive, oak doors of the sanctuary. As one door swung open, brilliant daylight flooded the sanctuary making it even more difficult to identify the running man.

At the last moment, though, the man paused and turned to face the priest. He shook his head slightly, a gesture of disapproval and then he was gone, swallowed up in the busy afternoon foot traffic.

The priest stumbled toward the prayer altar at the front of the room, a regal, ornate bench carved entirely by hand out of a massive mahogany tree trunk and knelt before it, clutching its railing with both hands. Sirens began wailing in the distance and then grew louder as local law enforcement responded to the priest's risky 9-1-1 call. They would be here any minute and there was nothing he could tell them. No crime had been committed, at least not yet. He didn't know the man's name and he didn't recognize him from any earlier confessions.

The cops arrived, impressive response time, and burst into the sanctuary. "Father, are you okay?"

He took a deep breath. "Yes, I'm fine. Probably overreacting. Had an intense moment in confession and got a little frightened but that's all. It's over. So sorry to bother you."

What was he supposed to say? *Someone's father is about to be killed but sorry I have no idea who it is*?

Los Angeles County had over ten million people in it and the police were already stretched to the breaking point with a shortage of officers and a steady stream of convicts being prematurely released back on to the streets because of the swollen, congested prison system. If he told them about the confession, he would simply add to their stress and sense of futility. No, he would just say a prayer and hope that the confession was merely a fantasy from a deeply disturbed mind and not the mind of an actual killer.

He shuddered though, as he remembered the little headshake the man had given him before disappearing into the street. He was probably being paranoid in light of the circumstances but if he wasn't mistaken, there was a clear threat in that look and without knowing who the man was and with only a shadowy glance at his face, there was no way to be on the lookout in case he returned for some payback. He thought of the man's flat, hollow voice, not the voice of someone merely looking for attention. A knot formed in the pit of his stomach.

"Yes, I'm sure, I'm fine. I'm truly sorry to take you away from your other work, officers. Thank you for your quick response and protection. God bless you for it."

They turned to leave with respectful, if a bit gruff, nods to the priest and as he turned back to the prayer altar, one of the officers called out to him, "Excuse me Father but for our paperwork can you remind me of your first and last name?"

The priest turned. "Stan Jeffries."

"Thank you, Father."

Father Jeffries turned back to the bench and began to pray for the protection of *two* fathers, himself and the father whose future murder had just been confessed to him.

Chapter Two

So there I was, leaning over the body.

Crimson stains streaked up and down my forearms as I worked frantically at reviving him; at least I think that's what I was doing.

The shouts were getting closer when his eyes fluttered open and a flicker of recognition crossed his dull, smoky gaze. That's when the panic kicked in and my heart started racing until I could hardly breathe.

He knew me and he knew what I had done.

He lunged up to grab me but his chest was spasming and I pushed him roughly back on to the concrete floor of the parking garage where he grimaced and groaned. He opened his mouth to speak but I clamped my hand firmly over it. I couldn't bear to hear him confirm what I suspected he knew.

The room started spinning and the bile of vomit was rising in my throat. My chest and arms were slick with sweat but then I realized it wasn't sweat. I was bleeding, almost as badly as he was, and I was clutching a bloody knife.

I wasn't hurting but I was very dizzy and I knew I had to get out of the warehouse. Fast. The shouting had stopped and I knew that wasn't a good sign. They must have found me.

I left him lying in a pool of our combined blood and as I sprinted away, I could still hear his shallow breathing.

Nothing made sense to me as I ran, except that I knew if they caught me, it would all have been for nothing and I couldn't let it be for nothing.

She deserved more than that and I was determined to give it to her.

That was why I killed him.

Yes, even as I skidded around corners and stumbled up the stairway to the street level exit, I knew that he was dead, or at least he would be momentarily. I just wondered if they would get him to talk before his shallow breathing stopped for good.

A shot rang out and chipped the plastered ceiling above my head and as I instinctively ducked, I tripped and went down hard, wrenching my shoulder. I could hear their footsteps and the deep growling of their dog. A Rotweiller. A vicious one.

I scrambled back to my feet and for the first time became conscious of the pain in my gut. It was like fire and I could tell that things on the inside of me were all messed up and out of place. I was in bad shape. Sheer terror has its perks though and as it gripped my soul it fueled my flight up the steps, carrying me out into the blinding light of day.

I burst out of the underground parking lot and staggered onto the Santa Monica sidewalk, oblivious to the shrieks and stares of the sandaled tourists and locals who were strolling along the 3rd Street Promenade, gaping at me as if I were a horror film come to life.

Had I been conscious of such things I might have noticed the extreme contrast between the lazy palm trees swaying above the So Cal beach scene and the bloody carnage that my life had become since I first met Stan.

Yes, I think that was his name, perhaps still was if they hadn't killed him yet. An unmarked van roared to a stop in front of me then, scattering a group of paparazzi that was hovering around some chic store that movie stars apparently frequented. The side door of the van flew open and a dark figure overwhelmed me and pulled me roughly into the confines of the van as it began to peel away from the parkade. I felt a momentary sense of relief to have been spared from the angry dog and its angrier master when a heavy weight pushed down on my exploding abdomen and the bile I had been choking back rushed upward in a burst. I wretched and gagged and then felt a dark bag being cinched firmly over my head.

I remember two things before I passed out, the smell of my own vomit and a sharp clicking sound, like a stiff ballpoint pen being repeatedly pressed and released. It's funny what your mind notices the moment before you die.

Chapter Three

Father Stan Jeffries' home was meticulously organized and despite its recent vacancy, it smelled fresh and clean. Detective Louis Stratton could even detect one of his favorite smells, birthday cake candles. He had followed his wife into dozens of candle stores over the years and sniffed more candles than he could count. His favorite scent had always been the birthday cake ones. They always made him hungry. Sure enough, there on the edge of a counter was a partially burned birthday cake candle.

The blinds were pulled, so the room was dark except for the sunlight that leaked in from the sides of the blinds. His partner, Robyn Macomber, turned the switch on a lamp and the room took on a warm glow. It was definitely the home of a bachelor but not as much so as one might have thought. While it lacked an artistic feminine touch, at least the furniture all matched and the curtains and tablecloth didn't clash.

A giant flat screen television set filled one corner of the small living room across from a worn, leather chair flanked by twin end tables that each held several neatly arranged stacks of books. Louis felt a strange urge to sit in the comfortable looking chair and read and perhaps even steal a nap. He shook his head and mumbled something to himself about how retirement couldn't come soon enough if he was actually getting this soft.

Robyn had wandered down a narrow hallway adorned with as many photos as one might find in the home of a married couple who had multiple children and grandchildren. For someone who had never having married or fathered children, Father Jeffries certainly had a lot of friends. One of them had reported him missing after he mysteriously failed to attend mass and then missed the following two days of work as well.

A swell of emotion bunched up in Robyn's throat and she turned back to her partner and said in a slightly choked voice. "Interesting home isn't it? There's something different about it. I feel safe here, like I could sleep through the night in peace."

Louis nodded silently. She had nailed it. Peace. That's what Louis felt as he looked at the photos in the hallway. It felt like home and he too had a lump of emotion catch in his chest.

He joined Robyn in the priest's bedroom, another simple but dutifully cleaned room with minimalist décor and a pile of books beside the bed. Robyn was staring at a painting on one of the walls. The caption said, "the anointing" and it was one of the strangest paintings she had ever seen. Two female angels were pouring a massive pitcher of oil on to the head of a prayerful man sitting cross-legged on the floor. His eyes were closed but even without seeing his expression, Robyn could tell that the stress and anxiety of his day, and maybe even his life, was being washed away from him.

"The anointing." She liked it and she realized that she liked everything about this little, unassuming home. "I wish I had known Father Jeffries." She said suddenly to Louis who had joined her in contemplating the portrait. "I bet he had been a wonderful priest."

Stratton nodded. "That's the word on him."

Since his disappearance, they had interviewed dozens of his parishioners and several of his fellow-priests and had yet to hear a negative or damaging word about his character or integrity. His reputation was impeccable and he seemed to have the respect of everyone who knew him. It reminded Louis of an old leadership adage that said, "The definition of success is when the people who know you the best, respect you the most." It seemed to be true of Father Jeffries and Louis found himself hoping that it really was. God knew the Catholic Church needed a priest it could trust.

It was hard for Louis to remain optimistic about human nature after spending an entire career in law enforcement, investigating scandal and controversy. He knew he had become jaded over the years but he still held out hope that not everyone was a liar or a thief. Surely, there were people who were genuinely honest and forthright.

He remembered something he learned in college in an obscure philosophy class, something about how the Greek word for "hypocrisy" meant "experienced in the art of acting." Despite spending his entire adult life exposing people who acted inconsistently in their public and private lives, he still wanted to believe that somebody out there could actually have a shred of personal integrity and so he was secretly pulling for Father Jeffries, desperately hoping that their investigation revealed nothing scandalous about him. He wanted this priest to be the real deal.

Even more than that he wanted him to be found.

"Here's something," Robyn said, picking up a black, leather journal from the top of the end table beside the neatly tucked bed. Their search warrant limited them to handling only those items that they found in plain sight, so she bent to open the journal, hoping its contents might reveal something that could help their investigation.

"Does it look promising, or is it just 'dear diary' type stuff?"

Robyn was already busily skimming pages and didn't respond.

"Let's hope he wrote as much as he read," Louis muttered to himself as his partner continued reading.

Chapter Four

Light. Blinding light all around me. For the briefest of moments I thought I was having a religious experience, moving toward the proverbial light but then the agony in my midsection ruptured that hope and brought me back to my senses, telling me I was still alive, at least momentarily.

Breathing was excruciating and, as strange as it sounds, I could literally feel the shifting and pulsing of my internal organs. I had never before been conscious of my kidneys but now I could tell that they were both damaged and badly weakened and my spleen (who can feel their spleen?), I knew that something was wrong with mine. At another time, it might have been a fascinating experience to be so aware of my insides but as I heard my heart beating feebly in my chest, I also became aware of another sensation that threatened to make me vomit again. I could feel the bullet that had torn into my organs, leaving them shredded and sloshing into each other. The bullet was stuck in my lower back, three vertebras up from my tailbone.

This bizarre knowledge of my internal anatomy was such a weird experience that I thought I might pass out from the shock of it but then I noticed that I wasn't alone. There were people in the room, at least three of them.

"I think the drugs are working."

Someone shifted the bright, interrogation lights out of my eyes and I began to make out the shapes of three men standing behind a table across from me. Their expressions were difficult to read, not cruel or harsh, just impassive. Waiting.

My heart rate slowed and I was distantly aware of how sluggishly my blood was moving through my veins. I was dying.

One of them spoke, "I think it's too much. It's going to kill him."

Another man responded without shifting his eyes away from mine, "A little longer, we're almost there." Then to me, "Do you know who you are?"

I nodded. Then shook my head, realizing that I didn't actually know. I'm sure on most days that revelation would have been terrifying but at the moment I was more frightened by what I *did* know. I knew that my heart rate was fluttering like a heart does before it stops beating forever and I knew that I was losing circulation in my extremities.

A voice spoke again. "Do you remember anything about yourself, or why we've brought you here?" I shook my head again, although as I looked at each of the faces of my captors, I had the distinct feeling that I *should* know, especially the man who was addressing me. I knew that I should know him, that I *did* know him but couldn't recall how.

"Are you aware of your brain?" What a strange question. It came from the third man, sitting a little farther back from the others. Yes, I realized suddenly, I was, but I wasn't aware of it in a personal way, I was aware of it in the same way I was aware of the formaldehyde-soaked brain that my high school biology teacher kept in a jar on a shelf in the back of his classroom. There, at least I could remember *that*. We used to pass it around and marvel at the mysteries and intricacies of the human brain encased in such a small package of flesh. Yes, I was aware of my own brain but it didn't seem like my brain. I was an observer watching my brain from arm's length. My thoughts didn't seem to be originating from me but from an outside source. I was just a bystander who happened to be hearing them.

I could read the data in my brain almost like one would read the ticker tape on the bottom of a news screen. The facts were all there but they were impersonal, like I was remembering someone else's life.

"I think he's ready."

"Then let's do it quickly before we lose him."

"I want you to think. Do you remember your name?"

I did. Well, I didn't actually *remember* it per se but I knew what it was. In a distant, unattached sort of way I saw it written on the wall of my mind's eye and that's when the bullet shifted. It rotated slightly downward until it pressed up firmly against my sacral nerves, causing more pain than I knew could exist. My legs instantly lost all feeling and the blinding agony in my lower back rushed upward in a consuming wave, and I was gone, either passed out, or dead but gone nonetheless. I hung around for a few seconds longer, registering the reactions of the other people in the room. The men lunged over to catch me as I was crashing on to the hard, stone floor. One of them had a syringe in his hand and the other held some oxygen tubing and began looping it over my ears and connecting it to my nostrils. Very precise, like they had done this before.

Then there was nothing but darkness.

CHRIS JACKSON

Chapter Five

Detective Louis Stratton was already losing interest in Father Stan Jeffries' journal. It was primarily filled with Bible verses, spiritual insights and numerous "notes to self," but that was it. There was nothing that shed any light on his mysterious absence.

After a few more minutes of reading however, Robyn finally looked up and said, "I might have something!" Her eyes gleamed triumphantly as she read a hastily scrawled journal entry from several days earlier.

"Rough day in confession today. Had to call 9-1-1. I can't stop thinking about him and I don't think he was merely looking for attention. He said he was going to 'kill the father.' I'm probably being paranoid but I can't help thinking that the 'father' to whom he was referencing is me."

Two days lapsed before the next entry. Father Jeffries had written, "The man came back to confession today. I recognized his voice, hollow, flat and menacing.

'Forgive me, Father, for I have sinned.' I didn't know how to respond. All I could say was to ask him to go on. He asked me what Elliott had told me in his confession and when I asked for clarification, he said I knew exactly what he was talking about. He said, 'We know that Elliott Blythe has spoken to you and we want to know what he said.'"

The notes were uncanny, almost as clear and detailed as if Father Jeffries were sitting in front of them giving a verbal statement.

Robyn kept reading, "I told him, 'A man's confession is among the most private things in the world. I cannot disclose what Elliott revealed to me in private.'" Louis and Robyn both noticed that he didn't deny having spoken with Elliott. Stan's notes continued, "But that wasn't good enough for him. He said he would be back and that I would only have one more chance to talk. I'm frightened and I need to go to the authorities. I should have gone to them the first time Elliott came to see me. It's just so complicated."

Stratton looked at Robyn quizzically and asked, "Did he ever report a second visit?"

Robyn shook her head. "Not that we're aware of and since there are no cameras or recording devices in Catholic Church confessionals, we don't have a picture or an audio clip to help us."

They sat in silence for several seconds until Stratton said what Robyn was already thinking. "We need to find this Elliott Blythe." Robyn's fingers were already flying over the touch screen of her iPhone as she googled him.

His name popped up instantly along with an array of glossy photos of his pleasant, smiling face and advertisements for his high-end law firm. Robyn was punching his address into her GPS application as Stratton began turning out lights and shutting doors.

"His office is only twenty minutes from here." She said as they headed out the door with conflicted feelings of hope and concern. Each of them was hoping that the confession of an intension to murder someone had yet to be committed but they also knew that five days of silence was a very bad sign.

Before Louis had even turned the key in the ignition of their unmarked cruiser, their radio crackled and the dispatcher's crisp voice interrupted their plans and routed them to an underground parking lot in Santa Monica. The dispatcher told them that there had been a homicide and that the victim had been identified as a Catholic priest named Father Stan Jeffries.

.

Chapter Six

"The balance is as thin as a razor's edge. Too little and he hurts too bad to stay conscious, too much and it knocks him out anyway."

The words pulled me out of a dream-like state and brought me back to the reality of the hospital room. I kept my eyes closed and continued my deep, if somewhat erratic breathing and just listened.

"What do you recommend?"

"Well, I don't think we have any choice but to pull him out and learn what we can before the pain becomes too much."

"How long can we expect him to talk before it hurts him too badly?"

"Not sure, probably no more than a few minutes at a time. We'll have to be patient."

"Be patient? To even pull one conversation out of him? It will take hours and it will require dozens of starts and stops. It will be nothing short of torture and for what? We're going to have to get rid of him anyway, so why not just do it now. Increase the dosage and let him fall asleep forever so we can be done with him."

"We have to find out what he knows."

"It doesn't matter what he knows if he's dead."

"Yes but we need to know if he set any safety measures in place, like the pre-planned release of some unfortunate information to a greedy journalist if he doesn't make it home by a certain time."

"Do you actually think he had time to think about something like that?"

"Who knows, but we can't do anything until we're sure and we can't be sure until we help him remember what he knows."

There was a pause in the conversation and my heart began beating so fiercely that I was afraid they would hear it rattling against my chest. My own heart was beginning to hurt me.

The pain came in such a sudden wave that I was totally unprepared for it and I gasped loudly while lurching up into a sitting position and clutching my rib cage. It was a coughing fit and as it wracked my convulsing body so that I distinctly felt, and heard, the middle rib on my right side crack.

The pain took my breath away and as my coughs dwindled into silent wheezes. Tears coursed down my cheeks. Funny, I noticed how very stubbly my cheeks were.

Mercifully, one of the men reached out to the I.V. bag and increased the flow of the meds, causing me to instantly slip toward a hazy sleep.

"Do you think he heard us?" one of them said.

"I don't know but this is going to be even more delicate than we thought, if it even works at all. The mayor has an event tonight and he'll be here as soon as it's over. We'll try it again when he arrives."

Then I was gone.

I awoke several minutes, or hours or days later, I had no idea of time at that point. I was alone in the room. When I opened my eyes, the room began spinning so wildly that a wave of nausea threatened me and I quickly closed them again. I wanted to think and concentrate on my surroundings, try to remember something but I kept getting distracted by the pain in my midsection and also by the shape of my eyeballs. It was maddening. I could feel the contour of my eyes as they turned inside my head and I could feel my cornea pressing up against my eyelid as I squinted against the urge to vomit.

They say that children and adults with Attention Deficit Disorder can't handle too much stimuli that an excess of external stimulation quickly frays their emotions and heightens their sensitivities to a point that becomes frightening and even dangerous for them. What I was experiencing was that sensation. My mind was absorbing minutia about my eyes, my pupils, my irises, my retinas, my eyelashes and the barrage of information was more disturbing than the bile that was quickly rising in the back of my throat.

My right cornea had a scratch right across the center of it. Without impairing my vision it was the source of the constant itching that I suddenly remembered I had experienced that past year.

The tear ducts in my left eye were slightly clogged and that, I knew, was the cause of its frequent bloodshot look. Memories about my eyes and their appearance were returning to me along with other alarming, new data.

My right eyeball was slightly enlarged, which was probably why I was afflicted with recurring headaches on that side of my skull and my eyes were wet. I was crying again and I noticed with alarm that the salinity level of my tears was dangerously low. I needed electrolytes.

With a frightening revelation, I realized that my mind was diagnosing my body, swiftly and efficiently assessing damage to body parts that I had never known anything about and certainly had never consciously *felt* before. What was happening to me? The room was still spinning and my tear ducts were still flowing and I began sinking into a vortex of confusion and despair.

Then the door opened and someone walked in but I was already gone again.

Chapter Seven

Rachel Parker's laugh was slightly forced but her new celebrity boyfriend probably didn't realize it. It was hard to notice certain details like that when you were with her. In fact, that was one of her constant frustrations with men in general. They seldom noticed *anything* when they were with her except for her lips, her eyes and her ever wind-blown hair. She sighed as she considered this, grateful for the oversized, designer sunglasses that shielded her true emotions from his view. Beauty had its perks of course and when she was honest with herself, she was less troubled with the dumb blonde stereotypes than she let on. Her multi-million dollar modeling and acting contracts offered sufficient rebuttal to anyone who viewed her as just another pretty face. Still, there were times she wished that someone would see past the sexy images of her that clung to every other billboard in Los Angeles and recognize the *person* that she was on the inside.

Father Stan had been able to see the real her and she loved him for it. She thought of him anxiously and wondered why he wasn't returning her calls.

"Are you okay?" Her date asked gently. Maybe she wasn't hiding her thoughtfulness as well as she imagined.

"Yes," she mumbled turning back to face her newest celebrity boyfriend. "Just stalling—these events are becoming increasingly tedious."

He smiled at her, showing perfectly straight teeth, whiter than any tooth had ever naturally been and made to appear even more so when contrasted with his smooth, tanned skin. He was a beautiful man and most other women would have been smitten with him. They were sure to be the talk of the tabloids after today, their first public appearance "together." His latest film was rocking the charts and People magazine was circulating rumors that he was destined to be their upcoming "sexiest man alive." Hollywood's golden couple—that's what the headlines would say—until they started saying that he was cheating on her with strippers and call girls.

She shook her head angrily, wishing she didn't always have to be so negative. A realist. That's what Stan had called her but she knew he was just being polite. He didn't know how to be anything else.

A gentle touch on her shoulder brought her around. It was time. She took his hand, lifted the designer sunglasses to a perch on top of her platinum blonde hair and flashed her million-dollar smile—*ten* million dollar smile to be exact. She smiled for real at the thought of that.

They made their way to their seats, another black tie gala for the Hollywood elite, some of which had genuine compassion to match the depth of their pocketbooks. This cause was a worthy one, raising money to fund the renovation of an entire village in Sudan, complete with water filtering systems, educational strategies and the launching of a massive mobile medical clinic that would service, literally, thousands of orphans. Yes, this one was a good cause. However, she knew it wasn't the only cause being promoted at the event.

She spotted the mayor from across the room and knew it would only be a matter of minutes before he made his way over to her and mugged for his usual, impromptu photo shoot. She didn't know of any other elected official with more celebrity contacts—including the celebrities themselves who had been elected to office. He was gunning to be the president of the United States even though he hadn't officially announced his candidacy. Yes, they would be raising money for needy children in Africa tonight but they would also be adding to the necessary votes and influence to, quite possibly, put Kevin Gunther in the White House.

Not that he would be a bad choice or an incompetent leader. He had already won national acclaim with his smooth handling of the L.A. hostage crisis the preceding year—the largest hostage showdown with local law enforcement in California's history, or in America's history for that matter. His unflappable leadership and tireless work ethic was reminiscent of Rudy Giuliani after 9-11 rocked New York City and the entire world. No, it wasn't his experience or credentials that worried her—it was the other part of his life.

"Rachel," he greeted her flashing his own million-dollar smile. His wife, Shelly, trailed behind him and Rachel noticed that despite her attempt to hide her pain, her eyes were flat and hollow, reflecting the knowledge that only two other people knew, Rachel and Father Stan.

Rachel embraced him with the appropriate Hollywood air kisses and mandatory compliments and then glanced over at Shelly who only briefly made eye contact with her.

Shelly Gunther, Kevin's high school sweetheart and the homecoming queen voted "most likely to become rich and famous" was a classic beauty, always mistaken for their daughter's sister instead of her mother. With her perfect etiquette and genuine compassion and empathy she was the perfect counterpart for the fiery, outspoken mayor who never backed down from any case of inequity or injustice. They, more than any movie star pair, were the true golden couple of Los Angeles and their fame and star power were augmented by the fact that they were genuinely in love with each other, with a seemingly healthy twenty-five year marriage to prove it. Rich, beautiful, athletic, educated, talented and devoted to facilitating positive change in the world, they were an easy choice for California's governor's mansion and even quite possibly, America's White House.

As long as America never learned what Stan had discovered.

Rachel found herself wondering again if everything was okay.

Chapter Eight

"What a mess." Detective Louis Stratton mumbled in disgust as he lit his customary crime scene cigar, a medium strength macanudo and began pushing his way through the crowd of paramedics, cops, onlookers and the gathering swarm of reporters. He lifted a burly leg over the yellow crime scene tape and made his way deeper into the underground parking structure. He puffed deeply on the mac as he and his partner moved to the center of the crime scene that surrounded Father Jeffries's mangled body.

Robyn was already writing copious notes in her little, black notebook. She took more notes than anyone he had ever worked with, far more notes than ever made it into her reports and he found himself wondering, as he often did, what she found so compelling. Young for a detective, she was a brilliant investigator, near genius according to her test scores from Stanford and he could never understand why a beautiful, young twenty-something with an I.Q. like hers would want to lend her skills to the gritty streets of downtown Los Angeles.

They had been partners for about a year and he only had another nine months before he could hang up his shield and retire with full benefits. He chuckled to himself when he thought about their unlikely pairing as partners. They were something right out of a movie, the gruff, experienced detective showing the ropes to the idealistic young partner before the old timer retired for good. He wondered if it would be a peaceful retirement or if they would be thrust into one last deadly case before he could ride off into the sunset. As he approached the dead body, an uneasy knot formed in his gut telling him the odds were against the peaceful exit. "Bring on the movie rights," he mumbled to himself as they bent down to look at the dead priest.

"There's quite a story out there somewhere," Robyn said after studying the body for a moment. "The perfect priest who's never made an enemy in his life hears a couple of confessions from an Elliott Blythe and then a few days later turns up dead. We need to find Elliott."

Stratton nodded his agreement and then noticed something odd about the priest's clothing. His pants were high waters.

Robyn had just noticed it too and she also noticed that his shirtsleeves were too short and that crisscrossed tattoos were peeking out from them. They bent closer and stared at the man's face. He certainly looked like a priest with his black suit and once-white clerical collar but his face was bloody and swollen and it was hard to tell if it was the same kind face that had smiled at them from the numerous photos they had just seen in Father Jeffries's peaceful, little home.

The collar was stained dark red from the deep puncture wounds that riddled his midsection and as Louis and Robyn looked closer they both saw that the collar didn't fit any better than the rest of the clothing. It was stretched around the neck as far as it could reach but it was unattached in the back. Someone had dressed this body to look like a priest.

Louis looked up and spoke to a uniformed officer, "Who identified the body?"

The officer looked around quickly and then a troubled look shot across his face as he realized that his witness had stepped away. He whispered to another officer who turned and began walking quickly through the crowd of onlookers. "I don't see him, sir. We'll find him momentarily."

"No, you won't." Louis replied grimly. "He's gone and this isn't Father Stan Jeffries." He took a long, thoughtful puff on the macanudo. "Call me when this body gets properly identified." And then to Robyn, "Do you still have Elliott Blythe's address in that little phone of yours?"

Robyn was already punching in the numbers and walking hurriedly back to their car.

Chapter Nine

So I wasn't dead, at least not yet and my legs were working again. I stretched them under my bed sheets, grateful to have a sense of feeling.

I must have been loaded with meds because my pain had greatly subsided even though I was still conscious of my torn insides and the bullet that was now lodged tightly against my left facet joint. My memories were blank again and my mind was trying to ramp up, searching for answers.

I had already scanned the clean, sparse, windowless room and surmised that I was not in a traditional hospital room. There were no curtains or windows and no noises emanated from the hallway outside. An array of monitors and machines hummed around me in a peaceful, soothing rhythm, while the IV bag kept its continuous drip into my tightly bandaged arm. The only other piece of furniture was a wooden chair and a small table with a medical chart and a pen on it. I was already reaching for the chart.

The penmanship was clean and tight, all the characters printed in crisp, block letters. A name was written on top of the chart (my name perhaps?) and below it was a time-log of sorts, broken into thirty-minute increments. As I read the time stamped entries, memories started flickering crosscurrent into my thinking and I recalled staring into interrogation lights while three men stood across from me. I remembered their odd comments, about being aware of my brain and then I remembered dying, well, not actually dying, just being brought *here*.

10:15 pm. We killed him. His vitals are still okay but it was probably too much.

10:45 pm. Yes. We've definitely killed him. It's just a matter of time.

11:15 pm. Still alive but barely.

11:45 pm. Interesting. His heart rate is getting *stronger* and he's showing what looks like a REM pattern of sleep.

12:15 am. Yes, it's definitely a REM cycle. He's dreaming.

The door opened and a white robed orderly entered loudly, interrupting my reading. He chuckled when he saw me holding the medical chart and shook his head ruefully. "What a head trip," he muttered as he set a thick envelope on my lap and said, "You're supposed to look through these to see if they help your memory," and then he was gone.

The icy fingers of fear spread their familiar touch (yes it was a familiar emotion) through my soul as I continued reading the time stamped entries.

12:45 am. He knows. Kevin woke him up and confronted him and even though he didn't respond, Kevin is convinced that he knows.

1:15 am. He's a dead man. Regardless of what we get out of him, it's just a matter of time.

They were right. I briefly considered trying to leave but with the consideration came the horrifying realization that I would probably never be leaving this hospital bed. The bullet had collided with my spine and left several of my vertebrae fatally weakened. The awareness of it crashed into my soul, bringing another wave of nausea with it. My heart began racing and a surge of adrenaline sent a tingling sensation along my spine. I was a dead man.

Fighting back the nausea and a headache that had started building around my temples, I picked up the envelope and emptied its contents on to my lap. They were pictures, perhaps a dozen of them, all close-up facial shots of people I had never seen before, or at least I didn't remember seeing before. The first one brought a twinge of anxiety to me as I looked into the smiling features of a plain but pleasant looking man. He wore a crisp, blue suit and his somewhat messy, wavy brown hair gave him a youthful appearance. I felt concern for him but he also troubled me deeply and I wondered if he was partly responsible for the desperate mess I was in.

The next photo brought an unexpected sense of relief to me and my fear slightly abated as I studied her features. She was a beautiful woman with flowing brown hair and laughing eyes that conveyed both innocence and delight. She seemed a little younger than me, since I was...well, I couldn't remember how old I was. Anyway, she seemed younger and kind, very kind. She was wearing a big, floppy hat like the kind that people wear at the beach and she seemed happy. I liked her I decided and I could trust her, if I could only remember who she was or where she could be found.

She showed up in the next photo as well but in this one she wasn't alone. She had her arm around a younger girl whose features nearly matched her own, except that the younger girl's hair was red and she had a smattering of freckles that brushed across her rosy skin. The younger girl was smiling and her sparkling blue eyes conveyed as much emotion and delight as her mother. Yes, I realized, they were a mother-daughter duo.

The good feelings left with the next picture however. It showed a very handsome man in a tuxedo whose style and smile could have been ripped from the pages of GQ magazine. There was something unsettling about his body language and the intense gleam in his eye, especially when contrasted with the woman standing beside him. She was the woman from the first two photos, the woman I knew I could trust, but in this picture, despite the smile on her lips, her eyes looked lifeless and flat, like she had witnessed things she would never forget, things she would have longed to forget.

I didn't like him and I suddenly wondered if he was the reason I was dying in this hospital bed without any memory of who I was or how I had come to this tragic end. "He is my enemy." I whispered aloud and then I flipped to the next photograph.

It was Rachel. I was startled with my sudden knowledge but yes, that was her name and I loved her. I knew it even before the words formed in my mind and I felt an acute concern for her safety. She was beautiful, the quintessential supermodel and that was all I knew.

I was groping for additional details, searching my blank mind to try to remember something else, when the door handle to my room turned and I was no longer alone.

Chapter Ten

"Ladies and gentlemen, we will begin momentarily."

Rachel was grateful for the chance to sit without being the center of everyone's attention, although she knew she would still be ogled and whispered about. She sighed. At least she could look straight ahead and pretend not to notice. She was less than eighteen months into her newfound fame and she was already wondering if she was cut out for celebrity status. She hadn't even done anything significant with her life. It wasn't like she had saved a life, invented something, or created soul-stirring art. She just looked good on a runway and in Los Angeles in the 21st century, where millions of young people yearn for stardom and never find it, others had the fortune, or misfortune, to become a household name simply because the tabloids decided to latch on to them and *make* them famous.

Her thoughts turned dark and jaded. Her photo from this fundraising event would be all over the Internet within hours and in the morning her face would grace the cover of everything from the L.A. Times to much less reputable "news" magazines and all the while she knew she was less significant than the lowliest child they were gathered to raise money for.

She wasn't anything like Father Stan. He was an unsung hero. *He* should have been the one being honored on the platform tonight.

Stan always hated it when she thought that way and he hated it when she downplayed her celebrity or belittled herself. She remembered a recent conversation when he had looked at her tenderly and said, "Rachel, you were born to be famous. It's part of the note in life that you were meant to play. There's a *reason* you are where you are today. Your job is to find out why, gratefully enjoy the experience and use it to make a positive difference in the world."

Stan always saw the best in her.

She quickly blinked back a flow of tears and wondered if he would still see the good if he ever found out about her and the mayor.

He was being introduced now. Rachel realized that her mind had completely wandered during the opening remarks of the banquet. "Ladies and Gentlemen, Mayor Kevin Gunther!" Applause ripped through the assembly and a spontaneous standing ovation swept through the room and continued for nearly a minute after Kevin raised his hand in humbled protest.

At least he seemed humble and maybe he really was. Sometimes Rachel couldn't be sure. In many ways, he was the most ambitious and the most dangerous man she had ever met. She was afraid of him even now, and yet in other respects she revered him. He was a born leader of men who could pull greatness out of people and rally them around a worthwhile cause. She believed in him and she was committed to following him and lending to his cause whatever influence her starlet celebrity possessed.

She stood and applauded with the rest of the guests.

His brilliant smile swept the room and he seemingly made eye contact with every gathered person. It was amazing how he could speak to a crowd of thousands while making each individual feel as if he were speaking directly to them. It was truly a gift.

"Thank you so much for the gift of your time, your presence...and your donations." He added with a charming smirk. People laughed good-naturedly as he continued. "Shelly and I would never be where we are today if it weren't for people like you who believe in the message and vision of our administration. We are not out to build a name for ourselves, we are not out to reclaim California's, or even America's, reputation as world leaders, we are out to help as many hurting people as we can while we still have breath left to breathe and strength left to give."

It was his standard speech. Many of the guests had heard him give it a dozen times but it sounded fresh and genuine each time and the reason it *sounded* fresh and genuine is because it *was* fresh and genuine. Kevin Gunther was not a politician at heart. He was a humanitarian and a change agent with a burning passion to see the world around him shift for the good and if there were some who still had their doubts about his methods and motives, no one doubted his wife, Shelly.

Kevin was introducing her now as he always did and she waved and smiled with all the poise of a beauty queen combined with the innocence of a Midwestern farm girl. Everyone adored her.

However, very few could perceive the incredible effort it took for her to smile and wave and champion the many causes that bore her name. Rachel was one of the few who knew what Shelly had gone through and she was one of the few who could read the pain in the depths of her violet eyes. Rachel knew that Shelly was flat, empty and cold and no matter how she laughed and tossed her hair and smiled at Kevin's wit and charm, Rachel could see that Shelly Gunther was dying inside and she wondered how long it would be before the rest of the world could see it too.

Her mood continued to darken throughout the rally, until, mercifully, the event ended and she asked her driver to get her home as quickly as possible. She said a brief goodnight to her date, claiming an upset stomach and left him to hail a cab at the event center. Despite what the tabloids would print in the morning, she was only with him because she needed to try to move on. She had to try to forget. She kept her dark glasses on in the backseat of her car to hide the tears that she couldn't hold back any longer. When she was finally home, she pulled the blinds, buried her head under her covers like she used to do as a little girl and wished that morning would never come.

Chapter Eleven

"Tell us about Stan Jeffries."

I knew I didn't really have any choice but to cooperate, laid up as I was in this pseudo-hospital room and unable to move but something in me was fighting for some kind of upper hand in the conversation, determined to resist these men who had entered my room with such indifferent, arrogant demeanors. One of them was the man from the photo, my "enemy," and viewing him in person evoked the same dreadful emotions as seeing his picture had done.

He wore an expensive, tailored suit with an unbuttoned collar and diamond cuff links glinting from beneath his jacket. His dark hair was slicked back and I could smell his cologne from across the room. As he impatiently flipped through the time-stamped medical chart, a wave of fear swept through me. He was the reason I was a dead man.

"I don't know anyone named Stan Jeffries."

He looked up quickly, his eyes flashing a hint of mirth. "Nice," he said. "Try again."

"I seriously don't know who you're talking about. I don't know who you are, I don't know why I'm here and I don't even know who I am."

He glanced sharply at the other man, a doctor perhaps, standing in the background. "How much did you give him?" He asked with an unmistakable edge in his voice.

"It was the right dosage. It shouldn't have suppressed his memory to this extent. I'll scale it back."

"When will it wear off?"

"It's hard to tell. He's pretty broken and it's tough to find a balance that will suppress his pain enough to keep him conscious without suppressing his memory along with it. It might take several attempts to find that sweet spot before the Velorum can work its magic. I think he needs to sleep through the night and then we'll prep him for questioning in the morning."

Although visibly upset with the doctor's recommendation, my enemy nodded and replied, "Okay but the meeting starts at 8:00 a.m. and I'll be here as soon as it's over. Make sure he's ready to talk." As he turned to leave, he patted the other man's shoulder, a forgiving gesture, then abruptly exited without looking at me again.

The door closed behind him and I turned to see that the remaining man was noticeably shaken up by the interaction. His fingers trembled slightly as he reached out to adjust the flow of the fluids in my IV.

"What are you giving me?" I asked him, hoping to capitalize on his moment of vulnerability.

He hesitated before answering gruffly, "This is just saline to help flush your system."

"Flush my system of what?" but that was all I was going to get. He turned and quickly left, dimming the lights behind him.

I lay in the dark room, stretching my mind in an attempt to remember something, anything about who I was and how I got here. There was a dull ache in my abdomen and when I reached down to touch it, the prickly tips of stitches met my fingers. I opened my hospital gown and felt jagged rows of hastily sewn stitches crisscrossing my midsection. The feeling of my swollen wound, still sticky from my massive loss of blood stirred a nauseous response and also awakened a dormant memory.

I suddenly knew who my shooter was.

CHRIS JACKSON

Chapter Twelve

It was 8:00 a.m and the lawyers crowded around the conference table small talking and glancing expectantly at the large, ornate clock on the wall, the one the vice president had given the mayor as a thank you for his discreet handling of his son's indiscretions while on a Spring Break trip to Los Angeles. The air smelled of polished leather and strong coffee from their flashy, designer briefcases and their early morning Starbucks runs. It was a powerhouse group that had gathered for this unusual meeting, leading attorneys from the largest firms in Los Angeles. On most days, they would be competitors, seldom being seen together unless it was in a courtroom or a judge's chambers but they were intrigued by the "summons."

Each of them had received the same, simple message: "Kevin Gunther would like to secure your services for a delicate but extremely lucrative matter, one that requires the utmost level of confidentiality. He has additionally reached out to some of your leading competitors in a desire to assemble a team of the most brilliant legal minds for this endeavor. He trusts that your sense of vision and enlightenment will transcend your rivalries, at least until this matter is resolved." The note concluded with the particulars of the meeting place and it was signed, Judy May, the mayor's personal assistant, who, some believed, carried nearly as much influence as the mayor himself in making things happen politically in L.A.

People never disregarded invitations from either Judy or the mayor and so it was that at 8:00 Monday morning, they were settling into the comfy, leather chairs in the posh conference room outside of Mayor Gunther's office.

He entered with a flourish, a whirl of energy and intensity. His eyes flashed around the room, taking in every detail of those who were present and accounted for, while simultaneously shaking hands and greeting each of the assembled law giants by name. More than one of them found themselves admiring the mayor. He was one of the most controlled, confident men they had ever met. Perfectly comfortable in his own skin, he was the consummate people-person, able to relate with anyone in a disarming, compelling way, regardless of his or her age or station in life.

He came around to the head of the table and greeted them collectively with a flash of his brilliant smile.

"Gentlemen and ladies," he began with a nod to the few ladies in attendance. "I know you are busy and I truly appreciate your time this morning."

Several of them concealed smirks, like any of them had anything better to do than parley with the mayor. Kevin Gunther was going places. Most considered it a done deal that his next home would be in the governor's mansion in Sacramento, although others, shrewd political analysts, thought he might skip the governorship altogether and move his family straight to 1600 Pennsylvania Avenue in D.C. No, none of them were too busy for this meeting. They were right where they wanted to be. Meetings like this were where careers were made.

The mayor continued. "I need a lawyer."

Chuckles broke out around the table. The mayor never did or said anything without consulting the legal advice of his best friend and long-time counselor, Ray Gibbs. Ray was in the room now, sitting in the corner studying each of the attorneys in attendance, his face an imperceptible mask. He and the mayor had been friends since childhood but he had already built a reputation as a fearsome attorney with his brilliant mind and bulldog tactics in the courtroom before Kevin had recruited him away from his big firm and asked him to serve as his personal attorney and confidante. No, Ray hadn't ridden anywhere on Kevin's coattails. In fact, many attributed Kevin's meteoric rise in politics to his relationship with Ray.

"Seriously folks, I need an attorney, a team of them actually."

He paused to look at each lawyer in turn, checking to ensure that they were the right ones. Judy had certainly done her homework, inviting only the best, only the ones with enough ambition to sign on to his proposal and with enough guts to stick it out when it got ugly because it inevitably would.

"I've recently come into possession of a piece of knowledge that could potentially change modern medicine as we know it. Handled appropriately, this information could also produce a significant amount of wealth. A *very* significant amount." He finished meaningfully.

Most of the lawyers leaned forward appreciatively in their seats, anxious to hear more and grateful for Kevin's no-nonsense approach to the meeting. Each of them was already rich by anyone's estimation so Kevin's emphasis on the words *a very significant amount* hooked their curiosity and their greed, just as Kevin knew it would.

One of them, however, an attorney named Elliott Blythe, shifted uncomfortably in his chair and made a pretense of looking at his calendar. Ray Gibbs made a mental note of this, wrote something in his legal pad with his full point ink pen and then he stood.

"Thank you, that will be all for today," he said. "We will be in touch." With that he was moving forward and escorting Kevin out of the conference room. "Feel free to show yourselves out."

The meeting was over just like that.

The gathered attorneys sat in bewildered silence for a few seconds and then began gathering their belongings and showing themselves out. They knew that something had just happened to spook Ray and they were desperately trying to discern what it was. They didn't speak to each other on the way out. Each was wrapped in his own thoughts.

Without a word being uttered, there was a shared knowledge among them as they entered the elevator and stood in awkward silence. Kevin was right to have approached them. Collectively, they were the best attorneys on the West Coast, a true legal dream team but individually they held an additional appeal. They were indebted to Kevin, some of them deeply and not just for trivial things like the mutual exchange of legal and political favors. Some of them were indebted to him in ways that could end their careers if word ever leaked out. Their initial excitement had dampened significantly and the rueful emotions of those who had climbed to the top by any means necessary, began to settle into their guts.

Then, to counter those negative emotions, they began the mental gymnastics attempting to convince themselves that they were overreacting about Ray's abrupt interruption. This was probably just Ray Gibbs' quirky way of screening potential talent and surely they would be summoned again.

They all knew it would never be that simple. Nothing with Kevin Gunther ever was.

Chapter Thirteen

Kevin stared into the television monitor watching them all crowd into the elegant, polished elevator. "So were we right?" he said to a grim-faced Ray beside him.

Ray didn't respond right away, he was too focused on what the hidden elevator cameras were showing on the faces of the dismissed attorneys: fear, stress and gallant attempts at covering it up.

He nodded finally, running a hand through his closely cropped salt-and-pepper hair. "Yes. He couldn't conceal it. I could practically smell the guilt on him. I hate it but at least we know."

Kevin nodded thoughtfully as his cell phone chirped and he looked down. "I've got to run, Ray. When will we contact him?"

"It's happening as we speak."

Seventeen floors below, the elevator doors were opening and the L.A. legal elite were emerging in their designer suits and Italian leather loafers, their confidence sufficiently restored. The joking that accompanies people on the inner circle of a profession continued again and a few overdue lunch appointments were scheduled, more out of courtesy than any real desire to connect. They were, after all, rivals and competitors, although most of them now carried the secret hope that they might soon work on the same team, Kevin Gunther's team.

They exited the building and dispersed along the crowded California sidewalks, some hailing cabs and others waiting for their drivers to pull up to the curb beside them.

All but one of them. Elliot Blythe stood off by himself, shading his eyes from the California sun with the morning's Wall Street Journal. He was looking into his hand at a note that had been stuffed into it as he had exited the elevator and pushed his way through the crowded lobby. He hadn't noticed whom it came from and he was shaking his head disgustedly, both angry and terrified that he hadn't been more observant.

He thrust the note inside the side pocket of his briefcase and hailed a cab, sliding on his dark sunglasses and looking over his shoulder nervously. How could the word have leaked out? He was certain that he hadn't been followed. He mumbled into his cell phone, ordering his assistant to clear his morning's schedule and then slid into the backseat of a yellow cab. The driver raised his eyebrows in inquiry and Elliot shook his head, "I don't care. Just get me away from here."

Ray Gibbs closed his office blinds as the yellow cab drove off, carrying Elliot to the nearest bar where Ray knew he would sit and drink and stress about his future. Then he pushed "send" on a new blackberry and the text message was shipped to Elliot's phone.

It had begun.

Ray took a deep breath, made an entry by hand in his little, leather notebook, paged his secretary and continued with his day.

In the meanwhile, Elliot's day was collapsing.

"Vodka on the rocks." Elliot ordered ignoring the smirking look of the bartender.

Despite his chosen profession, the bartender must have thought that nine o'clock in the morning was a little early for straight vodka. On the other hand, he was open for business at nine o'clock in the morning in the hopes that someone just like Elliott Blythe might wander in for some solace or escape. In some ways, he was like a priest offering absolution, only he didn't prescribe penance, he just poured a drink. He chuckled to himself, amused by his recurring thought, as he reached for the Grey Goose vodka and poured two fingers into an ice-filled tumbler. "Enjoy." He said blandly to Elliott who downed the drink and promptly ordered a second.

Elliott gulped the second drink in similar fashion and then slowed down with his third and began to consider his options. He looked at the note again.

"Elliott, we know you talked."

There were no instructions or threats, just the statement. "We know you talked." Questions were swirling. Who was "we"? How much did they know? Did they know about Father Jefferies?

Elliott's cell phone vibrated briefly, informing him of an incoming text message and instinctively Elliott knew that it didn't bear good news. He had lost his phone two days earlier and he was still using a cheap replacement Go Phone and had no idea how anyone would have been able to access this number.

His pulse began racing as he slowly flipped the phone open, clicked the messaging icon and read, "Stan is dead. We need to talk." He gasped and then nodded, knowing that the inevitable moment had come.

"Bartender." He ordered his fourth drink.

Chapter Fourteen

The boy was crying. He lay in his bed with the covers pulled up tight over his head so that no one could hear him sniffling. He was certain that his mother and sister would never forgive him for what he had done. Despite his mother's assurance that it was okay, he knew that she would forever blame him for ruining their family and it was even worse with his sister. She had actually told him as much. He felt so scared and alone and so he buried himself even deeper under his sheets and blankets even though it was a hot summer day outside and their air conditioner still wasn't working.

He started sweating almost immediately and had to surface for some fresh air. When he caught his reflection in the mirror on his dresser and saw his swollen, red eyes, he began crying even harder. What had he been thinking? He was just a kid. He was so stupid to think that he was old enough to handle such a horrifying situation. He thought he was helping her but he had actually made her life worse. He missed his dad terribly and another wave of emotion swept over him causing him to audibly cry like a baby.

Then something else happened. A different feeling started stirring in a remote corner of his heart and it forced him to stand up out of his bed and choke back his tears. He rubbed two grubby fists into his moist eyes and ran his shirtsleeve across his dripping nose. He cleared his throat and shook his head as if to force away the teardrops.

He hadn't been wrong to tell. He was the only one who had done what was right and standing beside his bed in his mismatched pajamas he realized that he would have done it again. She deserved to be protected and he had undoubtedly made the right call. If his family was now falling apart, it wasn't his fault and they would see that in time. He was the only man in the family now and he would stand by his decisions and he would always do whatever it took to hold his broken family together. His mother and sister might blame him today but they would eventually agree that he was their hero. No one would ever hurt his sister like that again. No one.

Even in that emotional moment, a compelling clarity settled over him and he realized, "This is who I am. I am a protector of hurting, defenseless people. This is my calling." If he had looked in the mirror, he would have still seen the same puffy eyes and twin tear tracks running down two dirty cheeks. He was still just a kid and yet he was also becoming something more. Though no one would have noticed it by looking at him, in that moment he was becoming a man.

I woke up and I was crying into my pillow. It was a dream.

Despite my amnesia, in the rare clarity that accompanies an abrupt awakening, I knew that the boy in the dream was *me*.

I slowly opened my eyes and through the blurring edges of my vision, I saw that I was no longer alone. The dream faded into forgetfulness as I looked into the gaze of several anxious-looking doctors in white coats. My enemy was there as well, in a designer suit, looking rested and refreshed and completely composed. He was speaking to me.

"Okay, let's try this again. Do you know who you are?"

I shook my head.

The previous clarity from my awakening was already gone and I sat in their presence under an increasing fog of confusion and fatigue. Thankfully, my pain levels were low but I could feel them building again and my nausea was returning as well.

"Why doesn't he know?" My questioner snapped at a man in a white doctor's coat. "I thought you said the dosage was correct."

"It *is* correct and he *should* know." He replied with some visible consternation.

Actually I *did* know and in my foggy, sleepy state of mind, I had enough of my wits about me to try and leverage my presumed amnesia to my advantage. There was something about my identity that was very important to these dangerous men and although I was helpless, physically shattered and immobile, I determined to forestall whatever demise was coming.

"Let's decrease the dosage and try again."

"But the pain will be too much. He won't be able to stay conscious long enough to talk."

"We don't have a choice. Let's try it anyway."

Why did they have to keep saying that?

Someone adjusted the flow of my IV and within a matter of minutes my midsection erupted in enough agony that I mercifully blacked out again.

CHRIS JACKSON

Chapter Fifteen

Elliott stared at his cell phone, delaying the inevitable. He had been found out. There was no point in running, no hope of escape. Secretly, he had known this day would come. Even before his confession, he knew that they would all be exposed and he knew that between him, Kevin and Ray, he was the odd man out. He thought about his family and the guilt ate him up inside.

How did he let himself get sucked into this?

He had asked the question repeatedly since things began spinning out of control and he asked it again as the Grey Goose vodka started clouding his thinking. While its warm glow crept through his extremities, he ran down the mental checklist he had prepared. If they killed him, his savings and life insurance would more than provide for his wife of twenty-five years. The college funds for their son and daughter, fraternal twins that never ceased to be embroiled in their love-hate relationship, were fully-funded and would provide them with a first-rate education. Yes, his family would be well cared for. He just wouldn't be there to do the caring.

Elliott shivered at the thought of his wife reading the headline of the L.A. Times: "Respected attorney, Elliott Blythe, found dead in a back alley, murdered in cold blood."

Then he shook his head. Kevin Gunther and Ray Gibbs would never kill him. They might isolate him and blame him and let him take the fall but even now he didn't believe they were capable of killing him.

Either way he wouldn't go down without a fight. Although he was a genuinely nice guy and he tended to believe the best in people, he hadn't been naïve enough to fully trust his partners. He had dirt on them too and in the event of his untimely exposure, or worse, the dirt would find its way to the Nightly News with Brian Williams. Of course they were probably aware of that too, which was why they were confronting him now, trying to get him off balance so they could "handle" him and regain control of the situation.

He shook his head again. Despite how he had tried to cover his own backside, insure for his family's financial wellbeing and silence his over-active conscience, it was all falling apart now. He never should have signed on with Kevin Gunther and having made that epic blunder, he never should have talked to that priest.

The cell phone vibrated with another text. "We need to talk."

Shakily, he texted back. "Tell me when and where."

A quick reply startled him. "We're on our way to you now."

He looked around sharply, expecting to see a dark SUV pulling slowly into the parking lot. He glanced down at the bartender who seemed to have forgotten that he was even there. He turned around on his stool and met the hard stare of a large man in a rumpled sports coat with a half-smoked cigar clenched between his jaws. The man was sitting in a corner booth and he motioned for Elliott to join him.

Elliott staggered over to him, the fear and the vodka doing a number on his sense of balance.

"Who are you?" Elliott whispered hoarsely as he slumped into the booth and looked warily at the man.

"Detective Louis Stratton." The man replied, sliding his badge across the tabletop and then covering it with a massive palm.

Elliott shook his head. A detective? This was not at all what he was expecting.

"How did you get my cell number?" He asked, trying to find his footing in the situation.

"I don't have your cell number." The detective replied.

"Then how did you text..." The question died off and Elliott altered it. "You didn't text me saying you were on your way to meet me?"

Detective Stratton shook his head. "No but if someone just did and if that someone is responsible for the stench of fear and vodka on you at 9:15 a.m. then I think you'd better follow me out back to my car."

Elliott shook his head and then buried it in his sweating hands, running them through his wavy, brown hair.

The detective spoke again, "Elliott, I know and I want to help you."

Elliott looked up. "You know?"

The cop nodded. "I know. I've seen the body and believe me, you would rather talk to me than to the people who will be here any second. I need you to get out of this booth and leave with me. Right now."

Elliott's head was spinning and he was regretting his decision to drown his sorrow and fear in Grey Goose vodka when what he should have done was gather his family and race to the nearest international airport. He started crying.

"Mr. Blythe, you're under arrest for drunken and disorderly conduct. Please come with me." Louis Stratton gripped Elliott's arm with the strength of a vice, clipped his wrists together in handcuffs and practically carried him out of the booth and down a hallway through the back of the bar.

The bartender watched them curiously as they slipped out a side exit and then his attention shifted to the front door as it jingled open and a pair of burly men in suits entered and scanned the dimly lit room.

CHRIS JACKSON

Chapter Sixteen

Elliott had stopped crying, his terror yielding to fear-laced curiosity. Detective Stratton was driving calmly but quickly down side streets, hardly slowing through the blind intersections of the residential communities. He was making his way to Highway 1, the Pacific Coast Highway and he hadn't addressed Elliott again, letting him lay curled up on the backseat of the unmarked patrol car. They rushed past the beautiful homes with their tennis courts and custom pools and Elliott felt his fear subside just a little.

"I'm not sure if I should thank you or be scared of you." He offered.

Detective Stratton paused before responding, "I would do both, but you can probably fear me a little less than the people who are after you."

"Do you know who's after me?"

"I have an idea."

"Are *you* after *them*?"

"It depends on what I learn from you. I know you're involved but I don't think you intended to be."

Elliott looked at him hopefully, "How do you know..." he began but he didn't finish the question. His head was still spinning but something in him told him that unplanned words could be his undoing at this moment.

"Where are we going?" He asked instead.

"Somewhere we can talk." They turned north on to the PCH heading toward Malibu.

"So who texted you?" the detective asked as he slipped into his preferred lane and paced the car in front of him.

"I don't know for certain, they didn't identify themselves and I didn't recognize the number. It just said, 'Elliott, we need to talk.'"

"Do a lot of people have your private cell number?"

"No and the crazy thing is that this isn't even my cell phone. I lost my phone two days ago and this is the cheap replacement I picked up until I could find time to shop for a new one. No one has this number, not even my wife. After they texted me they honed in on my location in a matter of minutes. Just like you did." He added a bit defensively.

"Yes but I don't have your Go Phone number either. I had to do it the old fashioned way. I sat down the street from your house this morning and followed you to your meeting at Kevin Gunther's office. How did that go by the way?"

"It didn't. The meeting was a screen to gauge my reaction to something."

"I'm assuming you didn't react well?" Stratton smiled grimly from the front seat.

Elliott ignored the joke. "As I left someone put a note in my hand with the message: 'Elliott, we know.'"

"And your first response was to rush to a bar and begin downing shots of vodka? Not what I would have imagined from someone like you."

"I needed to think and I didn't want to go home or to my office in case I was followed."

The logic didn't really make sense to Louis, so he shrugged and kept driving. Then he asked, "So how much trouble are you realistically in?"

Elliott looked up sharply and wished he hadn't been talking so freely. Cursing the vodka-induced fuzziness, he muttered, "I should probably call my lawyer." Stratton grinned broadly. "Probably a little too late for that, now isn't it?" He signaled and pulled off the PCH and squeezed into a tight parking spot, masterfully demonstrating his parallel parking skills and jerked the car into park. In a series of deft moves that belied his bulky appearance, he reached into the back seat, un-cuffed Elliott, grabbed him by the wrist and pulled him firmly from the car. He shut and locked the doors and began leading Elliott to a sharp cropping of rocks that jutted out above the Pacific Ocean.

After carefully making their way to the edge of the rock wall and pulling Elliott down beside him, Detective Louis Stratton leaned in until his face was less than an inch from Elliott's and whispered intensely, "Mr. Blythe, I don't know what's going on but I've already seen one dead body and I've heard about other murder threats as well. I don't know what your involvement is but I know that Father Stan Jeffries went missing shortly after you confessed to him and now it looks like they're after you, too. For your sake and for your family's protection, I need you to tell me everything."

Louis held his breath, hoping Elliott would cave in and start unraveling this mystery. His partner, Robyn Macomber, was attempting to secure search warrants for Elliott's office and he was hoping to save her the time by securing an immediate confession. A confession to what exactly, he wasn't sure but he knew that Elliott had answers.

Elliott nodded and spoke softly, the tears flowing again, as a cloud of despair settled over his world. "It all started with Kevin and Shelly Gunther's daughter, Moriah."

CHRIS JACKSON

Chapter Seventeen

"What is your name?" I asked the question through dry lips and the words came out like a raspy whisper.

The man in the designer suit smiled at me and then glanced at another man and asked, "What do you think?" The man shrugged his shoulders and replied, "I don't think it matters. He'll eventually remember anyway."

"My name is Kevin Gunther. Do you remember me?"

I didn't. Not exactly. However somewhere deep inside me warning bells went off and I knew that I should fear this man even more than I already did.

Kevin smiled broadly and asked a different question, shifting the discussion away from him. "What can you tell us about the state of your heart?"

In a different setting it might have been a relational question, or a spiritual one but lying in the bed with my itchy abdomen, crushing pain around my lungs and my trembling hands and arms, I knew it wasn't. It was a medical question, asked of me, the patient and I realized with the same dread as before that I *could* tell him about the state of my heart.

"My heart is beating at 111 beats per minute. But it's only pumping about 40% of the blood that my extremities need. That's why my fingers and toes are going numb." Yes, I suddenly realized, I was losing circulation. "The damage was first caused by the bullet. It nicked my left ventricle and was enhanced by a splinter from a broken rib. The rib was initially damaged as the bullet passed by it and then later broke while I was coughing. The splinter is still stuck into the bottom of my left lung (that must have been the source of the thick agony surrounding my breathing) and is also poking into the muscle of my heart."

"Unbelievable, it gets me every time," muttered one of the men in a white coat, while several others murmured their agreement.

Only Kevin was silent with a gleam of victory in his fiery eyes. "Tell us more," he said.

As I continued to speak in my weak, raspy voice, the doctors took copious notes and began hooking me up to a heart and lung monitor and prepped me for an immediate MRI and ECG, no doubt to verify if my self-diagnosis was correct. They were all over me in a flurry of assessment, checking vitals, looking in my ears, up my nose and not so tenderly, checking the stitches on my stomach and chest. Fluid was oozing through them but apparently the thread was holding because no one seemed too concerned.

Someone was tickling my feet and I could feel it. Despite the fear and anxiety I felt in these doctors' presence, a wave of relief at not being paralyzed washed over me. The relief was short-lived; however, because I knew that my spine was badly fractured and the bullet was in exactly the wrong spot, having traveled up from my facet joint and now lodged firmly against the weakest spot of my damaged spinal chord. One strong jolt or push and it could go all the way through, permanently destroying my spine.

My brain was computing these details faster than my emotions could absorb them. It was like the time delay on an international video teleconference wherein a speaker's lips move a few seconds faster than the sound can travel to the other end of the line. My mind would absorb the details of the conditions and then a few seconds later the weight of those details would register in my emotions.

I was dying and if by some miracle I was released and allowed to live, I knew I would never walk again. The damage was too severe. I felt myself slipping into darkness, which seemed to be my new default response to my broken condition and newfound self-diagnosing faculties. This time before I blacked out completely, I remembered something, a real memory, and I knew I could use it as a weapon.

"Kevin," I whispered hoarsely as his name came back to me and the edges of my vision blurred.

He looked at me sharply.

"I know." I barely got the words out and they sounded so faint in my own ears that I wondered if he could hear me. He leaned over me, his face a mere inch from my own.

"What do you know?" He whispered back at me.

I smiled dreamily as I slipped away and that seemed to enrage him. "What do you know?" He demanded again, this time raising his voice to a low growl.

"I know about *her*." The darkness was inviting, comforting even and as I slipped into its embrace, I felt strong hands squeeze my shoulders. "Who are you talking about?"

"I know about Moriah."

Then, mercifully, the pain and darkness overtook me again.

Chapter Eighteen

"Moriah?" Detective Stratton sounded confused.

"Yes." Elliott's voice was still shaking but he was beginning to feel a little bit safer. At least the big detective didn't seem bent on killing him immediately.

"She died a few months ago?"

"Three months and twenty-two days." Elliott confirmed softly.

Detective Stratton looked at him thoughtfully. "So tell me about her."

"She was one of the loveliest girls I've ever known. I loved her almost as much as my own daughter." His voice choked again as another wave of weeping swept over him.

Stratton shifted irritably, the first sign that he was getting impatient with Elliott's emotional breakdowns. "Elliott, this isn't over yet. Talk to me so we can deal with this."

Elliott sniffed and looked at the detective curiously. "I don't know if you can help me. I don't know if I deserve to be helped."

Louis was getting exasperated. "Well, you have three options." He said. "I can arrest you right now as a suspect in Father Jeffries' murder, I can leave you to answer their text messages, or you can give me a chance to try and help."

Elliott's pride drained out of him at that and he sniffed, "You're right. I'm sorry. It's just that it really is so overwhelming. I never dreamed it would have come to this."

Stratton nodded, trying to appear understanding. "You were telling me about Moriah."

"Yes," Elliott continued. "She was a lovely, delightful young woman, the light of her parents' lives. Shelly was never supposed to be able to have children and the birth nearly killed her, so she and Kevin were content to raise her as an only child. They poured their heart and soul into her and they were, by anyone's estimation, an amazing family. They adored her and she adored them, never giving them a moment's grief in her entire young life. It was almost like they were all God's gift to each other, a private little clique that could weather any political storm together."

"How did you know her so well?"

"You don't know?" Elliott asked surprised. "You said you knew. How could you not know my connection?"

Stratton looked momentarily confused but quickly tried to cover his expression.

However, even in his vodka-soaked state, Elliott caught the blank look and knew that Louis Stratton didn't know nearly as much as he had let on.

"Do you know how she died?" He asked the detective in an attempt to move the conversation into a more controlled direction.

Louis caught his intention but couldn't counter him without even more obviously exposing his lack of knowledge, so he shrugged, "I know what the news reports said, that she died from a brain aneurism that hit her while she was jogging."

Elliott smirked, inwardly pleased with how little the detective actually knew. He stalled for a second, trying to decide how much to tell and how much to leave out. He wished his thinking was clearer and he inwardly cursed himself again for clouding his senses at the bar.

Louis helped him. "Elliott, I might not know everything and I'm sure you're right that this is bigger than I realize but I know enough and I do know that you tried to come clean. Father Jeffries wrote everything down."

Elliott jerked at the mention of Father Jeffries' name and Louis knew he had hit a nerve and regained the upper hand.

"Tell me about Moriah," he said. "And then tell me about Father Jeffries."

Elliott nodded and then slowly, carefully, began again. "It all started when Moriah got sick."

Louis relaxed a bit, intentionally calming his racing heart. He glanced out at the Pacific Ocean dotted with surfers and paddle boarders and then quickly scanned the beach and the highway before leaning into absorb Elliott's every word.

"It was a routine sport's physical for her volleyball team when they first discovered the tumor. At first, the doctors thought it was providential that they had detected it so early and their initial assessment found it to be benign. They didn't think it would require surgery and the plan was to simply observe it while Moriah continued her freshman year of high school like a normal teenage girl, at least as normal as the daughter of a celebrity mayor could be." The last sentence was laced with a bitter edge.

"Go on," said Stratton.

"At first it appeared that the doctors had been correct and that the tumor was indeed benign. It wasn't growing and she wasn't having any adverse effects, at least none that anyone could detect. What they didn't know was that it was a very rare tumor that did its damage secretly, poisoning her organs and destroying her from the inside before there were any external signs that something was wrong.

"When she collapsed on her bike ride it was easier to call it an aneurism than to reveal what had actually happened."

"What happened?" asked Louis in spite of himself.

Elliott shook his head slowly. "It was too shocking to seem real. *Every* organ in her body had shut down, every one and when they did the autopsy, her father had insisted on one although the results were never published, the medical examiner estimated that her organs could have belonged to someone in their late eighties instead of a physically fit, fourteen-year-old girl. The tumor, whatever it was, had literally sucked the life out of her insides and aged her internally by about seventy years."

"So she died of old age?" asked Louis incredulously.

"It would seem so, with every organ shutting down simultaneously."

"What did they learn about the tumor?"

"I don't know. I was never privy to that side of the study. What I am familiar with is what happened during the months before she died. I know about Velorum."

"Velorum?" interjected Stratton.

Elliott nodded. "It's a super drug. It endows its patient with a heightened awareness of their own body, literally enabling them to assess and diagnose the condition of their organs, tissues, skeletal structures and nerves. Everything. Combined with a doctor's skill, this trio, drug, patient and doctor, become a nearly miraculous team, able to precisely treat ailments that would normally go undetected and untreated. It eliminates the guessing elements of medicine and provides actual diagnoses and remedies. In theory, it could be the cure for cancer, or even the HIV virus."

"Why do you say, 'in theory'?" interrupted Louis.

Elliott shook his head. Someone was walking in their direction, a beachcomber with a wide-brimmed, straw hat and a faded T-shirt with shorts. Louis shifted nervously, anxious to hear more but somehow aware that he didn't have much time. He sensed that he and Robyn had stumbled into a conspiracy that went way beyond the abilities of a rookie and her soon-to-be-retired partner.

Father Jeffries was still missing, at least one person had been murdered and if the mayor and his people were involved, they certainly had enough power and influence to eliminate a lowly detective that got in their way. He wasn't even sure where to go with Elliott. The mayor was a celebrity with law enforcement. He even had a standing, monthly tee time with the captain, Louis' boss. Although he trusted the captain's integrity, he knew he needed hard evidence before even suggesting that Kevin Gunther was involved with something like a murderous cover-up.

"Why did you talk to the priest?" He asked Elliott suddenly. He knew the question would probably be answered in due course but his curiosity prompted him. Elliott was about to answer when a voice got their attention.

"Hey, don't I know you?"

The voice came from the beachcomber who had shuffled closer to them than Louis had realized and he inwardly cursed himself for getting too engrossed in Elliott's story. He was about to reply when the beachcomber spoke again.

"Yes, I definitely know you. In fact I've been looking for you, Elliott." There was a friendly smile on his face as he said it but his clenched fist, covered suspiciously by a beach towel, was raised and pointing in their direction.

CHRIS JACKSON

Chapter Nineteen

"Kevin, be careful." Ray Gibbs was advising his client and best friend as he had done in hundreds of situations over the years. "Don't hurt him, he's more broken than we expected."

Kevin nodded, trembling and backed away from the man on the hospital bed, making room for the doctors who were crowding around him to implement a battery of expensive, invasive, confirming tests. "But he said he knows, Ray. It's just what we feared and he said her name."

Tears rimmed the mayor's eyes and his usually confident, controlled expression crumbled into a hollow, pleading look. "How did we ever get here, Ray?"

Ray took Kevin's arm and led him out of the room and down a dimly lit hallway before answering. They turned into an empty room and he said, "That's the wrong question, Kevin. The real question is, 'what do we do now that we *are* here?' You know the answer to that as well as I do. We move forward with the plan. This isn't about money or power. It's about the greatest medical breakthrough in the history of medicine, but no one will ever believe that unless we finish the plan."

Kevin nodded, internally compartmentalizing his grief, promising himself that he would revisit it when he had the chance, possibly even sharing it with Shelly. "Thank you, Ray. I know. I just miss her so much."

Ray nodded grimly, allowing the appropriate amount of silence to pass before speaking again. "We found Elliott."

Kevin looked up, renewed interest sparking his hazel eyes. "Why did it take so long?"

Ray shook his head. "He was picked up by a detective that snatched him out of the bar just a few seconds before we got there and drove him out near Malibu. I have no idea how the detective was on to him."

"Did the bug work?"

"Yes. We caught their whole conversation on tape. Elliott was spilling his guts all right but we got there before he said too much. We'll have to deal with the detective but we can probably do it without anything drastic, which would be nice because he's a great guy with exemplary service and multiple commendations. One actually came from you."

Kevin winced at the thought, hating the path they were on but knowing there was no way out of it, at least not if they still wanted to change the world, which they still did.

"So you think it's contained?" He asked.

Kevin seldom questioned Ray's judgment or assessment but Ray nodded affirmatively, understanding that Kevin's emotions and nerves were much more frayed than anyone on the outside could ever perceive.

"It's in process and I should be hearing back momentarily. I intended to check back as soon as we knew if the drug was working. I'll call him now." Ray's cell phone vibrated even as he was reaching for it and his eyebrows arched in surprise, a rare show of emotion and he answered. "Hello."

He listened silently for nearly a minute and then exhaled sharply and ended the call. He looked at Kevin thoughtfully. "He got away," he said. "That detective is impressive."

"What does this mean?" Kevin asked, knowing that Ray was never at a loss for a plan B.

"I think it will be okay. We'll obviously find him again and it might actually work in our favor to have Elliott tell his story to the police. We're covered, Kevin and if we can steer his investigation, this detective might end up becoming an ally. Worst case scenario, we let it fall on Elliott."

"Okay." Kevin replied and then, almost as an afterthought, he added, "Who's the detective?"

Ray paused. "Louis Stratton."

Kevin looked at him blankly. "Doesn't ring a bell."

Ray paused again. "He's the detective from the Spring Break debacle."

Kevin groaned and then smiled ruefully. "I remember him. You're right. He is a good man. I hope we can pull this off without hurting him or anyone else." Then he added, "But that's probably not likely is it?"

Ray shrugged. "We'll see."

There was a knock on the door and a white-coated doctor entered. "We have some preliminary results."

"Already?" Kevin was surprised and pleased.

"Come and see."

Chapter Twenty

"Thank God for rude tourists—I'll never resent them again." Detective Louis Stratton was muttering under his breath as he cautiously slid his car back into the flow of traffic on the Pacific Coast Highway and began speeding toward Malibu. Elliott was too shaken up to respond.

An obnoxious couple in their over-sized Hawaiian print shirts and wide-brimmed straw hats had been noisily chasing their two unleashed Golden Retrievers as they burst in between Stratton, Elliott and their assailant, tangling them up in a literal dog pile. In the moment of distraction, Stratton jerked Elliott to his feet and propelled him up to the street and their waiting parked car where he peeled out of their parking space and slipped quickly away.

Louis was watching the road behind him when Elliott tapped his shoulder weakly.

"What?" Stratton looked at him sharply through the rear-view mirror.

Elliott stretched a trembling hand between the front seats and Stratton grunted as he saw the tiny recording chip that Elliott had pulled from underneath his un-tucked dress shirt. Someone on the over-crowded elevator must have stuck it to him.

Stratton nodded silently, assessing possible scenarios. He gingerly took the bug and then punched a button on his cell phone and listened as it speed-dialed his partner. Robyn Macomber picked up on the first ring, her intense, uptight voice echoing in the receiver, "Where have you been?"

Louis smiled in spite of himself. He hadn't wanted her as a partner. She was too young and he was too old and the last thing he wanted in his remaining year with the force was to break in another recruit. He had done his share of handholding over the years and had objected mightily when she was assigned to his care. His reservation wasn't personal. She was very likeable, easy to coach and had a tireless work ethic. His concern was that she was climbing through the ranks too quickly and he was convinced that the upper brass was too enamored with her Stanford credentials and her beauty queen looks. Despite his concerns, however, she had already proven to be a strong, dependable partner and although he still questioned why she would have chosen this particular career path, he had decided that there were worse things to do with his final months as a detective than coach a recruit with her intellect, commitment and unswerving sense of justice.

"I'm heading to Malibu with Elliott Blythe." He smiled again at the silence on the other end of the phone, as he pictured her feverishly beginning a new entry in her ever-present note pad.

"Where can I meet you?"

"The Pepperdine University library. We can talk in one of the conference rooms where we hold our training seminars."

"On my way," she replied and with that, Louis abruptly changed lanes, pulled off the PCH and began backtracking toward Santa Monica.

Elliott looked at him questioningly and then understood as Louis cracked his window and flicked the bug outside the car and then motioned for Elliott to undress. After throwing his clothes out the window and leaving him naked on the back seat, Louis finally spoke. "We've never had a training seminar at Pepperdine University. Hopefully, this will buy us a little more time."

CHRIS JACKSON

Chapter Twenty One

Ray Gibbs spoke into the receiver, "They're not going to Pepperdine but send a car anyway just to be safe and keep me posted." He hung up and shook his head at Kevin Gunther's questioning look.

"They've got the jump on us for now."

Kevin nodded silently. They were sitting in a small but comfortable office, just a few doors down from where their patient drifted in and out of both consciousness and life.

"There's something else we need to talk about," Ray said.

Kevin looked at him questioningly, nodding for him to continue.

"Rachel just heard that they found Father Jeffries' body. She's on her way here now."

Kevin absorbed the words thoughtfully and then asked, "Should we tell her the truth? News will break soon and it will be better if she hears it from us first."

Ray shook his head slowly. "No, not yet. Let her get through her speech tonight and then we'll tell her when things are more contained. Just comfort her and help her pull it together for tonight."

As if on cue the door opened and the fashion model was there, her eyes ringed with grief and horror and tears streaming down her cheeks. She fell into Kevin's arms and sobbed out the grief of her broken heart.

"Kevin, how did this happen? He was innocent. He was the only one who was innocent." She pulled back from him, dropped her head into her hands and choked back her tears repeating, "How in the world could this have happened?"

Kevin didn't reply, he just reached for a scotch-filled tumbler and sat back in his seat, downing the fiery liquid. It was Ray who spoke next.

"Rachel, you're speaking tonight."

She gave him a horrified look. "Are you serious?" She looked at Kevin pleadingly, "You actually want me to speak tonight after hearing that he's dead?"

"This event is too significant to cancel at this late notice. We need to get through it and process everything else afterwards," Ray replied evenly.

Kevin winced, wishing Ray were less direct. He tried to restate what Ray had just told Rachel by adding his own words of perspective, but he immediately regretted it. "Rachel, the plan has to move forward, especially because this sacrifice must count."

"This sacrifice?" She shrieked at him. Her tears had stopped, replaced with a frightening, cold rage. "You're calling this a 'sacrifice?' This wasn't his cause, Kevin. Don't make it sound like his death is furthering something good. Father Stan's *life* was a good cause. His death will be a shameful tragedy. His death will make ..." but then Kevin interrupted her, his own voice blazing now, "Rachel, I know that you confided in Father Stan."

She stopped. The fire and anger drained out of her with that and she sank into a chair and leaned her head back futilely.

"I know you didn't keep my confidence." Kevin wasn't sure if he should have added that fact, but it had the effect he was hoping for. She began composing herself, steeling her nerves and squashing her raw emotions.

"What time is the banquet?"

Kevin tried to hide his visible relief. "The usual. I'll send a driver to your place."

She sighed, wiping her helpless tears and then asked, "Will Shelly be there?"

Kevin nodded.

She rose to leave without looking at him and said, "Ray, I need a car and I'm coming back here as soon as it's over."

Ray Gibbs rose and followed her grimly out of the room, leaving Kevin alone with his scotch and his thoughts.

The event would go well, Kevin knew. She would dazzle the crowd with her beauty and her innocent devotion to their great cause. His wife, Shelly, would also be flawless as usual and Kevin, himself, would be as passionate as ever, possibly even breaking down near the end when he talked about Moriah, and then he caught himself. When had he started scripting his emotions? When had he started planning how and when to feel? He had never forced emotions before and he knew that had always been his greatest strength. He was a believer, a reformer and he would have done it without the money and celebrity status. Those were just tools, means to help him with his humanitarian ends. Yes, he was aspiring for the governorship and the presidency after that, but the motives behind those ambitions were still pure.

He hated that he had to keep reminding himself of that fact.

Chapter Twenty Two

Detective Robyn Macomber smirked at Elliott Blythe's nude figure, covered only with detective Stratton's Kevlar, bulletproof vest. She tossed him the change of clothes that Stratton had asked for and then turned away to allow Elliott a modicum of privacy. She asked over her shoulder to Louis, "How long do we have with him?"

Stratton shook his head, "I don't think we were followed but I can't be sure. We need him to talk as fast as he can. If they shut this down, or if their plans go underground, we might never get another credible witness."

"How do we know that *he* is a credible witness?" She asked, turning around to face Elliott who looked terribly out of place in Stratton's oversized, dingy running suit.

"Because," Louis responded, "My gut tells me he's a good person and I believe that his conscience will get the best of him."

"Oh, your gut and his conscience." She laughed playfully as she deftly assembled the portable recording device and turned on the microphone. "I'm so glad our only lead hangs on the strength of your gut and this guy's conscience. That's encouraging." Then she added seriously, "Of course, I've seen conscience go out the window for a lot less than the threat of being associated with murder."

"I have too." Stratton agreed softly. "But don't underestimate the power of a clean conscience. It can be one of the strongest forces on the planet and I think Elliott here needs that power."

Robyn looked at him curiously. Maybe all of this focus on a missing priest had triggered Stratton's spiritual side.

Elliott's head was much clearer now that the effects of the vodka were beginning to lift. "Have you contacted my family?" he asked.

Robyn nodded. "They're safe and an officer is on his way there now with instructions to remain outside the house until he hears from us but we don't know how much time we have, so we need you to start talking. Quickly."

Elliott nodded. With his clearing senses his resolve had also returned and the calculating mind that had helped him build a hugely successful law firm was working overtime. He knew his situation was probably hopeless and that it was highly unlikely that he would ever get out of this without jail time, or worse but at least he would try. The detective was right. His full cooperation *was* his best course of action and he grimaced at that thought. It was his full cooperation with Kevin Gunther that had gotten him into this mess in the first place. Yes, a clear conscience would be nice but he was way past that. It would be a miracle if he and his family survived, with or without his conscience.

"Let's get started," he said.

Detective Stratton nodded and checked the lock on the hotel door again.

Detective Macomber moved a microphone up to Elliott's chin and instructed him, "If your testimony exposes corruption and helps us locate Father Stan Jeffries, we will help you cut a deal." She slid him a legal document stating the terms of his confession and verifying the detectives' promises of leniency and then she pushed the record button and said, "Please state the time, date, your full name and whether or not you are making your statement under any form of coercion or duress."

He paused before answering, his shrewd legal mind absorbing the minutia of the document and then he responded, "My name is Elliott Blythe." He scribbled his signature in several places and then continued, "and I am making these statements of my own free will, under no hint of coercion or duress."

Although the recorder was capturing his every word, Robyn began feverishly writing down notes and Louis Stratton leaned back thoughtfully, watching Elliott's eyes and the muscles of his cheeks and jaw while he made his confession.

CHRIS JACKSON

Chapter Twenty Three

"Moriah." The name seemed to fill all the space in my mind while staying just out of reach of my memory. Even while I couldn't consciously recall the person behind the name, the name evoked powerful feelings in me of empathy and regret. Tears wet my cheeks (not unusual in my new condition) but they weren't coming from my physical pain or my declining heart. They were tears of grief. Grief for Moriah.

Who was she? Where had her name come from and why had I told Kevin Gunther that I knew about her? Why had Kevin's tanned, composed face blanched in horror?

It was the last thing I remembered before they changed the dosage on me again. The pain had been unreal, fire burning through every fiber and nerve ending. I heard screaming and realized it was coming from me. My heart literally stopped and I felt the surge of electricity as they shocked me back to life. My skin still burned from where the defibrillator paddles had scorched me.

I was alone in the room now and although I was fading again, I forced myself to stay awake and think, no small task considering that I was still conscious of every organ, tendon and tissue in my body. My mind was backlogged with information about the state of my body and yet I couldn't even remember my own name.

Then suddenly I did remember Moriah. I remembered her face, her shiny red hair framing her large, questioning eyes. I remembered her smile and the splash of freckles that dotted her small nose and rosy cheeks. I remembered her laugh.

I remembered her confession.

Her confession? The memory startled me and I twitched roughly and opened my eyes to see if I had been dreaming. The machines were still droning around me, my IV bag was still dripping its power into my veins and the darkened room was still empty.

I leaned back and tried to enter the memory.

We were sitting in the shade and she was whispering. I assured her that she was safe and that she could trust me. The memories were returning and a sudden surge of hope hit me, relieving the terrors of amnesia.

She could trust me.

Couldn't she? My mind blanked again and I couldn't remember if I had been true to my word or not. Had I kept her confidence, or had I betrayed her? The grief that hung alongside her memory filled me with doubt. Had I hurt her?

"Do you want to talk about your father?" It was a real memory. I had asked her that question while sitting beside her in the dark. She had nodded almost imperceptibly and then whispered barely audibly, "He can never know that I talked to you."

"You have my word." I promised her.

I realized I was sweating as the memory came into focus. It might have been excitement at the possibility of a return of my memories, or it might have been fear of what I was starting to recall.

"You can trust me." I had told her again.

I hadn't kept her trust though. I had broken my promise to her.

I had even assured her a third time, "You have my word."

Then the door opened and someone was turning on lights and adjusting the settings on my IV. As I squinted against the light, the memory retreated and I could feel it slipping away.

"I'm fine." I croaked, fighting to hold on to the image of Moriah's face but it was gone. The frightening nothingness of amnesia had returned.

When I awoke, several white-robed men surrounded me. They were asking me about Stan Jeffries and to my surprise I heard my own voice answering them.

Chapter Twenty Four

"No, it doesn't go there!" The young man looked up as the priest waved him off.

"Over there." He was pointing to a card table with a sign that read, "Boys sizes eight to ten."

It was a pretty impressive display considering that all of the merchandise came from the local residents, with virtually no financial support coming in from any outside organizations. Father Stan Jeffries had started this "community mall" with the stated objective of "improving the quality of all of our lives by a mutual pooling of resources."

He had long been preaching the virtues of communal responsibility, reminding the citizens of the neighborhood that the quality of life in their neighborhood rested solely on their shoulders.

He espoused the "broken window" theory, convinced that dilapidation and neglect only bred further breakdowns and he could be regularly seen with groups of residents painting abandoned buildings, picking up litter and mowing patches of lawn that the city never seemed to get to.

Today was Saturday, community mall day and the participants were rather proud of their makeshift trading post. The old adage, "One man's trash is another man's treasure," proved to be true as streams of people brought in armloads of used clothing and household items and deposited them on long, rectangular, folding tables. While it was true that much of what was deposited would have been deemed "trash" by most accounts, at the end of the day there was usually very little left over to be disposed of.

There were toy sections and art sections and even tools and fitness sections. The categories changed weekly based on the needs of some people and the resources of the people who gave but there was always something unique and interesting to be seen and scooped up by some lucky shopper.

The unique item on this particular Saturday was a beer cap sculpture of the Eiffel Tower. When its proud owner deposited it on the "art" table, he gave Father Jeffries a knowing wink. "It took me longer than you might think to drink enough beers to build this Eiffel Tower."

Father Jeffries smiled at him and before he could even move the unusual sculpture, an elated shopper scooped it out of his hands and excitedly added it to her shopping cart.

That's the way it worked at this "community mall." Rather than sets of individuals struggling to make ends meet, the residents of 21st through 29th streets, eight city blocks, had committed to a radical degree of communal living.

It wasn't just the yard sale items. The residents pooled the little money they had, their possessions and their talents, individual skills and abilities. They developed community services such as home and auto repair and childcare. Very few of the children in the predominantly single parent homes were latch key kids. The families pooled their time and developed some home-made after school programs for all of the kids of their neighborhood.

The quality of life had drastically improved for these families and word was beginning to spread. One newspaper had even interviewed Father Jeffries and some of the residents for a supposed cover story and although the story was bumped to a back page footnote in favor of a celebrity scandal, it was still rewarding to know that their sharing-oriented approach to life and community was beginning to spread.

Father Stan scanned their little "mall" appreciatively, watching as the people gathered and shared their resources. His heart surged with sudden love for them and he allowed himself to drift through the shared memories he had built with them during many years of christenings, baptisms, weddings and funerals (yes, he had performed more than his share of those). Those events bonded people for life and he cherished his relational bond with his congregation. He had been offered larger, more respectable church assignments in the past. Even last week a denominational leader had approached him about a new possibility but these offers barely even registered in his thinking. He was a lifer and he had no ambition to climb the ecclesiastical ranks to attain some level of prominence. He would be happy to perform the christenings, baptisms, weddings and funerals (well, maybe not those) for the *children* and *grandchildren* of these families that he had grown to love so much.

He had counseled them, prayed for them, visited their children in prison and taught them to believe the best about themselves, life and humanity. They were more than a church congregation they were his family and when he was honest with himself, he knew that *he* needed *them* at least as much as they needed him.

Especially in light of Rachel.

His countenance darkened as he thought of her. She had called him that morning, asking to see him. He saw her number come up on his Caller ID but sent her to voicemail. Their last talk hadn't gone well and he still didn't know what to say. She hadn't left a message, so he cleared the screen and stuffed the phone into his pocket, forcefully stuffing his emotions away as well. He wasn't ready and he didn't know if he ever would be. His humor returned briefly as he thought, "Maybe *I* need to see a priest." He chuckled to himself and then shook his head briskly as if to clear it of unwanted thoughts and turned to greet a parishioner that had been repeatedly calling his name.

Chapter Twenty Five

"He is a Catholic priest and he's been working in the L.A. area for twenty years." I was reading the words off the wall of my mind as if they were data on a ticker tape. There was no emotion and no sense of personal attachment. They were just words, memories I suppose, except that I didn't *remember* any of them. I just *knew* them in the same way that I knew who some of the Civil War generals were.

"Does he have any hobbies?"

"No." I responded. "His ministry is his profession *and* his hobby."

"Does he have any close friends outside of his parishioners?"

"No, not really and I don't think his parishioners would really count as 'friends.' He loves them and he is committed to them. They're the center of his world actually but I don't think they're his friends. They're more like his children, his responsibility."

"And what about Rachel?"

Her name had the same unexpected effect on me that it had earlier and I couldn't completely suppress the flood of emotion that it released into my soul.

My questioner exchanged a glance with another man in the room and I knew that I had messed up. Despite my broken condition I was desperately trying to retain the upper hand in my interactions with my white-coated captors and I had just blown it and the frightening thing was that I didn't know *why* I had messed up, or what I had revealed to them. My memories were fading again and I really didn't know who Rachel was and I had no guess as to why my knowledge of her was so important to these men. What I *did* know, and yes this was a real memory, was that I loved her. Yes, that was the emotion. I loved her, but I couldn't remember her and that produced a fresh panic that threatened to strangle me.

Questions rolled into my thinking. Who was she? Where was she? How was I connected to her? Was she in trouble, too? Did she need me? Was she worried about me? Did she know the condition I was in?

"And what about Rachel?" He asked it again.

For a split second, I almost answered in the first person but then I remembered that they weren't talking about me; they were asking me about Stan.

"Yes, the father is close to Rachel but I think they've been recently estranged."

"Estranged?"

"Yes, their last interaction wasn't pretty." An urge to cough tickled my raw throat and with a growing dread of what it would do to my fractured spine, I had to give into it. The cough wracked my skeleton, jarring my badly damaged lungs and sent a pounding pain down my back and up to my temples but surprisingly left my spine intact.

"I don't know the details," I wheezed. "But it was ugly. Hurtful words were exchanged, words that went deep." I realized I was weeping freely again. "He didn't approve of her recent decisions."

The men in the white coats exchanged glances again and I could hear one whisper, "Call Kevin. I think he's ready."

Alarms went off in my brain and I really didn't want to be ready for whatever it was that they thought I was ready for.

"The room is spinning."

They looked back at me sharply and one of them touched the I.V. bag to assess the flow of the meds. "Get him here quickly."

"I can't see." It wasn't a lie. The room had suddenly darkened on me and despite the bright, fluorescent lights beating down on me, everything had grown dim and shadowy.

I think someone was flashing a light in my face and a faraway sounding voice spoke above me.

"I think we're losing him. His pupils are blown. I think it's too late."

My pupils *were* blown and I knew that I was stroking, with my body shutting down, finally giving into the fierce trauma it had undergone.

However in that moment, a strange surge of awareness settled over me, and my hope returned. I knew that it was only a mild stroke and that it wouldn't cause any long-term damage. I also knew how to treat it.

That's when I remembered.

I knew why I was here, and I knew what this whole project was about.

"I'm having a stroke." My words were slurred but audible and they evoked a flurry of activity.

"How do we treat it?"

"It doesn't need treatment. Just let me rest and everything will recover. Sleep will reboot my hard drive." I smiled weakly at my poor attempt at humor and a sudden surge of relief buoyed my soul.

I remembered.

"Get Kevin here *now*!" They were rushing around the room now, talking on cell phones, adjusting the leads and monitors all over my body, checking my vitals and replacing my IV bag. The room grew brighter and I smiled again knowing that my self-diagnosis had been correct. It *was* a mild stroke and I *would* recover from it, at least until my other injuries killed me, and then another flicker of hope hit me. If I could diagnose my stroke, perhaps I could diagnose the rest of my injuries and if I could accurately diagnose them, perhaps I could live.

I realized, suddenly, that I very much wanted to live.

Chapter Twenty Six

"It's all about Velorum." Elliott spoke into the microphone. "The super-drug that enables the user to self-diagnose even the most complex of medical issues."

Robyn Macomber stopped writing her notes and shot an incredulous look at Stratton who merely shrugged.

"Say again," she said to Elliott.

"Velorum. That's what this whole project was about. It was the medical miracle that was going to revolutionize modern medicine and make Kevin Gunther the most powerful man in the world. It still might if Kevin gets away with it."

"It still might? You mean it actually *works*?" Robyn asked in disbelief, her mind beginning to race with the possibilities.

"Yes," Elliott answered convinced. "It's still years away from FDA approval and word will leak to our competitors long before it legitimately makes it onto the markets but we'll be out front and we'll hold the rights."

"We?" Stratton observed.

"Well, Kevin and his people." Elliott amended.

"Do you seriously believe this can work and that a *city mayor* could have such influence in a project like this?"

Elliott looked at Robyn before responding to her question. "Kevin Gunther is more than a city mayor. He's the heir apparent to the White House and there are hundreds of leaders from the business, military and medical sectors that recognize that.

"Velorum's developer came to Kevin first, because he knew Kevin had both the political clout and the personal passion to make Velorum a reality. Kevin is more than a politician. He's a believer in his message and he really will use Velorum to change the world for the good."

Stratton checked the hallway outside the hotel room again as Elliott continued.

"Velorum does work. I've seen it personally. I've sat in the room while sick patients perfectly diagnosed their condition and gave the doctors precise treatment steps. It's both amazing and eerie."

Elliott's eyes took on a faraway look and then he shook his head irritably. "It's unnerving to hear someone with absolutely no medical knowledge describe details of organs and nerve connections that they've never even heard of. One patient was able to tell us that the source of her allergies was actually a virus that had lain dormant for twenty years until an odd chemical from a new brand of perfume reacted with it."

Both Louis and Robyn looked skeptical and Elliott raised his hands in innocence. "It's what I saw and the prescription she gave the doctor worked. Her allergies dried up within a few days."

"How do the patients know the medical terms?" Robyn asked.

"Sometimes they remember terminology from Biology classes from college and sometimes they don't know the terms. They just start describing what they know and the doctors have to interpret it but it's really amazing."

"So this drug, Velorum, enables patients to diagnose their medical problems and, in a sense, tell the doctors what to prescribe back to them for treatment?"

Elliott nodded at her. "Exactly."

"What's the catch?" Stratton asked bluntly.

Elliott smiled faintly and answered, "Yes, the catch. Other than financial concerns there are three primary challenges facing the project. First, Velorum reacts dangerously with any other medicine. Even the slightest mingling of Velorum with any other drug creates a poisonous toxin that can sometimes be fatal."

Stratton's skepticism was increasing. "And the second?" He asked with just a hint of sarcasm in his tone.

Elliott didn't seem to notice. "Since the patients must be weaned off every other med before receiving Velorum, the doctors only have a very small window of time to get the diagnosis from the patient and implement a new treatment regime. If too much time lapses, the sickness can spread and the patient not only loses the possible miracle from Velorum but also whatever time they might have gained from more traditional treatments."

Robyn looked intensely at Elliott and asked, "If the drug has these self-diagnosing properties, couldn't it be taken during routine physicals and check-ups to help with the early recognition?" Louis looked at her in surprise wondering if she was actually buying this testimony.

"Yes, that would be part of the plan." Elliott replied.

"How is it administered?" she asked again.

"Intravenously."

"How extensive has the research been?"

Before he could answer, Louis interrupted, "What's the third catch?"

Elliott nodded darkly and paused before answering. "Velorum is a peculiar drug that has the unique ability to both *enhance* and *subdue* pain. Given in small doses, Velorum amplifies pain levels to an extremely high degree however, once enough of the drug enters the patient's bloodstream it has the *opposite* effect and begins to minimize and anesthetize the pain. Unfortunately, we haven't yet learned how to bypass the initial painful stages and immediately get the patient to a curative one. For now, at least, Velorum hurts its users before it heals them."

He was about to say more when his cell phone vibrated. "It's them," he groaned. Robyn quickly turned the recorder up as Elliott flipped open the phone and heard a voice say, "Elliott, your family is worried about you."

Chapter Twenty Seven

"Kevin, it's working!"

Kevin looked up quickly at the interruption, his fatigued expression fading into a grin of triumph. "How long do we have?"

"No way to tell but he just accurately diagnosed a mild stroke."

Kevin was already rushing down the hallway. He caught up with a white-coated doctor who turned to him as he approached and said, "Wow, Rachel looked upset when she left. Is everything okay with you two?"

Kevin slowed slightly and offered a curious look at the doctor who kept staring resolutely ahead. "What do you mean 'you two'?"

Before the doctor could answer, Kevin's cell phone vibrated and a voice began speaking before he had even said hello. "Kevin, we've found him. I'll check back shortly."

Kevin closed the cell phone with a relieved sigh, thankful for Ray Gibbs' efficiency. He just hoped they had reeled Elliott Blythe back in before he shared too much with Detective Louis Stratton. He muttered a curse as he thought about Stratton.

Louis Stratton was a good man with an impeccable record and unswerving loyalty to law and justice. Kevin would have liked to garner his personal loyalty but despite Ray's optimism about winning him to their side, he knew that Stratton would never agree to participate in the Velorum trial. There were too many questionable loose ends and too many unanswerable ethical questions. Kevin respected men like Stratton but he also found them frustratingly short sighted. Velorum would change the world and provide miraculous answers to the frantic prayers of countless families. It would be worth whatever sacrifices it cost in the short-run.

Besides, he mused, Stratton and men like him couldn't understand. They hadn't had their only daughter die in their arms because Velorum *wasn't* available. No, he concluded, he didn't need Stratton. Ray was right to view him as an unfortunate casualty. He momentarily faltered in his stride though, as he wondered just how far the collateral damage would go and then an unexpected wave of sorrow for Moriah blindsided him, causing him to walk even slower.

The doctor looked at him with some concern. "Mr. Gunther, I'm sorry if I overstepped by asking about Rachel."

Kevin smiled weakly, grateful for the shift in thought. He collected his composure and answered stiffly, "There's nothing going on between Rachel and me."

"Yes sir," the doctor responded uncomfortably.

When they arrived at the dimly lit hospital room, they could hear a flurry of activity inside and both men were grateful for the distraction.

Their patient appeared to be drifting off to sleep. His eyelids were fluttering slits that threatened to close. "Keep him awake." Kevin demanded and a doctor adjusted the flow of the IV bag in response.

The patient's eyes opened slowly and a flicker of recognition passed through them, replaced almost instantly with the blank, pain-haunted look they had carried for the past 48 hours. The recognition passed so quickly that Kevin almost doubted that he'd seen it but no, it had definitely been there. He had identified him.

"Is he stable?" Kevin asked the team of doctors urgently.

"Yes, for the time being. I think we've gotten a handle on his pain and if we can keep him comfortable he should be able to begin diagnosing."

And remembering, Kevin thought wryly.

"How bad are his injuries?" Kevin already knew the answer but he wanted to know if there was any renewed optimism among the team.

There was a collective headshake from the medical team. "No hope for him. He's way too damaged but hopefully we can get what we need before he passes."

"How long will that be?"

"A day. Maybe two."

The words sounded harsh and grating to Kevin, even though he himself had just mentally discarded Detective Louis Stratton. He wondered if all of his colleagues sounded this cold and calculating and he suddenly longed for the earlier years of vision and inspiration when their mission had been cleaner and simpler and no one would have even considered any of the fatal consequences that now seemed inevitable.

He shook his head angrily, alarmed that he was so easily distracted, especially since they were closer than they had ever been to tying up this particularly dangerous loose end. He bent forward again to look into the patient's eyes. Yes, there was definitely recognition but the man was hiding it well and suddenly Kevin felt a wave of panic and he wondered how long the man had been feigning his amnesia.

"He knows." He snapped at the lead doctor who had walked with him down the hallway. "And he's known for a while. Find out how long he's known and then find out *what* he knows."

He turned back and found the patient's eyes closed and his chest falling and rising in rhythm.

He cursed again. Either this man was unexpectedly shrewd even in his deteriorating state, or they had pushed him too far and would never be able to extract what he knew.

Chapter Twenty Eight

I didn't know what else to do, so I kept pretending to sleep but I could feel Kevin Gunther's eyes burning into my face. He knew that I knew and I cursed inwardly, berating myself for being so careless and for losing the only leverage I possessed in this horrifying game. Broken and helpless, my only hope had been to prolong their belief in my amnesia until I learned enough of their plans to somehow use it against them but I had been careless and I had allowed my anger at Kevin to take over and now he would be relentless in wringing the information out of me. While they were convinced of my ignorance there was a remote chance that they wouldn't pursue it anymore and would perhaps let me go.

No, that was stupid, wishful thinking. I was a dead man after all and besides, Kevin would never let me go, *could* never let me go. Everything had changed after his wife visited me that night and I knew that I would forever be Kevin's enemy.

The memory came back to me, even as I felt Kevin's probing eyes on me and heard his voice barking orders above me.

"Wake him up, get him talking!"

Kevin's voice faded in to the background as I was drawn in to the memory. It was a warm autumn evening, as most autumn evenings are in Los Angeles. Shelly Gunther had called my private number and against my better judgment, I had answered it. Before she said hello, I knew she would ask to meet me and I knew I would comply. How could I not?

"I need to see you." Although expected, her words still startled me, as did my response.

"Where are you?"

She gave me directions and I was out the door within ten minutes, pulling into traffic on my way to see her.

The warning alarms were fierce in my head as I drove but I knew I didn't really have a choice. The time for walking away had long since passed and whatever consequences awaited me were now mine to bear.

Even so, my conscience argued with me and a sense of foreboding cautioned me.

I sighed deeply and signaled a left hand turn, failing to notice the headlights that made the same turn several car lengths behind me. I suppressed a smile as I lay in the hospital bed reliving the memory. In my memory I saw what I had been unable, or unwilling, to see in real life. I had been followed. I knew it now, although I had missed it in the emotion of driving to see Shelly.

Then another thought tumbled into my reverie. Did Shelly set me up or was I just randomly followed? She could have easily used me to force Kevin's hand but no, I realized that despite everything, I still trusted her. She was too broken and her grief was too real. Shelly wouldn't have set me up. It had to have been Kevin and his ever-present suspicion. He must have discovered our conversations and decided to have me surveyed.

I made the left-hand turn and looked down at my cell phone as Shelly called again, no doubt wondering how far away I was. I silenced the phone and turned into the vacant parking lot.

She was waiting.

Chapter Twenty Nine

Detectives Stratton and Macomber looked warily at Elliott Blythe as he repeated again more firmly, "I have to cooperate with them. They're threatening my family for God's sake."

Robyn looked at the cell phone that Elliott had just closed and shook her head. "Elliott, there's already been one murder and Father Stan is still missing. We can't let you walk back into their control until we know more of what's going on."

Elliott responded to her evenly. "I don't have a choice. They're desperate to keep Velorum under wraps and my only hope is to convince them that I've come back to my senses and won't cause them any more problems."

"And how will you do that?" Detective Stratton asked softly. "They had you bugged so they know you started telling me about the drug and you've already gone on the record testifying against them. They'll never trust you again."

Elliott stared at the big man for a moment wishing he had never confided in him or his eager, young partner. It was his fear and the alcohol that undid him. That combination had always been his downfall.

"I haven't told you anything that you can use against me." He said finally. "Nothing that I've disclosed up to this point is illegal."

Louis exhaled loudly and rocked back in his chair. It was true. Elliott hadn't shared anything illegal or incriminating before they were interrupted. Ambitious medical experimentation certainly had the potential to turn ugly but at this point there was no crime that could be proven. Elliott's legal expertise had seen to that.

Stratton's voice rose slightly, "Elliott, don't do this."

But Elliott interrupted him. "Please. This is the only way. Let me cooperate with them. Let me attempt to negotiate with them and then funnel information to you as I'm able. Believe me, I still want to help you but I *must* try to protect my family. Besides," he continued steadily, "if you try to detain me, I'll clam up. You can't hold me for anything and no laws have been broken today."

His voice was sounding more confident and lawyerly and Louis and Robyn nodded slowly together as they weighed the reality of his words. It was true that Elliott had been terrified when Louis met him in the bar and then the suspicious man at the beach had spooked him but beyond that, they had nothing. There was no proof that Father Jeffries had been murdered or even injured and there was certainly no visible connection between his disappearance and the mayor's office. Elliott's sensational story about a wonder drug conspiracy was interesting and even worth looking into, but there was nothing concrete to it. Unless they could capture the details of his testimony, or receive some other hard evidence of wrongdoing they were momentarily stuck.

"Okay," Louis finally said. "We'll follow you."

"No," Elliott said firmly. "There's something else you need to do." He reached his hand toward Robyn's note pad. She mutely handed it to him and he began to write.

An hour later Ray Gibbs was watching Elliott Blythe through the tinted, one-way glass. He had been naked when they found him, covering himself with blankets from the hotel bed. He said the cops questioned him and then left him when they didn't learn anything of substance but Ray knew that wasn't the case.

Elliott had told them plenty and there was obviously a reason that they had let Elliott be taken, especially after the fiasco on the beach. They probably knew their best hope for a bust was to have Elliott face Kevin and Ray, attempt to re-enter their trust and then begin funneling evidence to them on the outside. The question was how much had he already told them and how risky was it for Ray to play along? Although not personally involved in the Velorum project, Elliott had provided substantial amounts of legal advice and support from the beginning. He didn't know everything but he certainly knew enough to hurt them.

He knew about Moriah, Kevin's daughter, and Ray needed to know what Moriah had told Elliott. More than that, however, Ray needed to know what Elliott had in turn told the priest.

Ray studied Elliott's haunted, terrified expression and knew that despite his fear, Elliott was a shrewd and cunning man who knew exactly what to say and who to say it to. Ray needed to be careful not to underestimate him, not that he was likely to do so. Ray seldom underestimated anyone.

Ray slowly entered the room and merely nodded.

"So have you really contacted my family?" Elliott asked softly.

Ray shook his head, yes.

"And is he really dead?"

Ray nodded again without speaking.

Elliott felt his defenses crumbling and was overcome with a need to beg and plead for his family's safety but he forced himself to stay quiet, determined not to play that easily into Ray's hand. He bit his cheek and studied Ray in turn.

Ray Gibbs was an intriguing man, a brilliant lawyer with impeccable credentials, a superior business understanding and an uncanny ability to read people. He was one of the most respected and feared, attorneys in Southern California and possibly even the country. For all of his brilliance however he was extremely adept at avoiding the limelight, preferring to pull the strings from the background like Mario Puzo's Godfather.

Elliott smiled suddenly at the comparison and then quickly replaced his smile with a troubled look. The last thing he wanted was for Ray to employ Godfather-esque tactics with his family and he knew that Ray was capable of doing just that. Decapitated horse heads weren't out of the question with Ray.

It hadn't always been that way.

Ray and Elliott had actually been friends with a history dating back to their pre-law days. Elliott was one of a very few young men who could match Ray in his intellectual curiosity and personal intensity. They had bonded immediately, rented an apartment together in law school and pushed and challenged each other through the countless late nights of study and the agonizing preparations for the California State Bar exam.

They both passed the Bar with flying colors on their first attempt and briefly considered practicing in the same firm. Elliott respected Ray and despite a ruthless streak that he saw in him, Elliott would have never questioned his integrity or concern for law and justice. Ray was one of the good guys and his ambitions went way beyond making money and retiring rich. He truly wanted to change the world.

Kevin Gunther wanted that too.

Kevin and Ray had been friends even longer than Elliott had, their history going clear back to Jr. High where they played basketball and ran track and field together. Throughout all of the angst and emotion of high school and college their friendship remained constant. Ray and Kevin, two idealistic dreamers, stuck together, fueling one another's desire to contribute to the greater good and make the world a better place.

They were a compelling duo and Elliott had immediately sought the same type of acceptance from Kevin that he had found with Ray. Kevin had an innate charisma that at once inspired and intimidated. He was quick to laugh, quick to encourage and was able to turn the slightest injustice into a world-changing cause, like he did their freshman year in college after he became student body president and instantly set out to divert some of the school's funds to fighting poverty in the neighborhoods that surrounded their school campus.

Although never as close relationally to Kevin as he was to Ray, the three of them formed an unspoken alliance to become the best emerging leaders they could be and leave a lasting legacy of justice in their generation.

Those days seemed like a lifetime ago.

In the years that had transpired, Ray and Kevin had changed. Although they still possessed a fervent zeal to change the world, Ray in his quiet, behind-the-scenes way and Kevin in his dynamic, up-front way, their passion had consumed them. The big leagues of political ambition had taken a toll and by the time Elliott had veered away to found his own firm, he was already alarmed at the change he saw in the two men.

Ray had never married and instead buried himself deeper and deeper into the intrigues of his work. Kevin seemed driven, as if possessed, by a need to push the boundaries of what was possible.

It began with initiatives to eradicate poverty, a concern that was as deep in Kevin's nature as anything else and then it spread to medical cures and technology. Convinced that cures for such evils as cancer and HIV were not only possible but within reach, Kevin began a feverish campaign to attract world-class doctors and scientists to help him assemble "the generation that would change it all."

It was his work in these areas that had attracted the support he needed to assume the Mayor's position in Los Angeles, a position that most people rightly believed was a mere stepping stone to bigger and better things but it was mid-way through his second term as mayor that Moriah had become sick.

Elliott looked into Ray's eyes again, wondering if his old friend was thinking any of the same thoughts.

"Are they okay?" Elliott asked quietly, desperately hoping that old ties would garner some mercy for his family.

"For now." Ray answered.

Elliott sighed and conceded. "What do I need to do?"

Ray paused before answering, "Tell me everything."

Chapter Thirty

"I hope we made the right decision," Robyn Macomber said as she and Louis Stratton drove slowly back to their office. When Elliott took the phone call in the hotel room and learned that his family had been contacted, it had seemed like the best option; indeed Elliott had insisted it was the *only* option. The caller hadn't overtly threatened Elliott's family but even his veiled inference was enough to cause Elliott to shut down.

The caller tried to placate Elliott insisting that things had been needlessly blown out of proportion and that they simply needed to talk. The voice on the phone had said, "Elliott, one conversation can clear up any misunderstanding. We simply need to know what you heard, what you're thinking and also what you said to the priest." There were no names or details given, nothing incriminating if the recording were ever played in court.

Robyn and Louis hadn't bought a word of it but they also didn't have a scrap of evidence of any wrongdoing. The best they could do was keep snooping around on their own while Elliott tried to re-enter Kevin Gunther's trust and look for ways to funnel evidence to them on the outside.

Louis hated the plan and he wasn't at all sure they had done the right thing. Even though Elliott was insistent that it could work, as most desperate husbands and fathers would be, Louis was almost certain it would end badly. Even though it was difficult to picture Kevin Gunther and Ray Gibbs as cold-blooded killers, he knew that they had landed themselves in a desperate situation and he knew that desperation could turn men dangerous very quickly.

He grunted and responded to Robyn's statement, "I think it's the best option we have. Let's see what Elliott left us and pray that he contacts us soon."

She nodded, looking down at the address and locker combination scribbled in Elliott's handwriting and then glanced out at the houses and palm trees as they sped past them. "Do you believe his story?" She asked.

"Which part?" He sniffed.

"The whole thing, about Velorum and its potential to cure cancer and HIV?"

"I believe the day will come when doctors find those types of cures." He answered. "I have a harder time believing that a city mayor, regardless of his political potential, could be at the center of such a story and I have a hard time believing what Elliott said about Moriah."

Robyn nodded. Yes, she found that part of Elliott's confession to be especially troubling too. "That's why we need to find Father Jeffries." She said, "If Moriah went to him as Elliott suggested, then we would have two testimonies."

Stratton laughed, "Yes, from a lawyer and a Catholic priest, not the most appealing witnesses in some circles."

Robyn smiled in response but didn't laugh.

"I think Father Jeffries is different." She said finally.

Louis grinned and shook his head. "I think it's the best option." He repeated. "We need evidence and Elliott'll never be able to get it to us if he thinks his family is in danger."

"But what makes you think they won't just kill him?" she countered. "There's already been at least one murder and the guy you met in Malibu certainly wasn't there to have a conversation with you."

She was right but under the circumstances and with Elliott's refusal to consider any other options, it was the best they had come up with. They left him sitting naked in the hotel room, snuck quickly back to their waiting car and began driving back to their office. Stratton took the note from Robyn's hand and looked at Elliott's cryptic message. It listed an address, a locker number, a combination and instructions to be there at 7:00 pm sharp.

He shook his head and muttered softly "What a horrible plan."

Chapter Thirty One

Shelly was in my arms sobbing uncontrollably before her head even hit my chest. I remembered the moment so clearly as I lay in my hospital bed and the emotions of that night began crowding back into my soul.

Nervous to be seen together, I had led her to my car, opened the passenger door for her and prepared to merge into the light flow of evening traffic. As I pulled back on to the street, a car sped past us and a smattering of light bulbs flashed into my upturned gaze. Before I could begin speculating about who was holding the camera however, Shelly began to speak in a low, choked voice.

"I don't know if I can do this."

She faltered as her voice broke off and her shoulders shook with her sobbing and when she looked up at me, her face was filled with a mixture of agony and compassion. "I saw them," she whispered.

"Again?" I asked with mounting anxiety.

She nodded.

"And you're sure you couldn't be mistaken?" My words sounded hollow in my own ears but I had to cling to even a shred of hope that perhaps Shelly *had* been wrong.

Her silence discouraged me more than any affirmation could have.

I asked her again anyway, "Are you sure?"

She nodded, the tears still streaming freely down her face, and then it was my turn to fall apart. My insides were cold and I suddenly felt like I was going to faint. The road in front of me looked hazy and the sensations from the steering wheel in my hands felt distant and dull. I wasn't breathing so I inhaled sharply to catch my breath.

Shelly gripped my hand and in a blur of tears I pulled the car onto the shoulder of the road. I pushed the gearshift into park and turned to her as the same racing car sped toward us from the opposite direction threatening to collide with us. At the last moment it swerved and just missed sideswiping us but as it sped away I saw another scattering of flash bulbs as its mysterious driver continued surveying us.

I still couldn't think about that though because at the moment my heart had broken into a thousand pieces and disappointment was flooding into every crevice of my soul.

Rachel and Kevin.

Shelly was regaining her control and her voice was a little stronger.

"They can't know that we know, at least not yet. We can't risk damaging the project."

"Shelly." My voice sounded strangled in my own ears but she cut me off.

"No! We're so close and we can't de-rail our progress. We'll deal with it after."

There it was. That was why she was the perfect wife for Kevin Gunther. Their lives, quite literally, were not their own and despite her own pain Shelly was refusing to relinquish her and Kevin's vision of a better world but then her voice grew bitter.

"Our daughter dies and he decides to have an affair." She fell silent again and then looked at me tenderly and added, "I'm so sorry for you, too."

I nodded in the dark and she gripped my hand as we both wept silently. After several minutes of sniffing and coughing I told her. Before I could internally edit my words or apply wisdom to their timing, I blurted it out, "Moriah came to see me."

Even on the side of the darkened road, I could see her recoil visibly and I could hear her sharp intake of breath.

Her question was inevitable. "How much did she tell you?"

"Enough."

We sat in silence for several agonizing seconds before she whispered, "Was I right?"

"Shelly, I can't," I began but she interrupted me sharply.

"Don't you dare tell me that my daughter came to see you and then not answer my question! No matter what the answer is, I need to know."

She was right and I knew I would need to tell her everything and I also knew it would devastate her even more than her discovery of Kevin and Rachel's affair and I was disgusted with myself. Why had I chosen that moment to tell her? My head started spinning again and I felt like I was losing my grip on the situation and then a mocking voice laughed inside my head. What grip on the situation? I had no grip on the situation. I was running in front of an avalanche of events that were about to overtake me along with everyone I loved.

Shelly was staring at me from her tear-streaked eyes.

"Are you all right?"

The words weren't from Shelly they were from a white-robed doctor who was flashing another little light in front of my eyes. My pillow felt wet around my neck and I realized that I had been crying my way through the memory.

Rachel and Kevin.

Moriah.

Chapter Thirty Two

Elliott began. "I told Father Stan everything."

Ray nodded. He already guessed that of course but he was visibly relieved to hear Elliott admit it so easily.

"Why? If you were trying to take us down, why go to a priest?"

Elliott looked at him quizzically. "I wasn't trying to take you down. I hope you succeed."

Now Ray was confused.

"Ray, I still believe in Velorum. We *need* Velorum and I want it to work as much as anyone does. I didn't go to Father Stan to try to expose you. Father Stan's a priest for God's sake. Who is *he* supposed to tell?"

Ray considered that for a moment, inwardly amused with how he had overlooked such a simple possibility. Elliott hadn't set out to betray them after all. He simply needed a priest! He laughed out loud at the revelation and then exhaled a sigh of relief before resuming his lawyerly composure.

"It doesn't change anything, Elliott." He said still smiling bemusedly.

Elliott nodded. "I know."

Ray started another question then changed directions and asked curiously, "Did it help?"

Elliott looked confused.

"Seeing a priest?"

For the briefest moment Elliott felt the familiar emotions of friendship and brotherhood that he and Ray had enjoyed through their young adulthood. "Surprisingly, yes. You should try it."

Ray smiled grimly and shook his head. "I don't know if a priest could handle my confession."

Elliott wasn't sure how to respond. Ray was never given to much introspection. His skill set lay in the arena of cold, calculated analysis but still, every person has a conscience and a need for absolution.

"Ray, will you please keep my family out of this? I swear I won't hurt you or Kevin. Just tell me how I can fix this and then let me get out. I'll return to private practice, I'll shred all of my documents and I'll never breathe another word about Velorum."

Ray was silent for a moment staring hard into Elliott's pleading eyes. Elliott thought he saw a flicker of compassion in Ray's gray gaze until he shook his head and responded. "It's too late for that and you know it. That card possibly, *possibly*, could have been played in the beginning but after Moriah..." His voice cut off and he shook his head angrily.

"Elliott, there's no way. You're in this just as deep as we are and besides Detective Stratton was clever enough to find the bug before you spilled your guts to him so I have no proof of how much you actually blabbed." The flicker of compassion was gone. "How much did you tell him anyway?"

Elliott shook his head desperately, "I told him about Velorum. I told him that it wasn't just a fantasy but that it actually works but I swear I didn't give him details on how it's been tested and I didn't tell him about Moriah."

Ray looked doubtful but didn't press the issue. He shifted the discussion back to the priest. "Why Father Stan?"

"Sorry?"

"Why Father Stan? If your conscience was bothering you and needed to confess to someone why choose Father Stan? Why not go to someone completely removed from the situation? Why go to someone so close to everything?"

"I think I *needed* someone close to the situation. I needed someone who could genuinely understand the pressure and the trauma without being distracted by the incredible claims of Velorum. Father Stan was the safest person I could think of. He's a priest. He has to keep my confession confidential but he also knows Kevin, so he understands the pressure that prompted some of our decisions."

Ray shook his head. "We weren't pressured into anything, Elliott. Everything we have done has been carefully thought out, planned and necessary."

Now Elliott shook his head, anger building inside him.

"Necessary? You're really telling me that Moriah was 'necessary.' Does Kevin know you think so?"

Ray's voice blazed in response, "It was Kevin's idea, Elliott."

Elliott was stunned. The oxygen seemed to get sucked out of the room with that revelation and he grew light-headed and dizzy.

"It was *Kevin's* idea?"

Ray didn't answer, irritated with himself for divulging the information. Perhaps he was too close to Elliott and someone else should be handling his interrogation.

"Elliott, I will always view you as a friend but what you did was inexcusable. I'm sorry but I can't promise you anything until I *know*." He got up and walked briskly toward the door while Elliott called after him.

"Ray, stop! Let's figure this out. We can fix it. I know we can. Please, Ray. My family."

Ray knocked sharply on the door and it immediately opened to allow another man in the holding cell with them. He was carrying a stiff duffel bag and he had a grim, determined look on his face that made Elliott's pulse start fluttering rapidly.

He was done crying. His grief and fear were hardening into desperation.

And a plan.

After all he could be a dangerous man too.

Chapter Thirty Three

Back at their office, Detective Louis Stratton hadn't said a word although he had chewed through half of his cigar without lighting it. His partner, Robyn Macomber, had been equally silent as she listened and re-listened to Elliott's confession. One part in particular had captured her attention and she had replayed it at least a dozen times.

Stratton didn't seem to mind. A veteran detective with an impressive list of solved cases to his credit, he understood the unique habits and thought processes that accompanied the initial absorption of evidence. His personal approach was to quietly smoke his favorite brand of macanudo cigar while letting his mind ruminate without any structured effort. By allowing his thoughts to drift through the evidence on their own accord, he could usually identify anomalies that he might have missed if he focused too hard.

It had frustrated a lot of his partners who didn't understand his approach. By no means lazy or a procrastinator, he was known to sit in thought for an entire day chewing on his lit, or sometimes unlit, cigar, until something from the evidence jumped out at him and that was a pretty good description of how it happened. While other detectives would do endless research and review their notes a hundred times, Detective Stratton would let the answers come to *him*.

Robyn's approach was different but she didn't seem troubled by his. In fact, she barely seemed to notice that he was still in the room with her. She rewound the tape again.

Elliott was speaking.

"So I went to tell Stan everything."

Louis' voice interrupted him, "You mean the father?"

"Yes." Elliott sounded impatient with the interruption.

She rewound it again. "So I went to tell Stan everything."

She finally looked over at Louis. "Why did he call the father by his first name?"

Stratton's thoughtful eyes focused instantly and twinkled curiously. "What are you thinking?"

"He knew the father. Do you think the father was either in on it, or at least knew something about it?"

Stratton looked at his young partner approvingly. "So what's the next step, Sherlock?"

"I don't know. They took him too soon. We needed five more minutes with him but I don't think Father Jeffries was simply an objective outsider that Elliott confided in. I think he was more deeply connected." Then a troubled expression clouded her features and she asked quietly, "But do you think Kevin would actually have done that to his own daughter? He was crazy about her. Everyone knows that and I don't think it was a publicity stunt. I've seen them together and I can promise you their father-daughter bond was legit."

Louis looked at her thoughtfully, suddenly realizing that he had never bothered to ask her any questions about her own family. "I think that's where this is headed," he said grimly.

There was a perfunctory knock on the door to their office and then their boss, Captain Troy Majors entered brusquely and asked, "Got a minute?"

The young captain didn't seem happy.

"Why did you request all of the files we have on Kevin Gunther's administration?" He demanded.

Stratton's heart sank. "We're still looking for the missing priest and one of our leads seemed to indicate that at one point he was involved with the mayor."

"So you *suspect* the mayor's office of something?"

Robyn and Louis were silent.

Captain Majors continued. "Mayor Gunther is off limits. He is the best mayor this city has ever had and the last thing we need is to jeopardize this office's relationship with him by a slanderous, irrelevant investigation." He looked at them intensely. "Whatever lead you think you have it's nothing. Am I clear?"

"Yes sir." They said in unison.

He closed the door behind him and the two detectives looked at each other in shock and curiosity. "So we're on to something," Robyn said with a pleased smile.

Stratton nodded but felt a cold knot in the pit of his stomach. To be shut down this early in the investigation definitely did not bode well for his future and that, he knew, was because he had never been the type to be easily shut down.

Chapter Thirty Four

"My guess is twenty-four hours, tops."

The room fell strangely silent at the words. The only noise was the pulsing sound of the ventilator that was keeping me alive. They had hooked me up to it about an hour earlier after my throat collapsed and I had nearly suffocated.

I think I had been crying too hard reliving the memory of my conversation with Shelly. I felt my throat swelling and in an incredibly surreal way I knew that it was about to swell shut and cut off the flow of air through my trachea.

I also knew what they should have done to treat it.

Fluid had built up in the tissue and a simple lancing procedure would have allowed them to drain the area and restore enough space for the oxygen to pass through. Unfortunately, with my thickening airway, I had been unable to tell them that and in their urgency to keep me alive, they intubated me.

At first, I hated the experience. I could count all of the scratches that the tube caused to my larynx as it was roughly inserted and I knew (I was still curious about *how* I knew) that it wasn't likely that I would ever breathe on my own again. I think that's what the twenty-four hour thing was all about.

My body was shutting down and toxins were coursing freely through my bloodstream. Yes, twenty-four hours was about right.

Strangely though, I also felt some relief because dependent as I was on the breathing machine, there was no way that these men could force me to talk and I realized with sharp clarity that it was imperative that they *not* get me to talk.

My memories had returned.

All of them.

"Twenty-four hours? And how soon can we get him off the ventilator?"

It was Kevin Gunther's voice and I hoped to God that he wouldn't be able to get them to try extubating me. Kevin had a way with people though and he usually got what he wanted.

"Mr. Gunther, he's not coming off this ventilator. His organs are shutting down. He's done for."

Kevin's face radiated cold fury. "That is not acceptable. I need him to talk before he dies. You make that happen, no matter what it takes."

I expected the doctor to disagree, to tell Kevin that it was impossible but he didn't. Instead he reached for my I.V and increased the flow of Velorum that was dripping into my veins.

Yes, Velorum, that's what this was all about. It was supposed to be Kevin's swan song, securing his mark in history as the catalyst behind the greatest medical breakthrough of all time.

Kevin leaned over me and whispered fiercely in my ear. "I know you can hear me and I know you can talk to me. I need to know *everything*. I need to know what he told you and I need to know what you did with the information."

I opened my eyes and looked directly into his hazel ones staring at me from two inches away. A shiver of fear ran up my spine (a strange experience considering that I was already a dead man) and I don't know why I did it but it sent him into a rage.

I winked at him.

He probably would have struck me except that even in his emotional frenzy he stayed in control. That was an indelible mark of Kevin's character; he never lost control. He smiled grimly at me. "You're not dying until you talk to me."

I shook my head and made writing motions with my left hand.

Kevin noticed the movement and barked at one of the doctors, "Get him something to write on!" They pressed a permanent marker into my hand and held a yellow, legal pad beside me. My writing was barely legible but Kevin could still read the three words.

"It wasn't Elliott."

He blanched. He was losing his grip and I could tell the room had started spinning around him.

"Who?" He whispered hoarsely.

I scribbled a name.

He choked. "You're lying."

I shook my head. Even if I was betraying her by telling him it didn't matter. She would admit it as soon as he asked her. That was her greatest strength. There was nothing hidden in her character. She probably had the cleanest conscience of anyone I had ever met.

Kevin ripped the pen out of my fingers and tore up the page I had written on. He looked menacingly at the roomful of doctors. "Get him talking within the next hour."

As he stalked out of the room, I prayed in my mind that Shelly would weather the storm and I prayed that it wasn't a mistake to send him down that path.

Chapter Thirty Five

Shelly opened her journal, its polished leather scent mixing with the lighter, breezy fragrance that always seemed to permeate her office.

The room was perfectly suited for her personality. No overhead lights, simple yet elegant décor adorned the corners and bright, classy curtains and drapes covered the generous picture windows. The curtains were pulled back and they revealed a charming, sitting garden replete with birds of paradise (her favorite tropical flower), bougainvillea and twelve different varieties of palm trees but the real beauty was what lay just beyond her garden, the Pacific Ocean.

Although raised in the Midwest, she was an ocean-lover to her core. Crashing waves had always provided better therapy than what she received from the high-end counselors she had seen and until recently, a simple walk along the beach was able to provide her with at least momentary twinges of hope amid the many dark days that she and Kevin had weathered. Even today, she felt gratitude for being allowed to live in what she believed to be the most beautiful community in the world. The Southern California coastline would always have her heart.

As would Moriah.

Her picture was the only item on her all-glass writing desk and as Shelly looked at it thoughtfully, her resolve hardened.

She would go through with it after all. Earlier in the morning she hadn't been sure but now, looking once again into Moriah's twinkling, blue eyes she knew she couldn't live with herself any other way.

She held her favorite writing pen loosely, a well-used medium point ink pen with a refillable core, and smoothed the pages of her journal to begin a new entry.

Her penmanship was both bold and feminine, precise strokes connecting with gentle loops and curves. She journaled several times each week and she found the discipline to be nearly as rejuvenating as her moments on the beach.

"In all likelihood this will be my final entry before it all breaks apart. While I hope that isn't the case, the reality is that things have spun way beyond anyone's control. I still don't think Kevin sees it yet (or at least isn't willing to see it).

"Moriah, oh my sweet daughter, I am so sorry. No penance could ever be harsh enough to pay for what we did to you."

She was usually crying at this point but today, the steely determination that anchored her to her plan also held back the waterfall of her tears. She had written hundreds of such entries over the past few months, one of the only helpful assignments of advice her grief counselor ever gave her and Kevin never bothered to read them. He was just happy that *something* was helping her cope.

No, he never bothered to look through her journals. A pained smile hardened on her lips as she thought of this and that was why her journals held more than the emotional processing of a highly bereaved, slightly unstable mother.

They held the truth.

After today they would also hold the final piece.

She still wasn't sure how much difference it would make. She obviously wouldn't leak the information to the press. She didn't want to ruin Kevin publicly if it would jeopardize Velorum and with Stan still missing she couldn't take the risk of exposing him in the process.

Nevertheless, she would write it all the same and she would be ready for the backlash.

She re-read the last sentence. "No penance could be harsh enough to pay for what we did to you." Her flowing script continued. "Today I'm going to pay what I can."

Chapter Thirty Six

Elliott's screams could be heard several doors down but unfortunately for him there was no one around to hear them, at least no one who would be inclined to help.

Ray Gibbs swallowed a fistful of ibuprofen and chased it down with straight vodka. Elliott's fierce yells were affecting him more deeply than he had expected and in a rare moment of self-doubt he wondered if they were crossing an unnecessary line.

Elliott was no lightweight. He was certainly clever enough to put a plan in place to protect himself and his family. There would likely be some backlash. He rubbed his temples angrily trying to shut out Elliott's cries that had now turned angry and guttural.

The torture was necessary. Elliott couldn't be allowed any shred of confidence or leverage. He needed to know that his family would experience as much and more if he didn't cooperate.

It would work. For all of his vices and character flaws, Elliott loved his family.

He was one of the few high profile attorneys in Ray's circle of colleagues that had remained faithfully married for over twenty years and amid his multi-million dollar legal pursuits he hadn't lost his children's hearts either. His kids adored him as much now as when they were toddlers.

It would devastate Ray to have to hurt them. He and Elliott had been best friends for years and he had attended the christening services for all of Elliott's children. Ray's polished demeanor momentarily slipped and he hung his head in his hands and choked back a muffled sob but he quickly composed himself when he noticed that Elliott's screams had stopped. The introductory torture session must have come to an end.

Ray wiped his eyes, tucked in his shirt more tightly, cleared his throat and began walking down the hall to continue his conversation with his old friend.

He knocked on the door to give Elliott a moment's notice before entering and then pushed open the door.

Elliott was sitting at the table bent forward clutching his abdomen as if he were nauseous or ill. His countenance was drawn and pale and his hair was damp with sweat that was trickling freely down his temples. He raised bloodshot eyes to meet Ray's gray ones.

"You've made a mistake, Ray." His voice was harsh and cracked after having screamed most of it away. "You've gone too far and it's not going to work out for you in the end."

Ray was too cautious to disregard Elliott's warning. He looked at him questioningly.

"I have insurance."

Ray's heart sank at the words. "What insurance?" He asked softly.

"Detective Stratton."

Ray shook his head relieved. "No, I don't think so, Elliott. I just received a call from Stratton's captain letting me know that the detective is starting to sniff around Kevin's files. If he already knew, he would be beating down our doors right now, not starting from scratch like this."

Elliott nodded. "But he *will* know, within the hour. I've set things in motion."

"Elliott, think about your family."

"I *am* thinking about them, Ray and if you touch them, the whole project goes down!" Elliott's voice cracked again but there was enough authority in his look and tone to make Ray pause.

"If it's set in motion, can you call it off?"

Elliott shook his head. "No but it can happen quietly. Only you and Kevin would need to go down. Velorum can still go forward."

Ray laughed dismissively. "I don't think so. Kevin *is* the Velorum project and we wouldn't be where we are today if we were weak enough to be exposed by one rogue detective. I think we can handle Detective Louis Stratton."

"It's not just Stratton." Elliott said in a near-whisper. "It's Shelly. She has evidence too."

Ray sat down hard in the chair across from Elliott, his mind swirling. Elliott smirked enjoying the momentary upper hand.

"Elliott, we can stop her too."

"No way, Ray. Because despite how far you've gone, despite the torture and the cover-ups and the murder, I don't think there is any way that Kevin Gunther would hurt Shelly. Not after Moriah."

Ray was silent. Elliott was right and if what he said were true, it could all end within the hour. He needed to stop Shelly without hurting her and he prayed that it would be possible. He shut down what little empathy he possessed and began to think.

What evidence could she have? Her computer was bugged and their phone traces would have picked up on any suspicious conversations. For a moment he was baffled until a sudden revelation sprang into his mind and he almost laughed out loud.

Her journals.

She had written everything down, right under their noses. Marveling at her courage, he pushed the chair back and lurched toward the door.

"It's too late." Elliott called after him.

But Ray was already on his cell phone calling his driver.

Chapter Thirty Seven

The clock was ticking. I could hear its second hand clicking away even above the gentle hum of my life support machines and I could hear it inside my own body. With every beat of my heart, more of my vital essence was slipping away. It wouldn't be long now.

However, there were still some things I needed to understand.

I found myself wanting to talk to Kevin even though I would never risk that. To do so would unravel everything and I knew it didn't matter whether I received answers to my questions.

There was no doubt that I held the moral high ground.

I shifted my weight gently, maddeningly conscious of the breathing tube that had been slightly off-center as the doctors slid it down my throat. I needed to think. I opened my eyes to slits and gratefully saw that the room was empty.

With my memories restored, fear was gripping me in a different way. The fear that accompanies amnesia is an insecure fear of the unknown but this fear was directly tied to what I *did* know and I knew that with the many-layered traps and intrigues of Kevin Gunther the hope of justice prevailing was laughable at best.

One thing pulled at me, however, one thing that could possibly provide the remotest chance of redemption, Rachel.

I could see her clearly in my mind's eye, slightly wind-blown platinum blonde hair held loosely in place by the over-sized designer sunglasses that seemed forever perched on top of her head and sparkling blue eyes that took the breath away from most men. She was the quintessential supermodel and I still remembered the day she signed her first major contract. She couldn't believe it was real and her insecurities surfaced to undermine her like they so often did. It sometimes seemed like my full-time job was to reassure her of her value and identity.

Of course, Kevin Gunther hadn't helped.

A swell of bitterness rolled through my torn guts at the thought of their affair. It was one of Kevin's rare blunders. Certainly, he had been attracted to Rachel but attraction wasn't the issue. He was in a desperate, haunted place and Rachel was vulnerable.

She always had been.

Unfortunately, I had never been able to help her. My heart constricted with the conflicting emotions of profound love for her and then a sadness that went deeper than her fling with Los Angeles' dashing mayor.

I missed her and I wished she were here. I felt hot tears begin sliding down my stubbly cheeks but with the tears came a swelling sensation in my throat that caused the breathing tube to bind painfully against my larynx. I forced back the tears and tried to shift my thinking. I started coughing.

The ventilator's airflow became constricted and the alarms on my monitors started ringing loudly. Within seconds, white-robed orderlies dashed into the room and began punching buttons and examining tubing connections.

The coughing fit passed, so they simply fluffed my pillow and rearranged my tangled bed sheets. I lay as still as I could, overwhelmingly conscious of my broken state. It was truly a marvel that I was still alive, with my shredded organs, fractured spine, blood loss and a breathing tube that was now doing the majority of the breathing for me.

At least I was still lucid but I knew lucidity would abandon me soon enough and I desperately needed to think while I still could and before they came back to try one last interrogation. I forced back my feelings for Rachel and decided to start at the beginning.

Logical.

That's how Rachel had always described me and I needed that emotionless logic to rescue me now.

Okay, I thought. Let's review.

Chapter Thirty Eight

"Kevin, we have to intercept Detective Stratton. Elliott's insurance card is being played."

Kevin absorbed Ray's words. "Where are you now?" he asked.

"I'm checking out another possible leak."

Kevin decided not to ask. "I'm staying here, Ray. They say he only has another twenty-four hours at best and I need to get him to talk."

"Kevin, don't put too much hope in that. We pushed him too far and he's a dead man already. Besides, I don't think we need to be too concerned. I think Father Stan got in way over his head and I believe Elliott is a much bigger threat."

"I don't know, Ray." Kevin replied. "He said it's Shelly."

"Shelly?" Ray asked sharply. "What about Shelly?"

"I don't know." Kevin sighed wearily. "But if you can believe this, he winked at me and he said it wasn't just Elliott. He said it was Shelly too."

Ray was silent for a moment before responding. "It can't be Shelly." He finally said. "She didn't know."

"I think she knows more than we assumed. I'll have to talk to her tonight."

"Be careful, Kevin. I'm sure she doesn't know anything. Don't say too much."

"Talk to you soon." Kevin snapped his phone shut, while Ray's driver exited the freeway and turned down the road to Kevin and Shelly's beachfront home.

Ray shook his head grimly. He hated keeping things from Kevin even when they were for his own good but he had to find out what Shelly knew. He would be at the house in about ten minutes, so he leaned back in his leather seat, shut his eyes and tried to assess the potential damage. If Elliott and Shelly were both talking, then the odds were not good. Somehow the truth would leak out and Velorum would be shut down. He and Kevin would surely be investigated and even if nothing came of it, their political dreams would be over.

Ray was a bit surprised by Elliott's resilience. He and Kevin had specifically chosen him because of what they had perceived as a vacillating weakness in his character. Elliott was a people-pleaser to his core and he hated to disappoint. It was an unusual character trait for a litigious attorney in a high profile city like Los Angeles but it had actually contributed to his success. People felt they could trust Elliott and that he truly had their best interests at heart and it had helped him become a highly successful attorney.

It was that same people-pleasing nature that Ray and Kevin felt would work to their advantage. They knew that Elliott would believe in Velorum and they were convinced that he would remain loyal, even if things got a bit gray and unclear.

At first their assessment seemed correct. Elliott was ecstatic about the Velorum project and he immediately bought into their vision to change the landscape of modern medicine. His humanitarian side was apparent when they discussed how Velorum's mass production could change the entire course of underdeveloped nations and his greedy streak surfaced when he realized that his name could actually be associated with a legitimate cure for cancer. He was a believer, he was loyal and he wanted to please.

That was why they pegged him to be their fall guy.

He would never see it coming until it was too late. He believed too much in their histories together and once it struck, he would be in too deep to resist and then there was the fact that Kevin and Ray really did care about Elliott and they were convinced that they could protect him even after he was indicted and sentenced. Ray knew the right judges and he was certain he could secure leniency.

They couldn't afford to wait for all of the FDA red tape to be processed. They needed Velorum to be available sooner and so Elliott would be blamed for its mishandling and premature distribution and he would pay for it with a year or two of his life. On the other hand, his sentence would be served at the most comfortable, least strenuous, minimum-security prison in the state. His family would be granted liberal visitation rights and while incarcerated, he would receive the book rights for the Velorum story that would chronicle the wonder drug's development. It would sensationalize the drug and give it the grassroots swell of support that could force the FDA to approve it for legitimate distribution and application.

Velorum would be legalized, the world would be changed. Kevin Gunther would most likely land in the white house and Elliott would be a very rich man.

They never expected him to talk to the priest.

Ray rubbed his throbbing temples, a common practice on this never-ending day and ordered the driver to park several hundred yards away from the Gunther home, a charming beach house set in a gated, oceanfront community.

He needed a few more minutes to think before he confronted Shelly.

Chapter Thirty Nine

"If only we could locate Father Stan," Detective Robyn Macomber said thoughtfully.

Her partner, Louis Stratton, nodded his graying head absently and then responded. "What about Rachel? We might be able to get her to talk. Elliott said she was a part of Kevin's inner circle and she knows the priest as well as anyone does."

Robyn shook her head, "I don't think so. She's a true believer."

"Yes, in Velorum and Kevin Gunther" he persisted, "but not in murder. She's a wide-eyed schoolgirl who just got the biggest break in her life with her new celebrity status. The last thing she will want is to be associated too closely with Kevin when his star comes crashing down."

She shook her head again. "Louis, she's already associated with him. Rachel Parker is the Hollywood face for his campaign." Robyn looked up from her sleek laptop and spun it around for Stratton to see a photo of Rachel wiping tears from her eyes as she stood elegantly behind a simple podium.

"This was from Kevin's rally two nights ago and she's scheduled to speak on the under card again *tonight*. Apparently she brings the house down every time she speaks. I guess she's more than just a pretty face."

Stratton grunted his agreement as he peered at the screen, amazed at how Rachel could make a political event look like a fashion show.

"She'll be tougher than you think." Robyn said confidently. "I think our best bet is to get back to Stan's house and continue looking around. If she confessed to him he might have kept a record of it."

Stratton shrugged and agreed. "It's worth a shot." Then, with an edge in his voice he added, "If only we had five more minutes for Elliott to finish his confession."

Robyn was silent for a moment and then exclaimed, "But they don't know that do they? For all we know they think Elliott spilled his guts. They probably think he made a full confession." Her mind was racing but Stratton was frowning and shaking his big head.

"They're probably already shutting things down, Robyn. If we try to threaten them, they'll just move quicker."

"What other options do we have?" She persisted. "I think you should try to bluff them and then we should head back to Father Stan's home and look through every file we can find."

Stratton laughed in spite of himself. She wanted him to threaten Kevin Gunther and then she wanted them to violate the parameters of their search warrant. His esteem for his rookie partner continued to rise and he knew that if her enthusiasm didn't get both of them killed, which it most likely would, she would become a formidable detective. She was already gathering up her things and powering down her laptop.

Stratton glanced down the hallway but no one was paying any attention to them. He scrolled through his phone's contact list and paused when he came to the G section.

Gunther, Kevin. His finger hovered over the number. He respected Kevin, admired his leadership and agreed with the journalists who ranked his handling of the L.A. hostage crisis on par with Giuliani's handling of 9-11.

Kevin had never been a mere politician out to build his own legacy. He wanted to change the world and he had started by changing Los Angeles. From urban development programs, poverty reforms and single parent initiatives to increasing the pay, benefits, training and protection of the police force, he had won the hearts of citizens and law enforcement alike.

Stratton didn't fault his captain for shutting down the investigation. He understood. Every politician had skeletons in the closet and if keeping Kevin's locked safely away kept the police force at its current level of success, then it would certainly be a reasonable price to pay. Tolerating minor corruption at the top level to eradicate it in greater quantities on the streets definitely seemed like a no brainer, the much lesser of two evils. Most cops wouldn't think twice about looking the other way.

However, that had never been Stratton's style. Corruption at any level reproduced itself and had to be shut down.

He looked at the clock. They had two hours to kill before Elliott's information would be available. He glanced down again at the hastily scribbled message from Elliott: "1322 1st avenue. 7:00 p.m. sharp. Locker #55. Combination: 7-7-7. Any earlier and the contents won't be delivered. 7:00 p.m. sharp and everything will make sense."

The address was already cued into their GPS and they would be spinning the combination by 7:05 p.m. In the meantime he might as well threaten the mayor. He was retiring soon anyway.

He sighed deeply before touching the screen of his phone and then listened while it rang through to Kevin Gunther's private line.

Chapter Forty

"I need to see him, Kevin." Rachel's voice was strong but with a faint quiver in it that betrayed her near-breakdown state.

Kevin sighed deeply before responding on his end of the phone. "No way, Rachel. They need to conduct an autopsy first. You'll have to wait until they're finished. I'm sorry."

Her strangled cry tore at his heart but there was nothing else he could tell her. He listened patiently while she cried on the other end of the line.

His phone beeped indicating an incoming call but he ignored it as he listened to her muffled sobs. After a moment, he said softly, "You'll do an amazing job tonight, Rachel. You always do."

Despite the mixture of grief and outrage that shook her insides she replied, "Thank you, Kevin." She still wanted his affirmation. "It's just so unfair," she whispered.

He nodded and then realizing that she couldn't hear him nod his head he said softly, "You're right. This has been much harder than we anticipated and it's taken a toll on far too many people and Rachel, I'm not going to tell you that the toll it's taken on you or Shelly or others has been worth it. I'm tired of the 'greater good' speeches but I do want to remind you that the good that will come from this is going to be spectacular. Granted, we all might be crushed in the process but we are going to save tens of millions of lives."

It was more than a stump speech and Rachel knew it. That was why she signed on with Kevin in the first place and why she continued to work for him and why she loved him. Yes, she admitted to herself. She loved him and she hated herself for it. She hated herself for the affair and she hated herself every time she saw Shelly and her haunted eyes. At first, she thought that Shelly must have found out about her and Kevin but after she learned the truth about Moriah, she breathed easier, assuming that Shelly's grief was unrelated to their betrayal. Recently though Shelly's demeanor had turned icy toward Rachel and the unshakable sadness that clouded her eyes was now mixed with an almost frightening determination. Rachel could see it clearly. Shelly had come to a powerful decision about something.

Moreover, it frightened Rachel.

At that moment her phone vibrated as an incoming call interrupted her and Kevin. She looked down and exclaimed, "Oh my God! It's Shelly."

"Shelly?" Kevin's voice sounded as startled as Rachel's and he glanced down at his phone to see if Shelly had tried calling him first. The number on his screen wasn't Shelly's. It was an unnamed, unfamiliar number, which was odd because very few people had his cell number and Kevin knew most of their numbers by heart. His phone beeped again.

"Rachel, take the call and then call me back. Someone is trying to reach me too. Call me soon." He pushed the accept button on the incoming call and left Rachel to respond to Shelly.

"Kevin Gunther." The mayor spoke curtly into his phone.

There was a pause on the other end and then a gruff voice spoke. "Mr. Mayor, this is Detective Louis Stratton. Do you have a moment?"

Kevin paused momentarily, shocked at how quickly things had been set in motion. Ray must have been right about Elliott. He took a deep breath and replied. "Great to hear from you, detective. Unfortunately this isn't a good time. I'm very sorry but you'll need to try me back a little later." Then he flipped the phone shut, knowing full well that it wouldn't be the last call from Detective Louis Stratton.

Chapter Forty One

Ray cracked open a chilled bottled of distilled water and slugged back several swallows. He stretched his back, rubbed his temples and checked his watch. He needed a few more minutes to gather his thoughts before he confronted Shelly. He leaned back into the car's leather seat and took another icy swallow.

He had always admired her, even more than he admired Kevin. He understood Kevin and his incurable drive for significance. It was hard-wired into his DNA. Some people just had it and Kevin was one of them. He was the captain of every team he turned out for in school and he had led every organization he had ever been a part of since. The presidency wasn't a long shot by any means. It was practically a given. Ray understood Kevin's ambition and he respected it even though it was of a different nature than his own.

Ray had always fancied himself an advisor that whispered into the ear of the king, rather than the front man on the stage. The advisors were the ones with the real power. He didn't need to rub shoulders with reporters or get his mug in front of cameras at press conferences. He liked being an unseen influencer who held the strings of the men and women in front of the microphones.

Not that he ever pulled Kevin's strings. No, he never did that with Kevin. Kevin was not a man to be manipulated or controlled, not even by Ray. Kevin was his own man with clear aspirations and a sense of destiny that reminded Ray of men like Sir Winston Churchill. Ray loved Kevin like a brother and served him as loyally.

There was something different about Shelly, however. Something about her had always intrigued Ray and in his lonelier moments made him wonder if he *should* attempt to find a woman to journey through life with.

He understood Kevin but Shelly was a mystery.

She possessed the poise and elegance of a beauty queen and had walked the Red Carpet in Hollywood causing as much of a stir as any of the current movie sirens but she had never lost even a shred of her innocent, small-town roots. She was humble, honest and caring and never the least bit intimidated by the social elite. In many ways, she reminded Ray of a scaled-down version of Princess Diana who could parlay with the rich and powerful as comfortably as she could the poor and destitute.

She was the perfect match for Kevin in every way. Equally polished and poised as Kevin (probably from her *actual* beauty queen days), she also carried his authentic zeal to change the world but where Kevin had a fiery personality that could travel the full spectrum of human emotion in a single conversation, Shelly was the eye of a storm, perfectly peaceful in every situation.

Ray had watched her handle the pressures of political life with a grace and aplomb that disarmed the most hostile of critics. She was unwavering in her character and perfectly comfortable in her own skin. She could diffuse difficult situations, speak hard truth when it needed to be spoken and still convey unconditional love and compassion. Ray had always wondered where she learned to do that.

She was a simple Midwestern, schoolgirl and yet here she was married to a rising political star whose future could possibly be on par with Nelson Mandela's for its far-reaching significance and impact. She intrigued Ray, who made it his business to discover the flaws and weak spots of every person in Kevin's inner circle but could find none in Shelly. She was unflappable, loyal, steady and gentle to the core.

At least until Moriah.

That's when everything had changed. Shelly stayed strong during her daughter's illness but when Moriah died, Shelly broke inside and Ray knew it was unlikely that she would ever recover.

She was never supposed to know about Moriah's treatments and she never would have known if Moriah hadn't spoken to the priest. The priest must have broken his vow of confidentiality because somehow Shelly had found out.

That was Kevin's downfall. Even if Velorum worked and he made it to the White House, the internal damage would be too great. Yes, Ray realized it now. Even if all of their political aspirations came true, Kevin had lost where it mattered most and he would never get her back, especially if she ever found out about Rachel. That would be a final dagger to her heart.

Ray felt traumatized as he realized how quickly things could fall apart. He allowed himself to imagine what it would feel like if Shelly left. Other politicians had divorced and then continued to have brilliant careers, many of them remarrying with the public soon forgetting their former lives but Ray knew Kevin couldn't do it. His attachment to Shelly was too deep and Ray knew that Kevin would try to move heaven and earth to win her back.

He also knew it was over. Shelly would never recover from Moriah and a sudden tremor of fear ran through Ray as he wondered what he would encounter in her study. He shook his head abruptly and stepped out of the car. Time was up. He really didn't need to try and formulate a plan.

Shelly held the upper hand.

Chapter Forty Two

My first encounter with Shelly Gunther was engraved in my memory. Actually that might be a bit dramatic considering my recent amnesia struggles but at least I could remember it for the time being.

It was an early spring morning, the kind that made Californians remember why they lived in California and it already felt like summer. Birds warbled cheerfully. Trees exploded with new buds and the sunshine was casting everything in a happy, optimistic light. Smog was minimal and the light, offshore breeze was just strong enough to sway the palm trees without messing up her hair.

She was holding Moriah's hand as they crossed the 3rd Street Promenade in Santa Monica on their way to the pier and its famous roller coaster. They were wearing matching sundresses and carrying big, floppy bags over their shoulders. Their over-sized sunglasses and freshly pedicured toes completed their twin ensemble and I found myself thinking they should be in one of those celebrity mother-daughter coffee table books.

Moriah was adorable, perky and animated and from my view across the street I could tell she was a chatterbox. Shelly didn't seem to mind, though. She nodded and laughed as Moriah spoke, completely in tune with her little daughter, even while watching out for speeding motorists, cyclists, skaters and boisterous street preachers and performers.

I was a bit surprised to see them alone. Although I knew of Shelly's reputation as a simple, down-to-earth lady who was equally comfortable at a garage sale or a black tie gala with her husband, the newly elected mayor of Los Angeles, it was still surprising to see her leading their daughter in such a densely packed place without any visible security or bodyguards.

Of course, it only took a moment for me to realize that they *weren't* alone.

I mentally pushed pause on the memory as the door to my hospital room opened abruptly and a twinge of fear shot through me. It shut again just as quickly however and after a moment of slowing my heartbeat, I resumed my thinking.

Moriah must have dropped something because she abruptly let go of Shelly's hand and turned back into the middle of the street. The crosswalk light had turned red when she made her abrupt move and several cars had begun lurching into the intersection.

My response must have been involuntary because I hardly remembered hurtling my body in between her and the oncoming traffic. Tires screeched, Shelly screamed and Moriah looked up at me sharply as I lunged to her side, scooped her into my arms and yelled at the oncoming traffic.

Fortunately, the cars stopped in time and Moriah was safe but before I could appreciate her safety, a man rushed up and snatched her from my arms, while another threw me roughly to the ground and dug his bony knee into the middle of my back.

"Mrs. Gunther, she's fine." One of them called loudly to Shelly.

"Let him up for God's sake!" she responded in a frightened, angry voice. "That man just saved my daughter's life."

I was jerked unceremoniously to my feet and personally introduced to Shelly Gunther for the first time. Horns began

CONSCIENCE

beeping from the backed up traffic that hadn't seen what the delay was all about as Shelly shook my hand gratefully and gushed, "I can't thank you enough, sir." Then the burly bodyguards were escorting her and Moriah back across the street and toward the Santa Monica pier.

Moriah turned and waved as her little legs ran to keep step with her mom.

I waved back and then finished crossing the street myself. Although I was headed in their same direction, I felt funny about following them, so I sat down to catch my breath on a vacant bench.

A large shadow loomed over me and I looked up to see the guard that had body slammed me onto the asphalt. He was handing me something. It was a business card with Shelly Gunther's name and contact info on it, along with a hastily scrawled note. "Please call me when you have time. My family has been looking for someone like you."

I looked at the guard questioningly but he had already turned to catch up to Shelly and Moriah. I studied the business card again wondering why in the world Kevin Gunther's wife would need me to call her. To thank me again? That didn't seem right. I looked down the street but they had already turned a corner and were out of my sight. I pocketed the business card as an unexplained mixture of curiosity and dread began to settle into my gut.

I smiled grimly as I remembered the moment, my lips spreading out away from the breathing tube in my mouth. I had carried that curious dread nearly every single day since my brief introduction to the Gunther family. I tried licking my cracked, dry lips but the effort was too painful.

CHRIS JACKSON

Chapter Forty Three

"Hello, Rachel." Shelly's voice was measured and controlled.

Rachel's heart began racing as Shelly skipped the pleasantries and got right to the point. "Rachel, I want you to know that I know." A pause, then, "And I understand and I forgive you." Another pause. "I forgive Kevin too and I just wanted you to hear it from me personally."

The room began spinning around Rachel and her heart started pounding even more wildly. Shelly knew? Rachel gasped audibly, unable to find words for an appropriate response.

Shelly continued. "I know this must be very awkward for you, so I won't drag it out. I just wanted you to know before."

Before? Before what, Rachel wanted to ask but Shelly was ending the conversation.

"Goodbye, Rachel. I really do forgive you." And she was gone.

Rachel stared at the phone and then stumbled across the room and fell heavily onto a colorful sofa. She cradled her head in her hands and fought back the lump that had risen into her throat.

Shelly *knew*? And she *forgave* her? And she wanted her to know *before* something? She cleared the screen on her phone and hit speed dial #1, Kevin's number. It rang once but then she shook her head angrily and canceled the call. That was her problem all along. She was too dependent on Kevin Gunther.

She leaned back with her face to the ceiling and gave a strangled yell of frustration. The lump got the better of her and her tears came out in a burst. Once she started crying she wondered if she would ever be able to stop.

She did stop abruptly though when a strong knock rattled the door to her room. It would be Mark, her new celebrity squeeze and one of the people she *least* wanted to see at the moment. Forget what the tabloids said and forget that they had just made their public debut as a couple, there was no future with him. He was simply her rebound after Kevin ended things a few weeks earlier. Her heart ached at the thought and she wished that she had been strong enough to call things off with Kevin instead of leaving it to him to put the brakes on. He was right to do it and in many ways it made her love him even more but it also broke her heart.

She found herself longing for Father Stan, knowing that he would never judge her and that his heart would be breaking right alongside hers. He would also know what she should do.

The door shook with another loud knock. "Rachel, are you okay?" It was Mark's clear baritone.

"Yes, I just need a minute." She tried to sound natural but her nose was so plugged and her voice was so shaky that she knew he wouldn't buy it.

"Rachel, can I come in? You don't sound like yourself and I thought I heard you yell. Are you sure you're okay?"

Anger coursed through her then, not at Mark but at everything. She yelled at him to leave her alone and then instantly regretted her tone. She heard him mumble something and then heard his footsteps retreating down the hall but she didn't have the energy to follow him. She would apologize later. For now, she just needed to think.

It was the worst scenario she could possibly have imagined. To have gotten involved with Kevin while everything was happening with Moriah was bad enough but now this, being exposed by Shelly? It was too much for her. She curled up on the sofa like a baby and let herself cry it out.

Her phone rang a few minutes later and it was Kevin. He must have seen her attempted call. She let him go to voicemail and then cried even harder, wishing *she* had ignored *him* the first time he had called her. It had all started with a phone call and now it was ending with one.

Chapter Forty Four

Ray knocked softly on the door to Shelly's study. He had bypassed the main entrance knowing she would be waiting for him here. He glanced out at the Pacific Ocean while he waited and marveled at how often he looked at the ocean without really seeing it. He drove alongside it on the Pacific Coast Highway every morning on his way to work but he was usually so engrossed in his morning phone calls and his daily strategic planning that he didn't even notice it. People from all over the country saved their money so they could take a measly one or two week vacation in Santa Monica and see its massive beaches and famous pier and yet Ray drove past it every morning seldom even noticing it was there.

He shook his head, amused at what a random thing the brain could be. He was about to hear news from Shelly that could possibly destroy the entire project and he was wondering why he didn't appreciate the ocean more. He wondered if he was finally cracking up under the stress.

He rapped on Shelly's door again with a little more force, inwardly annoyed that his melancholy feelings hadn't lifted. If anything they were growing even stronger. He suddenly thought of

Elliott's pained, haunted expression and for the first time in as long as he could remember, his resolve started to waver.

Elliott hadn't cracked. For as easily as he cried and as broken as he was over the threat to his family, he was much stronger than Ray had expected him to be. Elliott was no pushover and he must have realized that if he spilled his guts he would lose any shred of leverage that he had in the situation. Even though Ray had indeed contacted Elliott's family, he had no intention of actually hurting them. What he wanted was Elliott's *knowledge*. Ray needed to know what Elliott knew and he needed to know what Elliott had *done* with that knowledge.

Ray analyzed the situation with his brilliant legal mind as he heard Shelly's soft footsteps approach the oak door. What he really needed was for Elliott to buy in. That was the plan all along and he and Kevin had thought it would be a much easier sell to get him to cooperate. They never expected him to have such a strong conscience. Ray smirked as he remembered Elliott's admission that he had needed to speak with a priest.

Shelly unbolted the lock and gently opened the door, interrupting Ray's ponderings.

"Come in, Ray." Shelly said as if she had been expecting him. The exhaustion was evident in her voice and around her eyes.

He looked at her thoughtfully and then asked, "Do you know why I'm here?"

She gave him a brittle laugh and said, "Oh come on Ray, the real question is do *you* know why you're here and do you have any idea what Moriah told me about you?"

His stomach twitched uncomfortably and he shook his head, "No, I'm not sure that I do." Then he added hollowly, "I would never have hurt her, Shelly," but he could tell his words fell flat.

Her voice blazed back, "Of course you would never have hurt Moriah, Ray. You were her godfather, her adopted uncle. She adored you and she trusted you."

The room was beginning to spin slightly around Ray so he tried leveling the playing field. "What did you want to tell me, Shelly?"

He intentionally put just a hint of impatience in his voice but immediately wished he hadn't when she turned on him fiercely. "You were her *godfather*, Ray, her *protector*. That was your sworn job. You promised her and you promised me!"

Ray noticed even in the moment that she hadn't mentioned Kevin's name and he realized that he was completely unprepared for where this conversation might be going.

He softened his voice as much as he could. "Shelly, please tell me. I don't know what you're leading up to."

She gave him a hard stare that he found difficult to hold and then she responded.

CHRIS JACKSON

Chapter Forty Five

Elliott curled himself into a tight ball trying to stay warm in the corner of the stark interrogation room. A strong fan blew a crisp sixty-degree flow of air through the vents and it had dried the lather of perspiration on his skin and left him chilled and shaking. Despite his frantic concern for his family, he was falling asleep. In addition to causing excruciating, although non-damaging, pain, the three electrical shock treatments they had given him had sapped his already depleted energy tanks.

It had been a long day.

As he fought to stay awake and calm the violent shivering that shook his muscles, he thought back on his 8:00 a.m. meeting with Kevin Gunther and could hardly believe that it had occurred *that* morning.

He had been both frightened and relieved to receive Kevin's invitation to the lawyer's meeting. He had been frightened because of everything he had learned about Kevin and yet relieved because he assumed that Kevin would never have continued to invite him into any project-related task if he suspected Elliott in any way. At least that had been Elliott's rationale ten hours earlier when he traipsed into the mayor's conference room along with his peers from the legal elite.

He had obviously been mistaken.

The lawyer's meeting had been a front, a chance to lure Elliott out into the open and then snag him and reel him in. For a moment amid uncontrollable shivers, he wondered why they had gone to all the trouble of a pseudo meeting if they were simply after *him* but then it dawned on him that it might *not* have been a front. Maybe Kevin really *was* gathering an elite legal force to help him with the launch of Velorum.

Elliott shook his head even as he rocked back and forth on the tile floor. No, there was no way they would start distributing Velorum yet. It was still years, maybe decades, away from being ready. He pushed himself into a sitting position and then heaved himself to his feet and tried pacing the floor to generate some body heat.

His mind was racing with possibilities. Were they actually preparing to go public with Velorum, even after all the damage it had caused?

His thoughts flickered unconsciously to Father Stan and as it always happened when Elliott thought about the little priest, his heart grew heavy with sorrow. Where *was* Stan? He disappeared almost immediately after Elliott confessed to him. It was almost like someone had bugged the confessional booth and alerted Kevin and Ray even while his confession was being made.

He reflected on that first meeting with conflicting emotions. Father Stan had indeed offered absolution but he also insisted that Elliott go public with his testimony and that was definitely *not* something he had been prepared to do. In some ways, he wasn't surprised by Stan's urging. After all, Elliott wasn't the first person to talk to the priest about Velorum.

Moriah had done it too.

Elliott wondered if Stan had encouraged *her* to come forward with her confession as well and then for the millionth time, Elliott wondered darkly if that was why it happened. He shook his head angrily at the thought. No, there was no way Kevin Gunther would do that to his own daughter. No way! Then again, Kevin had done a lot of things that Elliott would have sworn him incapable of doing.

He stopped pacing and leaned wearily against the wall, his thoughts returning to the bright sunny day when he first made his confession to Father Stan Jeffries. He remembered the cool, dim sanctuary and what a relief it was from the blazing heat and brightness of a late-summer California day.

Elliott had never been to confession before. He had never felt the need. He had always been a pretty decent guy. He had a nice marriage, better kids, and a lucrative job that kept him more busy than he would have liked but still left a little time for family vacations and building a few memories. He had always prided himself on his reputation for honesty. He was the antithesis of the sleazy, money-grubbing lawyer of his generation. He genuinely cared about his clients and although his rates were on the high end, they weren't exorbitant. Yes, his had been a pretty good life with no major traumas or failures. He didn't have any demons to exorcise and no pressing weight of guilt to try to offload in a stuffy confessional booth. He had never needed a priest.

Of course, that was before Ray Gibbs' job offer.

Something had been off from the beginning. Ray was too eager, something he had never been in the past. In all of their years of friendship, Elliott had never seen Ray frantic or desperate. He was always the picture of cold, intentional calculation but when he approached Elliott to join the Velorum legal team he was different, sort of like a duck that appears calm on the surface but underneath the water is kicking its little webbed feet for all its worth.

He had no idea at the time how accurate that metaphor would prove to be. By the time Elliott agreed to consult with Ray and his team, the Velorum project was already spinning out of control.

Moreover, Moriah's treatments were about to begin.

He choked back a strangled sob at the memory and slid to the floor, cradling his head in his trembling hands.

Chapter Forty Six

"Forgive me, Father, for I have sinned."

"How long has it been since your last confession?"

Elliott chuckled, "I guess the answer would be never."

The priest chuckled along with him and Elliott immediately liked him. "Well, son, I commend you for beginning today. Welcome to your first confession."

Elliott smiled in spite of himself. "Thanks," he said a bit self-consciously. He cleared his throat and asked, "So, how does this work?"

"It works however you want it to work." The father's voice was upbeat and even, a clear tenor with just a hint of humor in it, like he was ready to laugh at any moment. "You unburden your soul to another person, me, so the weight of guilt gets exposed to God's light and, hopefully, rolls off your back and stays here in the confessional."

Elliott exhaled deeply and realized he had been holding his breath and his pulse was beating unusually fast and he was sweating. He almost laughed out loud as he recognized how truly stressed out he was, a nervous breakdown in the making.

The priest sat silently on the other side of the panel as if he were aware of Elliott's internal angst. He spoke gently through the opening. "Sometimes it's helpful for people to start by talking about something other than their item of confession. It puts them at ease and helps them feel more comfortable before they blurt out their big sin."

Elliott could almost see the priest smiling in the dim light and he found himself admiring his ability to be so positive and non-threatening, despite the fact that he was about to hear the ugliest confession of Elliott's life. Elliott was glad that he wasn't a priest. He had already listened to his share of confessions as his clients invoked their attorney-client confidentiality privileges. He hated carrying all of those secrets by himself and he suddenly felt a longing to pour out his heart to this faceless voice on the other side of the confessional booth.

"What do you do for a living?" The priest interrupted his wandering thoughts.

"Attorney." Elliott said through dry lips.

"Ah, so you hear a lot of confessions yourself." He responded as if he had read Elliott's previous thoughts. "It must be tough carrying everyone's secrets without the ability to offload them."

"Well, isn't that what you do?" Elliott asked.

"Yes and no." The priest replied cheerfully. "Certainly, I hear a lot of dark, painful things that are hard to process but I don't carry them by myself. I go to my own confessional at the end of every day and I offload everything I've heard during the day on to God."

Elliott felt his defenses stiffen a bit at the God-talk. Even though he was here to see a priest, he wasn't looking for a spiritual experience. He just needed to talk to someone and he needed to be forgiven. Yes, he realized even as he thought it that he was longing to be forgiven.

For everything. For working too many hours, for being absent during some key moments of his children's lives and for Moriah. Certainly for Moriah.

The priest suddenly changed directions, almost as if he could sense Elliott's discomfort. "Do you have a family?" Elliott's pulse slowed a bit at the question and a sense of calm started settling over him.

"Yes, a wife and two kids, twins."

"Are you proud of them?"

Elliott nodded genuinely and then realized the priest couldn't hear him shake his head. "Yes, very much so. They're the best things in my life." That brought him back to Moriah and that set his heart racing again and dried what little saliva he had in his mouth. He cleared his throat and coughed uncomfortably.

"Is all of this confidential?" It was the same question his clients routinely asked him.

"Yes, son, completely confidential." The priest's voice was serious now and Elliott felt a little bit safer but even so, he stalled for several more seconds before continuing. The priest didn't seem impatient and finally Elliott began. "Father, I have a pretty high profile client and he is involved in some pretty outrageous things."

"Go on." The priest said.

"Also, I've done some things for him that are absolutely inhuman."

The priest was silent on his side of the confessional and Elliott wondered if his initial warmth was cooling a bit. After another moment of silence, Elliott realized that the ball was in his court.

"Okay, Father, here it is."

Chapter Forty Seven

Shelly took a deep breath and then pressed her lips firmly together, obviously intending to lead the conversation instead of being baited by Ray. She walked over to a plush sofa in front of the picture window and sat while gently lifting a delicate, china coffee cup to her lips. She sipped at it briefly and then let her eyes take in the view of the ocean outside her window.

Ray dropped heavily into a chair beside her and turned his own gaze to the beach. The wind had picked up but there were still some die-hard beach lovers stretched out in the sand with their coolers and books soaking up the remaining moments of sunlight. It actually looked pretty nice and Ray suddenly wondered how long it had been since he had sat down with a good book just for fun. He was a voracious reader. His favorites had been World War II memoirs but it had been all business for many years. He couldn't even remember the last one he had read just for the pleasure of it.

When he turned to face Shelly, he saw that she was staring at him intently.

"When did he start seeing her?"

Ray was startled by her question, fully expecting her to start by asking about Moriah. He stalled before answering, not sure if he should confess or play dumb since he still wasn't certain how much she knew.

Shelly read his mind and spoke quickly. "Don't bother playing dumb, Ray. I know that you know and I want to know when it started."

"Are you talking about...?" He began and then trailed off softly.

"Yes, Ray, I'm talking about Rachel! There, I said it first. You didn't betray Kevin's confidence. Now tell me when it started."

Ray took a deep breath and unconsciously looked around the room for a bar.

"Do you need a drink, Ray?" Shelly asked with an edge to her voice. "After all these years you can't just talk to me straight?"

"It began six months ago," he said softly. "But it's over, Shelly. Kevin knew it was wrong and didn't want to hurt you so he called it off almost immediately." He instantly regretted his last sentence when Shelly reacted harshly to his moralizing.

"He knew it was wrong so he called it off? Oh how noble of him! He gets to have his little affair and then take the moral high road while probably breaking Rachel's heart in the process? How nice for him. Did you know about it the whole time?"

He looked directly into her eyes and said as gently as he could, "Yes, Shelly, I knew and I'm so sorry..."

She cut him off. "Don't, Ray. I don't need to hear it. I'm sure you advised your friend to knock it off. You know an affair with a twenty-something celebrity would undermine everything we've been trying to build. I don't doubt your counsel, just your loyalty." Her last words hung bitterly in the air.

Her words stung Ray deeply, because despite the twisted paths he had been forced to walk during this whole fiasco, he was actually an incredibly loyal man and he had been every bit as loyal to Shelly as he had been to Kevin. She seemed to recognize this because her tone softened substantially with her next question.

"Why, Ray? Why did he do it?"

Ray was feeling off balance in this conversation. He had fully expected her to talk about Moriah but now he began to entertain the faintest hope that maybe she still didn't know that part of things.

"I think it was the grief, Shelly. After Moriah..." he paused to see if Moriah's name would evoke a response.

No visible response.

He continued. "After Moriah, I think Kevin lost it for a while. He held it together publicly but behind the scenes he was a wreck. I know you know this better than I do." He watched her closely knowing that a misstep here could be costly.

"When did her treatments start?" She asked him softly.

So there it was. She knew. Ray exhaled loudly then sank back into the overstuffed armchair and titled his head back against the cushion. He thought about playing dumb and forcing her to show her hand but he wisely discarded the idea. It was all coming out now.

Chapter Forty Eight

I think I blacked out. I think I was still blacked out but I could tell I was waking up and moving toward consciousness, the way an air-deprived diver kicks and struggles to break through the surface of the water.

The surface kept getting closer and I finally broke through. I was awake and my throat hurt and then I noticed that the breathing tube had been removed from my larynx and I was inhaling and exhaling on my own. A flutter of happiness stirred through my broken insides but it was abruptly cut short by the voices.

"He's coming around. How long do we have?"

"Maybe ten minutes and then the pain will take him out again."

The pain? Then it came back to me. They had stopped the Velorum and already its effects were wearing away. It seemed that it was a peculiar drug that almost instantly affected its user once administered and almost instantly wore off as soon as its flow was interrupted. The flow into my veins had been interrupted and even as I was coming into full consciousness I could feel the beginnings of some excruciating tremors.

I realized suddenly how unstable Velorum was and what a miniscule window it offered for any effectiveness. True, it enabled its user to self-diagnose at a mind-blowing level of accuracy accessing medical knowledge from somewhere deep inside the subconscious but even the slightest miscalculation in dosage could trigger memory loss, unconsciousness, or enhanced pain sensitivities in the damaged regions of the body. Not only did Velorum help its user identify what was wrong with a broken body part but it also enhanced the broken sensation. So, at the same time that a patient was miraculously assisting the physician in diagnosing his or her kidney for example, they were also experiencing profound kidney pain that they might have otherwise been unaware of.

For me at that moment, I not only felt searing abdominal pain from my gunshot wound and my hastily sewn stitches, but I could also feel each individual tear, stretching and swelling in my skin, muscles and my organs themselves. It was maddening, too much data to contain at one time. I felt my body shuddering and convulsing as waves of painful awareness gripped me and then he was talking to me.

"Tell me about Stan." His voice was calm and it brought a measure of distraction to the accelerating pain in my midsection and spine. "What did they tell him and what did he do with the information. That's all I need to know. Tell me what he knew and what he did and I'll help you. I can dull the pain. I can even treat you and heal you."

Even in my fractured state I felt a grim humor in his words. I knew I would be a dead man by the end of the day. I knew it in my gut, I knew it because of the Velorum and I knew it because these men kept saying it to one another. I tried to smile but it probably looked more like a grimace.

His expression hardened and the calmness in his voice started slipping away. "If you won't tell me, we'll keep you suspended right here. We'll make sure you feel *everything*." I shook my head. *No,* I thought. I'll be dying soon so I won't be in this state for long.

He seemed to read my mind because he answered, "You won't be able to wait this out. You haven't even begun to experience the depths of what Velorum can do. It's a wonder drug but it's also a nightmare and you don't want that nightmare to grip you."

I looked at him curiously even as my legs began spasming uncontrollably under my sweaty bed sheets. I was already in the center of the nightmare and it had all begun with Stan.

Stan. Maybe I should just tell them what he knew and what he had done with the information. It probably wouldn't change anything if I did. He was a dead man anyway, just like me. Maybe I should tell them everything I knew and then drift away in peace. It was over either way.

His eyes were boring into me. "Are you ready to talk?"

I nodded.

"Okay, pull him out!" he said and a flurry of activity began. Someone increased the Velorum flow. I could feel it almost instantly and someone else shoved a recording device in my face. Kevin looked at me with a curious expression, a combination of satisfaction and barely concealed terror.

I liked seeing the terror part in his face and I was determined to keep it there.

CHRIS JACKSON

Chapter Forty Nine

I couldn't breathe. I started choking and panicking and I felt my stitches tear as I started thrashing around in my sheets.

And then it happened. The wonder of Velorum did its thing. I suddenly had an acute awareness that I was choking because of an involuntary contraction of the muscles along my larynx and I knew how to relax them. So I did. Just like that and I could breathe again.

Everyone exhaled a collective sigh of relief, except for Kevin who smirked at me and asked, "Pretty impressive isn't it?" He must have realized that Velorum had given me the intuitive knowledge of how to save my own life.

Despite the fear of my impending death, I found myself deeply intrigued with this wonder drug. I looked around the room into the collection of eager faces and then turned back to Kevin who was still staring at me with a triumphant look on his handsome features.

"Are you ready to talk?" He asked me again and I realized I was. I was a dead man already. I could tell that even without Velorum. So, I determined to play along and learn what I could before the end. I nodded.

"Good." Kevin was visibly relieved and he turned to a white-jacketed doctor and asked, "How long do I have?"

The doctor appeared both surprised and encouraged. "Well, he's actually stabilized somewhat. You might have a few additional hours."

"Good." Kevin said again looking at his watch. "I need to leave for the banquet soon but we should have plenty of time."

I was thinking the same thing.

"Let's start with Stan. Tell us what you know about him." Kevin's expression was hard to read. He looked both impatient and amused. "You do know Stan don't you?" This last question was directed at me but with a grin toward the others in the room who all returned the grin as if they were all privy to some private joke.

"Stan is a Catholic priest. He's deeply tormented over the hurtful things done by some of his fellow priests in the name of the church. He has always been a bit of a loose cannon. In fact, he would probably be considered a liability to the institution of the church if he weren't so good at his job. He loves his people, his people love him and his influence on the community speaks for itself." I spoke these words as statements of fact, as if I were reading them off of a teleprompter.

Someone behind me muttered, "Why the third person?"

Kevin replied quickly, "Because he doesn't know." I looked at Kevin and saw his eyes gleaming eagerly. The muttering voice in the background continued, "But if he doesn't know, how is he telling us all of this?"

Kevin's voice shook slightly as he answered, "Because the Velorum is telling him."

A jolt of adrenaline shot through my system with those words followed by a sinking fear, a fear that I didn't want to hear any more of what they were saying.

Kevin spoke again. "He still has partial amnesia. He doesn't know but the Velorum is restoring the memories. Folks, this could be the beginning of a cure for Alzheimer's."

There were collective gasps and murmured approvals at the words and then everyone was silent again as they stared at me with renewed interest. Determined to maximize my remaining hours, Kevin spoke again, "So, tell us more about Stan."

I was momentarily speechless after hearing what he had just said. I still had amnesia? And somehow my amnesia was covering my knowledge about Stan? Then I startled myself with my next statement, "Increase the Velorum so I can tell you everything."

Kevin smiled again and nodded to an assistant. "Do it! Increase the flow. Let's see where this will take us."

CHRIS JACKSON

Chapter Fifty

"It's all right here, Ray." Shelly pointed to a stack of leather journals on the edge of her desk. "Dated and arranged in order. No one else has seen them and no one else needs to. I'm not looking to ruin you and Kevin. I just want out."

Ray then noticed for the first time that there was a suitcase and a purse stacked near the front door. "Where are you going?" He asked her softly.

"Home, at least for a little while. After that, I'm not sure." She paused and sipped from her delicate China cup before continuing. "I just need a break, Ray. I need time to think."

Ray's mind was racing, already several steps ahead of what Shelly was saying. "We should release a public statement," he said. "To explain where you are."

She laughed gently, a bright, innocent laugh that Ray had always loved. "Ray, you don't even know what's in my journals yet. You need to read them and *then* decide what kind of press conference you'll need to have." She abruptly stood and walked toward the door, gathering up her suitcase and purse and positioning them on the front steps. She shut the door softly behind her and began walking bare-footed toward the beach leaving Ray alone in her study.

He watched her briefly, the wind whipping her dark hair around her and then he turned to face the waiting journals. He didn't move to immediately open them but instead looked at them thoughtfully, allowing himself a moment of contemplation before discovering what they held. He considered calling Kevin and informing him of Shelly's plan to leave but then thought better of it. Shelly was right. He needed to know what her journals contained before he did anything else.

He reached for the first journal and glanced at his watch knowing that time was slipping away. The banquet would begin soon and Kevin would expect him back for it. He opened the first journal knowing he couldn't afford to waste any more time.

As the journal slid open he caught the scent of Shelly's perfume mingled with the smell of the journal's genuine leather binding. Her first entry had nothing to do with Velorum but he read it thoroughly anyway. It was the saddest thing he had ever read. Unmarried and without children of his own, Ray had never personally known the depths of love that Shelly's entry conveyed.

It was all about Moriah and how much Shelly missed her. As he read, Ray felt a pang of guilt about the way he had secretly judged Shelly's incessant journaling. He understood that she was grieving and needed to find a healthy release but he had always thought she carried it a little too far and was a little too obsessed with capturing her emotions in written form.

All of his critical feelings seemed very foolish; however, as he read the raw, heart-wrenching sentiment of a mother who had held her teenage daughter in her arms as her life ebbed slowly away. Despite their money, fame and power, there was nothing that Kevin and Shelly had been able to do to save their little girl and it was unlikely that they would ever fully recover. At least that was Ray's assessment as he finished the first entry and moved on to the second.

Shelly wrote about Moriah and she wrote about Kevin and she expressed her love for each of them. She was grateful for Kevin and was deeply proud of him. She worried about his ambition but never wavered in her belief that he was a man that could be trusted. She was lucky to have him and he was lucky to have her. She knew that as well. That was one of the strengths of their relationship, a mutual respect, appreciation and realization that they were each needy and needed in turn.

Even though he had read tomes of personal documents during his career as an attorney, Ray still felt self-conscious at reading such personal, vulnerable sentiments. He glanced out the window to see that Shelly had reached the beach and was staring out over the Pacific Ocean as the waves washed over her toes and up to her mid-calves.

He thumbed through the remainder of the first journal quickly enough to accelerate the process but slowly enough to avoid missing any critical information. The first journal appeared to contain nothing more than the powerfully expressed grief of a newly bereaved mother and he was about to set it aside and move on to the next one when his eyes scanned a minimal entry near the very end. His name was in it.

He glanced at the beach nervously and found to his alarm that Shelly had turned to face the house and appeared to be staring directly at him. A chill traveled up his spine and along his arms as he looked down to read.

"Something is wrong with Ray. He will barely look me in the eye. I asked Kevin about it and he ignored the question. Kevin knows too."

Ray looked out the window again and saw Shelly still staring in his direction. He looked down again but there was nothing more. The final two entries ended the same way that the journal had begun with expressions of love and sorrow that were both inspiring and heart-wrenching.

He skimmed the second journal then snapped it shut with an angry grunt. He wasn't finding anything. It, too, was simply filled with Shelly's grief and innermost thoughts and evaluations. He sighed deeply when his cell phone vibrated in his jacket pocket. He ignored it, knowing it was probably Kevin urging him to hurry back.

The phone vibrated again and he ignored it again. He glanced out the window and couldn't see Shelly any more. She must have been taking a final walk along the beach before flying out to her parents in the Midwest. He glanced at his watch and felt his stress level rise. He also noted in alarm that storm clouds had rolled in while he had been reading and were creating an angry, dark mass above the choppy water.

The few sunbathers who remained were busily packing up their belongings and calling it a day. Ray noticed that the office felt hotter and muggier than it had before. He looked around for a thermostat as his phone vibrated a third time. This time he glanced at the Caller ID before silencing it and was surprised to see that it wasn't Kevin. It was an unnamed number and an uneasy premonition swept through him as he felt the abridged vibration telling him that this time the caller had left a message.

He hurriedly pressed "listen" and to his surprise heard Shelly's voice but calling him from a number he had never seen before. She must have purchased a new cell phone. He moved to the window and looked out at the beach and the increasingly darkening sky. He still couldn't see her and a flutter of panic joined with the stress that he was already feeling. He punched redial without paying any attention to her message.

She answered on the first ring and said simply, "You've already passed the information. I'm disappointed, Ray. I was convinced you would be able to see it." He looked around quickly, wondering how she knew how much he had read. He scanned the corners of the ceiling for obscure cameras. "I've just finished the second journal." He said in a rushed voice. "I know." She replied. "And that's the one with the key. Good bye, Ray." And she was gone.

His phone went off again almost instantly. He answered without looking at the number, "Shelly?"

"No," came Kevin's curious reply. "Why would you think I was Shelly?" Ray heard the sound of a car pulling away from the house and he identified Shelly's silhouette in the back seat. Her luggage had been moved from the porch.

"Ray, what's going on?"

Chapter Fifty One

Applause filled the packed out banquet room and continued until Rachel smiled and raised her hand in protest. This would be an Academy Award performance tonight. No one in this supportive crowd would know that she was dying inside.

Correct that, Shelly would know, but there certainly wouldn't be any sympathy coming from her.

Rachel grimaced slightly and then covered it with her polished smile and leaned into the microphone.

Her seventeen-minute speech was another home run. She struck the perfect blend of humor, empathy and, when necessary, intensity. She informed the audience of the horrors of poverty, horrors that Americans (making up only 4% of the world's population) could never comprehend. She appealed for more than contributions. She asked them for their hearts. She asked them to connect with the "innate compassion for humanity, the compassion that *makes us human*" and pledge to see poverty eradicated in their lifetimes.

She didn't normally crunch the numbers for them. She was merely the celebrity face of the cause but tonight she deviated slightly from her rehearsed notes and delved into the numbers and statistics, showing the audience how a joint-effort really *could* eliminate this scourge from humanity with only minimal effort. She regaled them with the incredible possibilities of a poverty-free world and smattered it with just enough painful statistics to get them stirred up without overwhelming them too badly. It was a rare gift to get people stirred to action around a great cause without making them feel too badly about themselves in the process.

She switched gears then, focusing their attention on a smiling face on the giant monitor behind her. "Sometimes one face can say more than pages of statistics," she said. "This little girl has lost her parents and grandparents and is currently raising her five little brothers and sisters in an HIV-infested village. We can help her. Kevin Gunther's proposal can help her." Her final words ended with a strangled pitch that bordered on heartfelt intensity and emotional collapse.

And with that, she was done. She flashed her million-dollar smile, sniffed slightly and dabbed at the stream of teardrops on her cheeks and exited the stage in a graceful rush.

Kevin watched her go, knowing that on this night her tears weren't for the orphans in Africa. He cautiously took the stage and momentarily faltered in beginning his speech. Fortunately for him, it produced a very positive effect for the audience. This is what they loved about Kevin and Shelly Gunther. They weren't merely politicians promoting a political cause. They were the real deal. They were humanitarians first, politicians second and despite their poise and polished elegance, they were *humans* who personally understood the pain that they sought to alleviate in their world.

Moriah had been their passion in life and now in death, she gave them even greater fuel for their cause. The public had loved them before her death but now they positively adored them. The Gunthers were devoted crusaders bent on changing the world despite their own brokenness and they weren't about to let their goals take a backseat to partisan loyalties. No, if they were elected to higher offices of power, their passionate concern for the most unfortunate members of society would follow them. They were the only political ticket today that would follow through in their promises to change the world and everyone knew that the world desperately needed changing.

Kevin's speech was a little more subdued than usual. He noticed with some irritation that both Shelly and Ray were uncharacteristically absent but otherwise it was perfect, another performance that raised incredible financial capital for worthwhile causes, while also securing another wave of firm political supporters. There had even been overwhelming chants of "2016" clearly suggesting that the Gunthers had a support base strong enough to lay siege to the White House in the next election.

Kevin waved appreciatively as the chants grew louder. Once upon a time the presidency had been his dream, the ultimate platform from which to serve the world but now the dream had become a necessity, a crucial part of a plan that was swallowing up everything he had ever lived for. Irritation filled him as he wondered where Shelly was but his irritation was instantly replaced with familiar feelings of guilt and regret. He left the stage abruptly and went to find Shelly.

Chapter Fifty Two

"So what did the mayor say?" Robyn asked her partner as she slid their oversized Crown Victoria cruiser into the flow of traffic that never fully died down in Los Angeles. They were on their way to Father Stan Jeffries' house prepared to violate the clear terms of their search warrant by rummaging through files, drawers and boxes that weren't sitting in plain sight. It was a significant violation and if they were caught, none of the evidence would be able to help them in court but they were desperate for information and if Father Jeffries had made one significant journal entry then he had probably made others.

"He hung up on me." Stratton replied grimly.

Robyn was silent as she absorbed that. Finally she said, "Well, at least we know we're on to something."

Louis nodded as he stared thoughtfully at the lights rushing past them outside the car.

The traffic was flowing nicely so it wasn't long before they pulled onto Father Jeffries' block and parked several houses down from his. They sat alertly in their cruiser, carefully staring at its darkened windows to see if anything looked unusual. After a few minutes of evaluation, they quietly exited their car and moved quickly down the street. Their pulses were pounding a bit and a tingle of adrenaline tickled their skin. There were so many unknowns in this case that they had to be ready for anything.

The home looked undisturbed and there wasn't any unusual activity on the street. A few kids were shouting as they scooted around on bicycles and skateboards and Louis wondered cynically if there were any parents in the homes keeping their eyes on them. Some music drifted out of a neighboring window but otherwise everything was pretty quiet. Robyn had the key and was efficiently opening Father Jeffries' front door.

Everything looked exactly as it had earlier that morning when they first read Elliott Blythe's name in one of Father Jeffries' journals. Louis shook his head, hardly believing that this case was only one day old. He replayed the events of the day beginning with their search of the house, the mysterious dead body, Elliott's near-confession and cryptic statements about Moriah Gunther and then his hand-written note about where to find all of the necessary evidence to blow open the Velorum operation.

Velorum. He shook his head again. What a crazy day.

He and Robyn didn't linger this time as they moved through Father Jeffries' home. They moved straight to the bedroom where they had seen a simple file cabinet in the corner of Father Jeffries' closet. Robyn moved the hanging clothes items, jeans, sweat pants and athletic shirts away from the file cabinet. Louis chuckled as he noticed Father Jeffries' choice of attire. "Hard to picture a priest in a Los Angeles Lakers T-shirt," he smirked.

Robyn nodded absently as she pulled on the first shelf of the file cabinet and felt it slide easily open in her hand. She looked at Louis hopefully and then started rummaging through the files. Fortunately, they were cleanly alphabetized and labeled. Since she didn't know which label to look under she started reading all of them. There were files on finances, important documents, old tax returns and one on original poetry. She was tempted to peruse Father Jeffries' poems to see what, if any, insight they would give into his character and worldview but she moved past it until her fingers landed on a file in the back labeled "Velorum." She pulled it out and passed it back to Louis who voiced her exact sentiment, "Surely, it can't be this easy."

She finished rummaging through the files then closed the drawer and opened the next one. This one held the mother lode. Not only was there a file marked "confidential confessions" but there were three individual files marked with the names: Blythe, Elliott; Gibbs, Ray; Gunther, Shelly and Moriah. Robyn scooped the files out of the drawer and spread them out on the neatly tucked bed.

"Louis, you're not going to believe this," Robyn said to him with a fierce gleam in her eyes. "Father Jeffries kept a file of key confessions."

He looked at her hopefully and brandished his own lucky find. "I found his calendar." He said with a grin.

She glanced at the clock beside the bed and commented, "We should probably head downtown to be at the drop site on time."

Stratton nodded, "You drive. I'll read."

She began to protest but then deferred, knowing that her soon-to-be-retiring partner wouldn't budge. "Okay, just read fast, old man," she said. He feigned hurt, then grinned at her as they rearranged Stan's closet, turned out the lights and moved quickly back to their waiting patrol car.

Chapter Fifty Three

Ray Gibbs' pulse was pounding as his eyes devoured the entries in Shelly's second journal. Her first journal hadn't revealed anything that could damage the Velorum project. It was simply filled with the heart-wrenching grief of a mother who should never have had to watch her daughter die. One entry in particular had pierced Ray's heart. Shelly had written, "I wanted to be a mother not a saint." Ray was moved by the sentiment and was curious about what might have prompted such an unusual statement.

A knot of guilt spread through Ray's stomach as he read her continued words of anguish and horror. "How could this have happened so quickly? How could we not have known she was terminal?" The words were a frequent refrain written in almost every entry of the first journal and Ray felt sick as he read them. "How could we not have known?" He moved on to the second journal.

Most of the second journal read like the first. Shelly was a beautiful writer and Ray thought that she would be effective at writing self-help or coping books. She expressed her grief in such clear, compelling terms that Ray found himself empathizing with her like he never had before.

She wrote about a gray pallor that seemed to cloud even the brightest of summer days and of a dull ache that spread from her heart to her furthest extremities. She wrote about the paranoia and panic that so often accompanies grief and about the social awkwardness that bereaved people stumble over. "No one understands," she had written. "And I don't mean that in a 'poor me' kind of way. It's just the reality. If they did, they wouldn't make shallow grief comparisons or try to placate my sorrow with trite, pat answers. I know everyone means well but what most don't know is that I'm dead too. I died with her and even though my body is still walking around, giving speeches and doing my duty, there's nothing inside. There are a few people who have walked this path before and they understand but they don't say much. They know better. They just show up."

Ray looked away momentarily, feeling like he was invading her privacy. Reading journal entries of this depth of raw transparency was unnerving but he had to keep reading; he had to know what she had recorded.

"Parents aren't supposed to bury their children. It isn't natural. I was supposed to teach her to drive and move her in to her college dorm and help her choose her wedding dress." The entry ended abruptly and Ray noticed a faint ink smudge where Shelly's tears must have fallen.

"Kevin knows I'm hollow inside and he is trying so hard to help me. I pray he'll have the strength to be patient, because I have no hope that I will ever really live again. I'll never again be the woman he married twenty years ago. That woman died with Moriah." Ray wondered how she had functioned as well as she had with all of these emotions bottled up inside her.

He felt another intense pang of guilt as he turned to the next entry and subconsciously glanced around again to see if there were any strong, adult beverages he could drink. He kept reading and just when his own emotions grew raw and threatened to strangle him and he wondered if he could handle any more of Shelly's processing, he came to the last entry of the second journal. "The walls are closing in on me and I wish I were dead. I looked through Moriah's journal today."

Ray blinked as he read those words. *Moriah* had kept a journal? That was Shelly's key. He immediately glanced down the hall toward Moriah's bedroom and was tempted to rush to her bookshelf to try and find it. Instead he opened the third journal and scanned its first entry. "There are no words for this horror. I don't deserve to live. No mother has ever failed her child more tragically than I have." There was a full page of frightening, self-deprecating comments.

Suicidal didn't begin to describe it.

Then his heart turned cold and his worst fears were confirmed. The next entry was a single sentence with a mere five words: "Kevin is going to pay."

Chapter Fifty Four

"I bet there's not a misplaced paper in this guy's life," Detective Stratton said as his partner weaved in and out of traffic en route to the strip mall that housed the locker with Elliott's "insurance" information. "I think he's the most methodical, organized person I've ever met," he continued.

"Of course you haven't actually met him yet," his partner said demurely. His expression darkened a bit and he answered gruffly, "True, but I feel like I know him. You should look at this calendar."

She arched her eyebrows at him as she kept her attention on the road in front of her. "Oh sorry," he said. "I'll read it to you." Robyn glanced at her watch as Louis read crisp, concise sentences that summarized Father Jeffries' various thoughts, tasks and appointments. According to Elliott, they had a very brief window of time to retrieve the items from his storage locker but they were slightly ahead of schedule so she relaxed just a bit as Louis continued reading.

"Hospital visitation day today—one birth, a sprained knee and a hysterectomy. I wasn't quite sure how to comfort that last one." He had written a smiley face at the end of the sentence. "I still marvel that I am privileged enough to be in these people's lives. Few individuals get to be there for the highest highs, the lowest lows and for the mundane days in between."

As the reading continued, Robyn found herself wondering what it would be like to have her own priest. Never religious, her family had never had any significant contact with clergy members from any religion or denomination but listening to Father Jeffries' unembarrassed love for the members of his congregation, she suddenly longed for a priest or a pastor to confide in.

"Have you ever been to confession, Louis?" She asked her partner suddenly.

He looked at her quickly. "Are you getting all sentimental again thinking about Father Jeffries?" he said with a soft smile.

"Seriously, Louis, have you?"

He shook his head. "I'm not Catholic. Presbyterian but sometimes I think I could use a visit to a good confessional after everything I've seen on this job."

She nodded wordlessly. They had never ventured into these waters in any of their conversations over the past eighteen months and now seemed like an inopportune time since Elliott's life potentially hung in the balance and time was of the essence. "Any word in there on Elliott?"

Stratton nodded, realizing like Robyn had, that they needed to stay on task. He began hurriedly flipping pages and said triumphantly, "Yes, ma'am. It looks like he had a meeting scheduled with Elliott at 7:00 pm two days before he disappeared." His voice trailed off as he read a brief note that had been penciled in beside the appointment time. It was the exact same locker information that Elliott had given them in the hotel room.

"Robyn," he said cautiously, "Father Jeffries knew about Elliott's locker too."

She gaped at him quickly as a flicker of hope stirred in each of their hearts but just as quickly they pushed it away. It was crazy. There was no way Elliott was actually sending them to meet with

Father Jeffries. "You don't think..." Robyn began and then dropped the question even as she was voicing it.

Louis shook his head. "No way. It couldn't be that easy." Then, he looked at the digital clock and asked, "How far away are we?"

"About ten more minutes," Robyn responded with a faint hope that continued to tantalize her. How wild would that be if they not only had Father Jeffries' files but found Father Jeffries himself? Detective work seldom had big breaks like this but they did occur once in a while. Perhaps this was their "while". Her eyes gleamed a little brighter and she pushed the accelerator more firmly. This could be their break.

"Robyn, there's more." Father Jeffries had filled the margin of the page with a vulnerable entry and Stratton began reading it slowly. "I don't think I can carry all of these confessions. It will probably cost me my collar but I have to step forward. If it had just been Elliott, I could possibly have offered a prayer and hoped for the best but not after Moriah. I have to make the call. I'll do it first thing in the morning. God help us all." The entry ended there.

"Did he make an entry the next day?" Robyn asked before Louis had a chance to turn the page.

He shook his head. "Nope. That's it." The calendar contained a clever mix of time stamps, filing systems, to do lists and space for copious notes and entries. Despite the need to keep reading, Stratton flipped to the back of the book to see who the manufacturer was. Perhaps using a calendar like this could help *him* organize his life. His wife would sure like that. He chuckled softly as he thought about her constant frustration with his lack of personal organization. Brilliant as a detective, he was usually out of organizational motivation by the time he got home at night.

"Louis, we're here." Stratton looked up as Robyn was signaling and merging into the turning lane that would take them into the parking lot nearest to the storage lockers. "Don't pull directly up to them," he ordered his young partner who was already thinking the same thing, a cold determination lining her youthful expression.

Despite himself, Louis half expected to see Father Jeffries waiting to greet them.

Chapter Fifty Five

Ray sat frozen on Shelly Gunther's leather couch. Outside, night had fallen and he could just make out the forms of the crashing waves as they continued their relentless assault on the Southern California coastline. The combination of dark skies and pounding surf was normally a magical, romantic pairing but Ray felt anything but magical.

His eyes were locked on the twin journals that sat side-by-side on his lap. He had found some Scotch and was already on his second drink but he was smart enough to take it easy. He needed to think clearly.

Kevin and Shelly had left Moriah's bedroom unchanged since her death and the journal had been easy to locate on her bookshelf. As he stared at it now, a cold fear latched on to his rapidly beating heart. Shelly's most recent journal, the one with all of the damaging entries was on his other knee. Which one should he read first? He didn't want to read either one. He wished he could throw them both in the Pacific Ocean. For a fleeting moment he wished he could throw *himself* into the Pacific Ocean.

He glanced at his watch. Kevin would be leaving the rally. His speech had undoubtedly been another home run and he was probably on his way back to the hospital room for a final evening of interrogation.

In a rare moment of self-doubt, Ray was at a loss on how to proceed. Should he tell Kevin about Shelly now, or let him finish his business in the hospital? Should he make the call and shut the whole project down, or should he see what Shelly and Moriah had written and perhaps learn what they had said to the priest?

He reached for Moriah's journal first. This one would provide the context for whatever it was that Shelly had written. A cold sweat had broken out on his forehead and he felt a shiver run down his neck and arms despite the muggy heat in Shelly's study.

He opened Moriah's journal and immediately recoiled as if a large fist had crashed into his chest. They say that the sense of smell is the most potent of the five senses at unlocking memories and it certainly seemed to be so now. He could smell Moriah's signature perfume and it nearly undid him. A huge lump of emotion bunched in the back of his throat and before he could stop it, a strangled cry slipped through his parted lips. He was already emotionally frayed from his role in endorsing Elliott's torture and now he felt himself unraveling even more. His usual composure was melting as the tragic events of the past few months began catching up to him.

He had always loved Moriah. She was his goddaughter, the closest thing he would ever have to his own flesh and blood. He remembered her christening and how honored he had been when Kevin and Shelly asked him to stand with them that day. Secretly he had been more honored than they would ever know.

Memories began washing over him of birthday parties, family gatherings where he would tag along with the Gunthers and of course, the time that Kevin couldn't break away from work to attend Moriah's career day in elementary school. Ray had gladly stepped in and attempted to wow the classroom of second graders with his tales of corporate law. He still remembered their confused stares as he tried to explain what it meant to be a lawyer. It was one of the toughest crowds he had ever faced but he had loved every minute of it. He loved all of the perks associated with being Moriah's godfather.

He especially loved the trust and confidence she placed in him.

He had always been one of her confidantes and it was one of the things in life that he valued the most. He had always been adept at garnering and retaining the confidence and confidentiality of his clients but he was especially proud of his special relationship with Moriah.

Moriah had always had his heart and he had always had hers.

At least, until the end he did.

He turned to the first page of her journal and began reading. He had always known she was a tremendous student but he was still impressed with her penmanship and clarity of thought. Her entries, primarily about typical adolescent angst and ambition were clear, concise and polished. She definitely had her mother's knack for writing. One entry in particular caught his attention. It had a boy's name in it and even now, Ray felt a surge of paternal protectiveness swell within him, but it was immediately followed by feelings of self-loathing. How dare he feel protective about a teenage crush after he had betrayed her so badly?

He felt like throwing up.

For a few seconds he started panicking and he seriously wondered if he was losing it. He stood up abruptly and walked to the large picture window as both journals fell to the tiled floor. He stared out at the dark skies above the choppy waves and stretched his aching back and neck. He reviewed the events of the day and could hardly believe that everything had changed so quickly.

Earlier in the morning, he and Kevin had a plan. Elliott would take the fall; they would all offer their penance in their respective ways and the greater good would be served. It would never undo Moriah's tragedy but at least it would make the tragedy count for something.

At least that was how they had justified it and it was how they were able to continue with their deeply layered plans but it was also before they learned about Shelly's plan to leave. Correct that. It was before *he* learned about it. Kevin still had to be told.

He looked back at the journals and steeled his resolve against the tidal wave of emotion that threatened him. He retrieved the leather books and re-opened the one that was labeled, "Moriah's thoughts."

Chapter Fifty Six

Detectives Louis Stratton and Robyn Macomber moved furtively toward the row of shabby lockers in the run down strip mall in East Los Angeles. The place was largely deserted and had a disturbing, frightening feel to it. Relieved to be wearing bulletproof vests, the partners walked closely together with frequent looks over their shoulders. There were so many unknowns in this case and so many close-calls, that they were both a little on edge. A car backfired in the distance and Robyn flinched and grabbed Stratton's arm as he instinctively ducked and reached for his nine millimeter. They looked at each other after that and grinned sheepishly. It had been an incredibly long day.

It began with a call to investigate the disappearance of a beloved Catholic priest and it had instantly taken them down a path of assault, corruption and sensational stories about super drugs that people were willing to kill for. Detective Stratton had been accosted on the beach, they had interrogated and then lost, Elliott Blythe and they had violated their search warrant orders in Father Jeffries' home and now, based on Elliott's tip, they were slinking into a public locker outlet with the hope of retrieving some incriminating evidence that would blow the whole case wide open.

Stratton had never had a day like this one in his entire career on the force. He glanced at his youthful partner and wondered if this would make her career.

Or if it would get them both killed.

He shook his head roughly and then hissed at her as he identified the section they were looking for. Elliott's locker with its damning evidence was just around the corner. "What time is it?" he whispered softly.

She glanced at her watch and mouthed, "7:05." The drop should have occurred five minutes ago.

Stratton looked at the wrinkled paper with the locker combination even though he had already committed the numbers to memory. It was the simplest locker combination he had ever seen: 7-7-7. For information as delicate or dangerous as what they were likely to find, it wasn't the greatest combination.

The locker area was deserted but they each had that unmistakable feeling of being watched. Despite their anxiety, Louis couldn't help but feel like they were living inside a cliché: the gruff, soon-to-be-retired veteran and the idealistic rookie sneaking into a locker in a rundown part of town without any idea of what they were about to find. Yes, this was definitely the stuff of a worn-out cops and robbers television show.

"Here it is." Robyn began spinning the combination. The clicking of the combination lock sounded ominously loud. Louis glanced around cautiously as his partner made the last few turns of the lock. It clicked open and as if on cue a bedraggled looking homeless man shuffled up to them so quickly that Louis flinched abruptly.

"Spare any change?" The man asked in a hoarse, gravelly voice. Stratton grunted a negative while eyeing him warily before turning back to his partner who was waiting to open the locker door. The panhandler backed away from the detectives but still hung around closer than Louis would have liked.

"Sir, can you please vacate this area?" Louis asked him less than kindly. The man stared at him with an amused smile that was mildly unnerving to Stratton. Something about him wasn't right and Louis was too seasoned to ignore his internal warning system. He moved purposely toward the man while his eyes scanned the surrounding area to see if anything else seemed odd or out of place. "Sir, I need you to leave." He whispered just a few inches from the man's face.

"Are you sure?" The man asked as he backed up and began shuffling away. "Don't say you weren't warned."

Robyn's head jerked toward him. "What did he say?" The homeless looking man chuckled to himself and began walking away. "You won't want to be here in the next five minutes. This is where the gangs come out to play," he called over his shoulder as his awkward gait carried him away.

Stratton's mind was racing. "Robyn, check the locker," he ordered but she was already a step ahead of him. She pulled open the ancient locker door then spun around to see where the homeless man was going. "Louis, it's empty."

Chapter Fifty Seven

For a hobbling, homeless man he moved surprisingly fast and the detectives had to hustle to catch up to him. Even as they warily approached him from behind, Louis could tell that something was very wrong. Both of the man's hands were hidden inside the folds of his oversized coat and Louis felt a cold pit in his stomach as he imagined what might be concealed there.

"Sir, I need you to stop!" He ordered for the second time but as with the first order, the man ignored them and merely quickened his pace. Robyn and Louis were forced to do an awkward trot-walk to keep up and gain on him. As they moved almost close enough to touch him, Louis un-holstered his gun and again ordered him to freeze.

The man's reaction was blindingly fast, far faster than they would ever have imagined from such a pitiful creature. Something glinted at the end of his arm and Stratton saw too late that it was a finely sharpened steel blade. The blow was intended for Stratton but in his wild swing the man missed him completely and instead buried the knife up to its handle into Robyn's ribs just behind her shoulder and above her bulletproof vest.

Her shock preceded her pain and she looked at Stratton with wide eyes before raising her arm to see the flow of blood that had begun gushing through her jacket and down her right side. Louis caught her as she slumped to her knees on the decaying sidewalk. He looked up at the homeless man who had stopped several feet away and was looking down at them with an unreadable expression. The knife was still clenched in his fist and Stratton noticed that his other hand gripped a thick manila folder held shut by a wide rubber band. He exhaled thoughtfully and then tossed the file in Stratton's direction before turning and walking quickly away. "I was going to give them to you anyway."

Stratton would have shot him in the back but Robyn began gasping and choking and crying out in pain. The knife had gone straight into her side at the exact angle of her heart. Stratton fumbled for his radio while sliding her gently to the ground. His hands were shaking and his voice was choked and strangled as he called in the situation and the need for immediate emergency backup.

"Stay with me, Robyn," he whispered fiercely as he pressed his jacket up against the flowing wound. She tried smiling at him and he was shocked at how quickly her face had turned ghostly white. Her lips were moving and a raspy question came out of them, "Did you get Elliott's info?"

The question startled him and he became overwhelmed with a father's love for his younger partner and her sincere devotion to her cause as a police detective. "I think so," he answered gently, his eyes scanning the folder that had been dropped nearby. He looked after their assailant but the man had already disappeared around a corner and Stratton noticed that the entire strip mall area was still eerily deserted.

Police and ambulance sirens began wailing in the distance and Louis felt tears of relief rush to his eyes. "Robyn, you're going to be okay. They're on their way." She pulled him close to her and said in a failing voice, "Go after them, Louis."

He shook his head gruffly. "Robyn, we'll go after them together. We're going to get you treated and then we'll bring Kevin Gunther down."

She shook her head, "Don't wait for me. Go now!" Her voice broke off in a whimper as slicing pain set her insides on fire.

"Hang in there, Robyn. They're almost here." His pulse was pounding erratically and he wondered if he might be going into some mild shock himself when the paramedics arrived and coolly took over the scene. Robyn was connected to oxygen and IV drips and loaded quickly into the waiting ambulance.

Stratton climbed into its cab and strapped himself in for the frantic ride to the nearest emergency room. The events from the last eleven hours tumbled around in his angry, fearful brain and as he started analyzing and prioritizing them, he also double-checked to see that Elliott's information was still with him. The file was there, tightly tucked under his arm. As soon as Robyn was safely in surgery he would see if its contents were worth the price to obtain them.

Chapter Fifty Eight

"For the first time since they found my brain tumor, I feel happy, hopeful. Dad said the medicine would make me sick and that it might hurt a little bit, but that it would most likely help the doctors figure out how to get rid of the tumor. The treatments start tomorrow and even though I'm a little nervous, I'm also very excited. Dad said Mom can't make it to this first round of examinations but that's okay because Uncle Ray is picking me up and driving me to the hospital." The journal entry ended with a little prayer to God for a positive doctor visit and it devastated Ray Gibbs to read it.

He remembered the day Moriah had referenced. Just as she had written, he had picked her up early in the morning for the first round of her treatments. Shelly was out of town and didn't know that Kevin had decided to use the experimental drug Velorum on their daughter.

Ray certainly had misgivings and had vocalized them to Kevin. Ray had never been afraid to speak his mind to Kevin. It was one of the things Kevin respected about Ray. They were friends and peers long before Ray had ever worked for Kevin and Kevin wanted it to stay that way. Ray closed the journal while using his finger as a bookmark and recalled the details of that fateful conversation.

Kevin had never looked so discouraged in his life. When Ray entered his office, he instantly noticed that Kevin looked like a man that had wrestled with a terrible problem and had reached a weighty decision. Kevin was usually indefatigable, a model of energy and strength. He never called in sick, never looked worn down and always seemed able to summon the internal strength to rise to any new crisis or challenge. He had the perfect makeup and internal fortitude for high-level politics.

Now, he sat behind his desk with a haunted, fearful expression on his face and a deep sorrow emanating from his puffy eyes. His appearance unnerved Ray, who wasn't used to seeing his friend and co-crusader this low. Of course, it was understandable considering that his daughter had been diagnosed with a fatal, inoperable brain tumor; however, Ray still had the eerie sense that it was something more.

Kevin had reached a decision about something and it was frightening and Ray knew in his gut that before their conversation was over he too would be in on it as well. "Kevin, are you okay?"

Ray paused the memory momentarily and sat back on Shelly's leather couch. It was too dark to see outside now and his own reflection peered back at him when he turned to glance out of her office windows. He looked horrible, exhausted and shrunken and he laughed at his appearance in spite of himself. His friends and colleagues would be shocked if they could see him at this moment. In the past, he had been famous for his consistent demeanor. Where Kevin was the fiery, passionate leader, Ray was the unreadable stoic with ice water in his veins. During his career as an attorney, he had heard gruesome details of the most inhumane crimes without changing his facial expression but tonight he looked haggard and old, like a president several years into his first term.

He thought back on that first conversation when Kevin had told him that they were going to try Velorum on Moriah and his shoulders started shaking uncontrollably. He knew it was cruel and unthinkable but he also knew that Moriah had no chance of survival without Velorum. At best, she had a few months to live and Ray loved her enough to understand the fanaticism and grief that would drive a father to employ such desperate measures to save his little girl.

Velorum could save her and that was why Ray's opposing argument was weak. True, he had voiced all of the appropriate concerns, the pain it would cause Moriah, Shelly's outrage when she discovered what was going on and the fact that it could fail and actually hasten her death but in the end he knew that he would still help Kevin go through with it.

He flopped heavily into the chair across from Kevin's desk and stared into his eyes for a long time. A dozen conversations passed silently between them during that stare before Ray asked softly, "When will we begin?"

"Immediately. Tomorrow morning. I've already told her that you would be picking her up."

Ray nodded. He wasn't angry that Kevin had presumed on his support. Kevin was right to count on him and even though this would hurt Moriah, it was for her own good. It really was her only hope.

As Ray pulled out of the memory and looked back down at Moriah's feminine journal, he shook his head bitterly. How naïve he and Kevin had been! In their defense, they honestly didn't know what the drug would do to Moriah but he wondered if their incessant commitment to "the greater good" hadn't clouded their senses.

Greater good sentiments made for good political sound bytes but they didn't justify torturing one's own daughter. Ray suddenly remembered the cold, decided fury in Shelly's eyes as she left earlier that afternoon and a deep dread settled over him again. He lurched up from his seat on the couch and reached for another pour of Scotch.

He guessed what was coming next in the journal and he needed some liquid courage to help him face it.

Chapter Fifty Nine

"Okay, Father, here it is." Elliott Blythe took a deep breath, threw caution to the wind and decided to trust Father Stan Jeffries. Elliott was still curled up in the corner of his makeshift holding cell as he reentered the memory. It wasn't hard to do. He vividly remembered their every word.

"Father, I have a client that has discovered a bona fide medical miracle. He's not a doctor but he's highly connected in both the medical and political world and he has assembled a team around him that has developed a probable cure for Alzheimer's, cancer and even the HIV virus." He paused for a moment and waited for the priest to laugh him out of the confessional booth. When the priest didn't, he continued.

"The drug is called Velorum and as crazy as this story sounds, it really works. I've personally witnessed its curative powers from minor maladies to life and death situations. It's still not ready for FDA approval, but it's close, at least relatively speaking, perhaps a few years." He paused again and this time the priest interjected from across the dividing partition.

"Son, this sounds like cause for a celebration not a confession. I take it this Velorum isn't quite as miraculous as it initially sounds?"

Elliott nodded in the dark and smiled to himself. Something about this priest had a soothing effect on his frayed nerves. He knew how to strike the right balance between sensitive silence and ice-breaking humor. Elliott liked him and he was glad he was confiding in him. His confession began to flow more freely.

"Sir, my client is Kevin Gunther, the mayor of Los Angeles." The father's silhouette nodded. He knew who Kevin Gunther was; nearly everyone in Los Angeles and the rest of the country did. Kevin's smooth handling of the nation's greatest hostage situation a couple of years earlier had earned him national fame as well as the "Rudolph Giuliani excellent leadership under fire" award.

Mr. Gunther was a friend to anyone who cared for the poor or underprivileged and that included Father Stan Jeffries.

Father Jeffries had met the mayor on numerous occasions and found him to be one of the few politicians whose stump speech platitudes had actually translated into effective policy. "I know the mayor." The priest repeated softly.

Elliott continued, a twinge of reluctance poking him again. He faltered at first and then blurted out, "Things aren't as great as they seem in the Gunther administration."

The priest chuckled mildly and said with a tone meant to encourage Elliott to continue, "Things are usually never as great as they seem."

Elliott nodded and continued. "Six months ago I would have said that everything was fine. Kevin and Shelly were as in love as ever. Kevin was on track to be credited with empowering the research that would provide the greatest medical breakthroughs of this generation and most political analysts felt he was a shoe in to become our next president. Tragically, all of that changed when Moriah, their only child, was diagnosed with a terminal, inoperable brain tumor and then died three months later under bizarre circumstances."

The priest nodded as if he was already privy to the news and Elliott recoiled slightly wondering how he could have known. Kevin's administration had kept extremely close wraps on the findings from Moriah's autopsy. Perhaps the priest was just a very good listener.

"Kevin is a wonderful father," Elliott continued. "He was a better dad to Moriah than I am to my own kids and I totally get his desperation. If my kids had a terminal condition, I can only imagine what I would be capable of doing..." His voice trailed off and this time the priest waited silently until he was ready to continue. "I have no judgment for Kevin and Ray..."

"Ray?" The priest interrupted him gently.

"Sorry, Ray Gibbs is Kevin's attorney and friend. He's my friend too actually." The priest nodded so Elliott went on.

"I honestly don't have any judgments against Kevin. I just needed to process this whole thing with someone. Again, I would probably have done the same thing myself if I was in his shoes and had access to Velorum." Elliott's communication was beginning to break down, as was often the case when people were trying to confess something that they were still processing.

The priest gave him a helpful prompt. "So did Kevin give the Velorum to Moriah?"

Elliott squinted at the priest in the dark, shocked at how quickly he had come to that conclusion.

The priest responded to his reaction. "It's a logical conclusion based on what you've shared so far."

Elliott inhaled deeply and nodded. "He started giving her Velorum treatments a couple of months before she died and I can't keep quiet anymore. For all of its amazing abilities, Velorum tortures the person who uses it."

Elliott was on a roll now. "Father, I've never seen anything so shocking. Apparently, Velorum makes the patient's nerve endings so hypersensitive to pain that the person feels like their skin is on fire. You would not believe the screams of agony that I've heard from people who were experimenting with the wonder drug. They beg us to make it stop. They say they would rather die than feel Velorum's fire in their veins.

"Again, let me be quick to say that the drug works and these doctors are not fundamentally cruel or inhumane. If they can figure out a way to minimize its painful side effects, it will provide hope for millions and millions of people. In the meantime however, it is nothing short of torture for the people who take it. People are desperate enough to try it, because they don't want to die and when compared to certain death, the prospect of a few hours of physical pain seems palatable. What most people can never understand though until they actually take the drug, is that death becomes a welcome houseguest compared to the way Velorum hurts them."

When Elliott fell silent the priest asked softly, "How many treatments did Moriah receive?"

Elliott's reply was a hoarse whisper. "Seven and I will never forgive myself for participating."

Chapter Sixty

Father Stan was shaken up by Elliott's confession. They had remained in the confessional for another thirty minutes while Elliott gave voice to the horrendous guilt that he was carrying. Elliott desperately needed forgiveness but didn't feel he could ever receive it. He talked about his own children and how he regretted being absent from far too much of their lives. He wanted to change and make a fresh start but he felt as if his world was collapsing.

Father Jeffries let him talk and assured him that no one was beyond the reach of God's forgiveness and grace. He didn't assign any penance. Elliott's guilt was already a heavy enough weight to carry but he was haunted by the story and he was still having trouble getting his head around it.

Kevin Gunther was a great man. Sure, he was extremely driven and could be as arrogant as any other political giant but he truly cared about people and he was crazy about his daughter. Stan tried picturing Moriah screaming in agony as Velorum set her young nerve endings on fire and he shook his head to clear the mental image.

Father Jeffries was sitting in his over-stuffed armchair in the corner of his modest, little home and he decided to do what he often did when the burdens from the confessional were too heavy for him. He reached for his simple laptop, opened a new blank document and began to type.

After filling several pages with his thoughts and emotions, as well as a detailed account of his conversation with Elliott, he retired early and fell into a dreamless sleep.

The next day he arrived early at the church and attempted to catch up on his never-ending pile of busy work before taking another stint in confession. For the better part of the morning, he returned emails, filed important documents and discarded papers that he had been holding onto for far too long.

He had two meetings with brand-new parishioners and another meeting with the lay leader of the church's community mall outreach. After that, he was finished except for his hours in confession.

He was dreading them.

It was never easy to listen to people confess their anger, lust and fear. It's not that he judged them. He was too aware of the ugly corners of his own heart for that but he did grow weary of constantly hearing about the negative and the shameful sides of life. Sometimes he wished there were "happy hours" in confession, where people had to talk about all of the *good* things they were experiencing. Perhaps that was why he was so driven in his community service projects. He was an optimist who wanted to make a difference in the world around him.

He didn't realize it, but that optimistic, hope-filled worldview had made him a favorite in Catholic Church circles. He had an unusual knack for communicating God's complete forgiveness without downplaying the tragic consequences of one's sin and consequently, people felt *liberated* when they were around him. Some people from other parishes would even drive across town to his confessional because they loved his gentle, humorous demeanor but today he felt neither gentle nor humorous. He felt heart-broken for Moriah Gunther and he was haunted by the sense that he needed to speak out on her behalf.

That's what he had counseled Elliott Blythe to do.

From everything Elliott had said, there would be many more Moriahs undergoing experimental treatments during the Velorum campaign. It wasn't a sadistic thing it was a medical pioneering thing.

Elliott had poignantly said, "The first surgeon to cut open a patient's chest cavity to perform heart surgery was viewed as a monster and yet history has proven him a saint." Despite the haunting that had driven him into confession, Elliott sincerely believed the same thing would be true for Kevin Gunther and his team of doctors and scientists. Velorum would change the world.

Elliott had said it at least a dozen times but after nearly every utterance he had also added the words, "but Moriah is such a steep price to pay."

"Are the other patients who have participated in the Velorum trial happy with the results? I mean despite the pain they had to go through, if it saved their lives, they must feel that it was worth it right?" Elliott had paused for nearly a minute before he answered Stan's question. Finally, when Stan thought that perhaps Elliott hadn't heard him the first time, the reply came.

"The ones who lived are happy."

Father Stan shook his head to clear the memory. He had pleaded with Elliott to go public with his story. Gruesome experimentations on living patients could not be the way to go about curing cancer, but then, another memory flickered cross current in his thinking and he pictured his mother's agony in her final days before pancreatic cancer violently took her life. She had been tortured *without* Velorum and still died a premature death. A part of him could understand Velorum's appeal.

With the moral dilemma building inside him, Father Jeffries forced himself to trudge down the aisle for his time in confession.

The massive oak doors at the lobby opened to allow a wave of afternoon sunshine to splash into the dimly lit sanctuary.

His first appointment had arrived.

Father Jeffries settled into his spot in the confessional booth and waited patiently while the other man took his seat.

"Forgive me, father, for I have sinned." He had a flat, emotionless voice.

"How long has it been since your last confession?"

"I was here this morning."

"And you needed another dose of forgiveness?" Stan forced just a hint of humor into his voice to try to put the other man at ease.

"I'm not here about my sins from this morning."

"So you did something else this afternoon?"

"No, father but I'm about to."

Stan's skin crawled at the words. Even though he had heard more than his share of delusional and even dangerous confessions over the years, he knew that something was very wrong with this one. He could tell immediately that this man was disturbed.

"I don't understand," he responded.

"I won't be able to come back here afterwards so I wanted to confess my sin in advance. Will you let me do that?"

Father Jeffries' mouth was dry and his pulse rate quickened significantly. "What are you going to do?"

"I am going to murder the father."

Chapter Sixty One

After talking to the priest, Elliott Blythe reached a decision. He couldn't handle the pressure anymore. He had to silence his screaming conscience and the only way to do it was to come clean.

About everything.

He had already established his contingency plan but he had never actually considered using it. He was simply doing what any smart lawyer would do, making sure his own backside was covered along with his client's. In this case however, it was his client that he wanted to protect himself from.

The Velorum project was not technically illegal. Ray Gibbs would certainly never let Kevin Gunther participate in anything that was. It was just immoral and while the finely worded disclaimers might keep the doctors and scientists out of prison if sued by an irate family member, they wouldn't be able to stop a public massacre of Kevin Gunther's image.

Kevin had built his political platform on his passion for humanity and it was more than a brand or a trademark; it was authentic. That was why the revelation of his cavalier approach to human pain during Velorum's research and experimentation processes would be a political nightmare. He would be deemed a hypocrite of the highest order and even if the public was forgiving about other kinds of indiscretions, they were loathe to forgive a candidate that built his life on publicly proclaimed ideals and then privately violated them.

If Elliott went public with Kevin's dirty laundry, it would likely be the end of the mayor's career and it would significantly set back the development and distribution of the Velorum wonder drug.

It would also ruin Elliott in the process.

His name was on all of the questionable disclosures. In fact, as his conscience grew more petulant and he seriously began considering speaking out, he knew that there was no way he could distance himself enough from Kevin and Ray to avoid the fallout himself. He had helped prepare all of the legal loopholes to allow Kevin's team to stay legally sound while delving into the morally murky waters of human experimentation. If the darker side of Velorum ever became publicly known, his name would forever be associated with it.

Elliott's heart had been in the right place, just like Kevin's and Ray's probably had been. They all believed in the good that Velorum would bring to the world; their problem was that they didn't want to use the right methods to introduce that good. They wanted to rush its release and thereby ensure that their names were linked to a medical miracle and Elliott couldn't continue with it.

Even before Moriah had confided in him, the pain they were causing their trial participants was already sickening him and after she told him what she had experienced his resolve had hardened even more. Even if it meant the end of his reputation and career, he would shut the Velorum project down.

So for several weeks he had been assembling enough documentation to draw a high profile investigation into both the Velorum trial and the Gunther administration. He hated doing that to his long-standing friend and he was especially grieved about what it would do to Shelly. She didn't deserve any of this. She was the heart and soul of the Gunther family and also of everything wholesome and good in their administration. Kevin was not without virtue himself but his virtues had long been overshadowed by his ambition.

The Gunthers would certainly never forgive him and he might regret his decision for the rest of his life but also knew that he couldn't live with any more blood on his hands. Even if the patients that had agreed to participate in the trial were terminal, Elliott still couldn't get the guilt of their deaths off of his battered conscience.

He assembled his files and arranged them in a way that would mandate an investigation. It was possible that once the investigation was over, Ray Gibbs' due diligence would rescue Kevin and they wouldn't be deemed criminals. In theory, they might even be able to continue with their political aspirations but at least the nightmare of Velorum would be reined back into more humane efforts.

He considered giving Ray and Kevin a chance to back down and voluntarily forego the Velorum testing but he knew they never would and he also knew that if he threatened them, they could shift tactics and allow the burden of responsibility to fall on *him*. He was, after all, their attorney. It wasn't the doctors' fault that they pushed the boundaries in their experimenting. That's what cutting edge doctors and scientists do. That's the only way that medical science was ever changed.

It dawned on him that perhaps they had even been planning to make him their scapegoat all along. They could streamline Velorum's release and then blame *him* for its premature distribution. Once circulated and the miraculous cures were readily apparent, there would be a demand for the drug. The side effects, no matter how heinous, wouldn't discourage everyone from trying the drug. Desperate people are always willing to take risks.

Yes, he realized as the pieces began fitting together, that was probably Kevin's plan all along. He would fast track the drug's release, create a public demand for it and then when the critics reacted, he would blame his attorney and then graciously offer to slow down his testing. The slowdown would be met with public outrage, however and he would very quickly garner enough grassroots support to legitimize Velorum's testing and distribution.

It was brilliant and it might even take a decade off the standard timeline for a new drug's release but to accomplish that end, they were going to let Elliott take the fall. He was their pawn. He shook his head and smiled grimly, determined to be a pawn that pushed back. He flipped open his cell phone and punched in a number. When a voice answered, he said simply, "Okay, I'm ready. Set everything up. If you don't hear from me by the arranged time, release the information to the authorities. All of it."

Chapter Sixty Two

Detective Louis Stratton sat in the corner of the E.R. waiting room as a horde of doctors and nurses worked feverishly on his partner. The homeless man's metal blade had nicked Robyn's aortic artery and she had almost bled out en route to the hospital but the paramedics had worked a miracle in the ambulance and now the E.R. staff was working another one. She was going to make it.

He was breathing slowly and deeply, trying to lower his highly elevated heart rate and blood pressure. His young partner's brush with death had prompted him to call his own kids, two sons and a daughter and tell them how much he loved them. He got three voice mails and left his sniffling sentiment on each of their phones. They would understand. His wife was on her way to the hospital and Robyn's parents would be boarding a flight from New York City within the hour.

The waiting room was filled with police officers and reporters. Somehow they had already heard the news but at least for the moment everyone was leaving him alone with his thoughts.

The contents from Elliott Blythe's locker were in his hand. He briefly wondered if Elliott had set him and Robyn up to be hurt or taken out but he quickly discarded that thought. The file from the homeless man contained a stack of computer disks and since he didn't have access to a laptop yet, Stratton set them aside momentarily and began perusing Father Stan's calendar that he was still carrying.

Almost immediately his eyes fell on a lengthy inscription crowded into the margins of one of the pages. It began: "So this is what a moral dilemma feels like." There was a little smiley face drawn after the opening sentence and Louis smiled back in spite of himself. He was starting to feel the same warm emotion for this missing priest that Robyn had expressed. He looked down the hallway to where they had taken her for her surgery and a pang of emotion stabbed at his exhausted heart.

He looked down and continued reading. "Of all the painful, nasty things I've heard in confession over the years, this one was the worst and it will also be the hardest to keep quiet about."

There was another paragraph in which Father Jeffries expressed the angst of someone bound by oath to keep secrets. The weight of all those confessions rested heavily on someone as compassionate as Father Jeffries and yet the thought of breaking trust and exposing those secrets was unthinkable to him.

Louis knew about the power of priestly confidentiality. He had had run-ins with priests during past investigations and he was well aware that they were bound by the strictest of oaths to never violate the confidence of a confessing sinner. The words from their Code of Canon Law were clear: "The sacramental seal is inviolable. Accordingly, it is absolutely wrong for a confessor in any way to betray the penitent, for any reason whatsoever, whether by word or in any other fashion." To do so would be an unconscionable sin against God Himself and no human agency, including local or national law enforcement, could force a priest to do so.

A cop to his core, Louis had always felt conflicting emotions about the whole confession thing. He understood that sometimes people needed a safe place to come clean. He had needed that safe place at times in his life but he didn't get how a priest could hear the details of heinous crimes without reporting the perpetrators. Forgiveness was fine but justice still had to be served.

In the event that a priest was uncomfortable burying a crime in the safety of confession, there was only one loophole they could attempt to use. They could refuse absolution until an appropriate penance, such as confessing the crime to the authorities, was completed. Louis had never heard of this happening and he was sure that most people would either try another priest, or conclude that a shady conscience was easier to live with than a jail sentence. In any case, it was the only slight option available to a priest during confession.

An "inviolable sacramental seal" was impossible to dismiss. Any priest who attempted to do so, even if his motives were righteous, would be subject to immediate de-frocking and that was why Father Jeffries' next words were so riveting. He had written, "If Elliott fails to step forward and confess, I will do so myself."

Louis blinked his eyes and read the words a second time and then he read the next sentence: "I'll get him to speak to me off the record and then I'll tell the police what he says in *that* conversation. I hate to betray him like this and I know it might end my career but there has to be a better way to cure the world. If Mr. Blythe fails to do the right thing, I will have no choice but to do it for him. Moriah is much too steep a price to pay."

CHRIS JACKSON

Chapter Sixty Three

Father Jeffries had been praying for nearly an hour. After his frightening ordeal in confession, he had uncharacteristically canceled the rest of his day and locked himself in his home office to pray. He muted his phone, drew the blinds shut on all of his windows and kept the lights down low while he knelt beside his desk and prayed for wisdom and protection. Deep in his gut, he knew that his frightening visitor had been directly connected to Elliott's confession and he also knew that both he and Elliott were in danger.

Elliott must have been followed and his followers were now attempting to intimidate himself. They were probably trying to shake him up so he would eventually reveal whatever it was that Elliott had confessed to him. Kevin Gunther's people must have known that Elliott was conflicted about the Velorum operation and was at risk to betray them all. As his analytical mind continued connecting the dots, Father Jeffries came to the inevitable conclusion that the man would return. They needed to know what Elliott had shared and they would most definitely make contact again to find out.

He remembered the little headshake the man had given him before exiting the sanctuary and disappearing into the Southern California crowds and a sinking discouragement spread through him, draining him of his courage and resolve. The man would return and Father Jeffries wasn't sure what his response should be.

Should he have a heart-to-heart talk with the man and try to get to the bottom of this whole thing rationally? Should he make an appointment to speak directly with the mayor and confront him with the information, or should he march to the nearest police station and bare his soul? A chilling thought struck him then. Would the police even believe him? Kevin Gunther was a hero in law enforcement circles and Stan had no evidence other than some easily denied words whispered to him in a dark confessional booth.

No, if what Elliott had shared was true then these were desperate, controlling men who undoubtedly had contingency plans for any possible setback to their agenda. History was on the line and in the big picture of history a lone priest was a very minor obstacle to overcome. Father Jeffries knew that he couldn't be there when the man returned.

He suddenly felt very small and decided to disappear for a few days to contemplate his options. He would immediately clear his schedule under the pretense of visiting some family members or friends but then he would secretly make contact with Elliott Blythe. It had to be in secret since Elliott was probably being watched. He needed to know what Elliott was thinking and if he had decided to step forward and blow the whistle, preferably before anyone "murdered the father."

When he remembered the man's cold, emotionless voice he wondered if he should leave that very moment but then he shook his head roughly and forced himself to rein in his quickly escalating fear. He needed to move quickly but he didn't need to make a mistake.

He stood and reached for his desk phone to start the process of clearing his calendar. As his secretary greeted him warmly, another pair of undetected ears tuned into the conversation and carefully recorded their every word. After Father Jeffries hung up with his assistant, another phone number was dialed and the same cold voice that had spooked him in confession spoke into the receiver. "He just cleared his schedule. He's leaving tomorrow. I would bet anything that he plans to snag Elliott again before skipping town. We'll have to move fast."

There was a pause on the other end of the line and then Kevin Gunther's voice spoke softly. "Do you think he plans to skip town, or do you think he plans to do something with Elliott's information?"

An uncomfortable silence was the only response on the other line. Finally, Kevin spoke again, "Very well. Make sure he doesn't get close to Elliott unless you're able to capture their entire conversation."

As the undetected eavesdroppers finished their conversation, Father Jeffries walked to his kitchen and slid a coffee packet into his fancy Keurig coffee maker, his one extravagant possession. He stared blankly as the machine sputtered; then hummed; then poured a steady stream of evenly brewed coffee into his waiting cup.

He blew a cooling breath into the cup and noisily sipped the steaming liquid, while rehearsing his plan to make sure he was acting instead of reacting. He was a methodical thinker who prided himself on living an intentional life versus a reactionary one. No, he decided, he wasn't overreacting and he wasn't being rash. Things were every bit as serious as he suspected.

After all, Elliott Blythe was not the first person to confess to him about the Velorum operation.

Chapter Sixty Four

"Thank you so much for seeing me on such short notice." She smiled graciously at me when she said it and as always I was instantly disarmed by Shelly Gunther's poise and grace. As I lay in my sweaty hospital sheets thinking back on that interaction, I knew that the frequent news articles about her were correct. She was one of those rare celebrities whose real life persona was just as kind and genuine as her public one. From her opening greeting and smile, I was again reminded that Shelly Gunther was the real deal.

She was a radiant woman, as pretty as a fashion model but humble and gentle enough to be non-threatening and disarming. She was beautiful and enchanting but without a hint of seduction. I was convinced that broken hearts probably piled up wherever she went. Kevin Gunther was a lucky man.

She seemed slightly hesitant that day and genuinely concerned about presuming on my time, which, to me, was humorous because as the wife of a White House-bound mayor she was one of the busiest women in Los Angeles.

"Oh, it's my pleasure." I replied with a weak attempt at matching her kind disposition. "How are you doing, Shelly?" I asked gently as I showed her to an overstuffed armchair across from my small desk and handed her a box of Kleenexes.

"I'm trying." She answered with a soft smile that melted into a heart-broken expression. "I just miss her so much and I can't believe that she's really gone."

I nodded as I took my seat across from her. She began talking then, the heart-wrenching anguish of a newly bereaved mother pouring out of her like a fountain. After several minutes she covered her mouth with her hand and said apologetically, "You probably weren't expecting all of that." and then she added with a gentle laugh that broke my heart while also brightening the entire atmosphere in my tidy but somewhat drab office, "Well, you did ask."

I chuckled politely and waited for her to continue. After a moment, she wrinkled her brow and said, "I do need to speak with you about something specific if that's okay." It was more of a question than a statement so I nodded an affirmative and encouraged her to continue.

"I need to insist on an extreme level of confidentiality." There was enough authority in her voice to remind me that she was more than a disarming wife and mother. She was a political activist that could hold her own against critics and opposition parties. She carried a rare balance of strength and grace and again I found myself being smitten by Shelly Gunther.

"Certainly." I responded with a forced smile. "I'm pretty good at confidentiality."

She smiled back at me and said, "I figured as much."

She took a deep breath and then began. "Something horrifying happened between Moriah and her father near the end." I raised a questioning eyebrow and she quickly clarified, "I don't think he personally hurt her in any way. Kevin would never do that. They were best friends since the moment of her birth. She adored him and he was always helplessly wrapped around her little finger. Kevin was possibly the greatest father in the world but even so, something was very off during the final months of her life." She paused with an anguished frown.

"What do you mean 'off'?" I asked gently.

"Whenever Kevin would enter the room and approach her she would clam up and get very quiet and distant and she also stopped confiding in me like she always used to."

Her voice faltered for a moment and she glanced briefly around my office sizing up my minimalist décor. She looked back at me after a moment and I saw tears standing out in her violet-colored eyes. I noticed that she looked like a young Elizabeth Taylor but I wasn't distracted anymore. Her story had my full attention.

She continued. "I asked Kevin about it and his response was completely uncharacteristic. In the past, if anything ever concerned Moriah, it went to the top of his priority list to fix but with this, he just sloughed it off and attributed the change in her demeanor to her failing physical condition. A few days before Moriah died I finally decided to press her about it and her response was horrifying. She said, 'He made me promise not to tell.'"

I was leaning forward in my chair and I pursed my lips and began shaking my head skeptically when she interrupted me. "No, I seriously don't think it was anything like that. I would never suspect him of that. It was something else."

I nodded for her to continue then and she said, "When I continued to probe Moriah said, 'the medicine hurts so bad.'"

"The medicine?" I asked.

Shelly nodded. "The public doesn't know this yet but Kevin has gotten involved with a group of scientists and doctors that are researching a potentially miraculous drug that will one day be able to save people like Moriah."

"Do you think your husband used this drug to try to help Moriah?" It was the obvious question in light of the direction of our conversation but it hit her like a punch to her stomach and she began trembling.

Her face blanched noticeably at the question even though it was exactly what she was insinuating.

"I think he might have." Her voice trailed off into a strangled whisper with the words. After a painful moment she spoke again, "And if he did, then it's inhuman to even think of what he put her through."

I looked at her questioningly and for the next several minutes she told me horror stories of Velorum's painful side effects. Kevin's people were working feverishly to find a way to minimize and control them but in the meantime it was a very unstable drug that sometimes helped, sometimes harmed but *always* hurt.

I pictured Moriah in her weakened state experiencing the kind of pain that Shelly was describing and I felt like *I* had been punched in the gut too. "Shelly, if he really did use Velorum on her, it was only because he was trying to help. You know that right?" Even as I said it I knew that if Kevin Gunther had indeed allowed his team to experiment on his own daughter, Shelly would never recover from it.

Chapter Sixty Five

"So this is what a moral dilemma feels like."

Father Stan's written words kept repeating in Louis Stratton's head. He was sitting near his partner's bedside now. She had successfully survived the surgery and was now recovering in the ICU. Visitors were usually banned from there but an exception could be made for a cop's partner. He would wait by her side until her parents arrived from New York City.

Louis had carefully read and re-read Stan's account of Elliott Blythe's confession and had felt himself being drawn even deeper into this "dilemma." On the surface it seemed horrifying that Kevin Gunther would actually experiment on his own daughter with a drug that was still several years away from FDA approval and no amount of justification could make his decisions palatable. However, when he superimposed his own family into the scenario things weren't quite as clear.

He imagined one of his own children being diagnosed with a terminal brain tumor and he wondered if, in that situation, he would be desperate enough to try Velorum even though it would hurt them in the short run. Would he torture them physically to save them from certain death? Physical pain would heal and its memory would eventually fade but death? It was forever.

He remembered one of his favorite Denzel Washington movies called "John Q" in which Washington's character, a frantic father, held a surgeon at gunpoint to get him to perform a surgery on his terminally ill child. Insufficient insurance coverage had prohibited the surgery so John Q took matters into his own hands and risked everything to try saving his precious son and it worked. His son survived the surgery, evaded death and as Denzel's character was led away in handcuffs at the movie's end, it was obvious to every viewer that any loving father could be tempted to do what Q had done.

Kevin Gunther was not unlike John Q. There had been no hope for Moriah apart from some devastatingly drastic measures and he had unapologetically taken them. Where John had held a surgeon hostage at gunpoint, Kevin had simply applied a medicine with enough curative powers to give the doctors a fighting chance to save his daughter's life.

Nevertheless, in doing so, he had also hurt her more than anyone would know.

The tumor was already too far advanced to save her. Elliott Blythe had told Father Jeffries as much in their off-the-record conversation. If doctors had discovered the tumor even a few weeks earlier, the Velorum treatments would likely have saved her life. However, with the late diagnosis, not even Velorum's powerful effects could provide the doctors with enough information to save her life. Consequently, her little body had been tortured for nothing.

That was the haunting. If she had lived, Kevin could have begged for Moriah's forgiveness and then pampered her for the remainder of her long, healthy life. He could have pointed to her *alive*, sparkling, blue eyes as justification for his decisions but since the treatments had failed, Kevin was forced to bear the guilt of having hurt her in her final days instead of holding her in them.

In addition, the agony of his actions was driving him mad. At least that was Elliott's assessment. Although Kevin was delivering speeches, gaining supporters and conducting himself in his usually polished demeanor, he was dying inside. He couldn't forgive himself and his failure with Moriah had driven him to an even *greater* determination so see Velorum perfected and distributed to the masses. Here again was another of Kevin's paradoxes: in the middle of his deepest grief he still wanted to help the world.

Detective Stratton shook his head as he reflected on all of it. Yes, he thought, he could understand Kevin Gunther. He nodded to himself as he realized that he could quite possibly hurt his own children if he knew there was a chance of saving them. Was that selfish, he wondered? It didn't really matter. He could easily be John Q.

He could easily be Kevin Gunther.

However, that was the father in him talking. The cop in him saw it differently. No matter how desperate Kevin had become, he had experimented on multiple people (Elliott hadn't told Father Stan exactly how many) with a dangerous, unapproved drug that was known to severely damage its recipients.

Cops weren't allowed to practice the greater good philosophy. They had to protect the innocents that got crushed along the way. In the big picture, Velorum was a wonderful thing that would undoubtedly transform modern medicine but in the little picture it was an illegal source of wounding for people who were desperate enough to allow themselves to be experimented on.

He hoped Kevin was successful but he also knew that Kevin and his mad scientists needed to be taken down.

He glanced at Robyn as she lay in her hospital bed all propped up with pillows and looking like a human electrical outlet with cords attached to her arms, nose and chest. She looked so sad as she slept. The pain from her knife attack was manifesting in her sleeping expression despite the steady drip of morphine that was flowing into her veins. He checked the time. It was nearly midnight and her parents would be arriving within the hour. He continued reading.

Chapter Sixty Six

"I talked to Father Stan again today. He is still insisting that I talk to my mother and tell her everything. He also said he wanted to talk to my dad but I begged him not to. Hopefully he won't." After that, there was a written prayer of thanks for Father Jeffries and a hope that nothing bad would ever happen to him.

Ray Gibbs looked up from his reading and momentarily closed Moriah's journal. Her wish for Father Jeffries' safety had brought last night's memory to mind. He reflected upon that horrible conversation.

Kevin had been furious. His eyes gleamed fiercely and his jaw kept clenching and unclenching in a violent attempt to stay in control of his emotions. He turned his back on Ray and the other man in his office and exhaled deeply. He waited long enough for his initial outrage to subside and also for his guests to feel incredibly uncomfortable. Finally, he turned to face them and even though he had regained a measure of composure, they could both feel a hot fury radiating from him.

"So tell me again what happened." Kevin said as he sank slowly into his plush leather chair and leaned menacingly over his desk in their direction. He wasn't angry with Ray; he was angry with the other man, the man that Ray had warned him not to hire.

Ray was never one to say "I told you so," but he certainly had the right to say it now. Everything he had warned Kevin about this young hired gun had come true.

The man glanced cautiously at Ray and then back at Kevin. He was young, maybe thirty years old and had a slouching, unimpressive appearance. He was in desperate need of a shave and he didn't look anything like the intimidating contract killer that he was. He appeared weak and insecure with a shifty, unsure expression. Of course, that was all an act. Kevin knew that he was frighteningly proficient and competent at his trade.

The left side of his face was swollen and his right side was covered with a blood-soaked bandage that had been hastily applied to a nasty puncture wound. Fortunately for him it was a flesh wound and hadn't caused any lasting damage.

Ray had nearly come to blows with Kevin in his insistence that they not go down this particular path. "Nothing stays quiet or hidden in politics!" It was one of his favorite mantras and he had practically screamed it at Kevin when he had been informed that Kevin had contacted the killer. Both men remembered the interaction.

Ray had shouted. "Kevin, this is the end of your career! There is no going back from here. We are not criminals and no matter how badly we miss Moriah and want to make her death count, we are not doing this."

Kevin's entire body had started quivering with rage as he stared into Ray's fierce expression. Normally Ray would have backed down at this point but he knew too well how much was at stake. Kevin's grief and regret over Moriah was clouding his thinking and Ray was not willing to let his best friend ruin himself as a result. "We are not doing this." Ray had said firmly and then turned to walk away.

"It's too late, Ray." Kevin's words had brought Ray sharply around.

"What do you mean it's too late? Tell me that you did not authorize a hit on Father Stan Jeffries."

Kevin responded quickly, "Don't be ridiculous. Of course I didn't order a hit on him. He's not even going to touch the priest. He's simply going to send a message, shake him up a bit emotionally so we can eventually get him to talk."

Kevin had made a colossal mistake. The man had indeed touched the priest and now Ray was standing silently beside Kevin's desk while the killer stared at them from his slouching position in the chair across from them. A vein was visibly throbbing along Kevin's temple and his molars were grinding audibly. "Clay," he addressed the younger man through gritted teeth. "Why did you do it?"

"You told me to do whatever it took." Clay's voice was surprisingly steady despite his nervous, shifty appearance.

Kevin practically shouted in response, "Yes, to get him to talk to me! I never ordered you to kill him!"

The young man shrugged. "At least he won't be talking now."

Ray feared that Kevin would fly over his desk and tear at Clay's eyes so he interjected quickly. "Tell us everything that happened. Don't leave a single detail out." He nodded at Kevin, a calming, steadying look.

When Kevin sank back into his chair, the young man started talking again in his flat, hollow voice.

"I dropped in on him at confession. I thought it would be fitting to talk to him there." He smirked as he admired his own creativity. "I told him I needed to confess my sin in advance."

"What sin was that?" Kevin asked with a snarl. Ray shook his head at him and nodded for the man to continue.

"I told him I was going to murder the father." Clay paused for dramatic effect until Ray prompted him, "And after that?"

"After that, he got all courageous on me. He tried to get me talking while he dialed 9-1-1. I could hear his phone beeping though so I high-tailed it out of there and left him to wonder if I was a harmless crackpot or if I had actually been threatening him."

Ray and Kevin both nodded. They were aware of the shaky 9-1-1 call that Father Jeffries had made and they also knew that no official report had been filed on it.

"And you returned a couple of days later?"

The killer nodded at Ray's question, which was really more of a statement. They all knew that he had returned and they knew what had happened after he did.

After Clay surprised Father Jeffries again the very next day in confession, Father Jeffries disappeared without communicating any clear details to his assistant or his staff. The young hit man feared that the priest was planning to run to the authorities to blab his information about Kevin, so he felt he had no choice but to use his considerable skills to locate his whereabouts and track him down. It wasn't hard to do. Father Jeffries hadn't gone far. He was still in Santa Monica when Clay found him and then murdered him in an underground public parking lot on the 3rd Street Promenade.

Kevin looked at him with a frightening intensity and said, "I need you to tell me everything."

Chapter Sixty Seven

"One mild black coffee coming right up, Father!" The barista's cheerful baritone greeted Stan Jeffries as he entered the quaint little coffee shop. The employees could practically set their watches by Father Jeffries' punctual morning routine and on most days he didn't even need to stand in line to get his coffee. It would already be waiting for him and they never bothered to charge him for the order, since he always put triple the price in the tip jar. Everyone at the coffee shop loved him.

He was like a big brother or a second dad to most of the employees and even to some of the regular customers who frequented the place at the same time he did. He knew nearly everyone by name and he never seemed too busy for a smile and a genuine "How do you do?" More than a few of the coffee shop employees and even an occasional customer had pulled him aside to ask for a free, impromptu counseling session and they quickly discovered that nothing was taboo. He was always available and he seemed comfortable discussing anything with them. In some ways, they were like a second congregation to him and several of them had even begun attending his "official" congregation as a result.

Seldom discouraged and never too rushed to encourage others, he was a bright spot in their weekly routines and that was why on this particular morning the barista could tell that something was very wrong.

Father Jeffries had indeed greeted him with a kind smile but instead of creasing his face in deep laugh lines like his smiles usually did, this one faded quickly, replaced with a deeply troubled expression. He seemed unusually preoccupied and distracted, possibly frightened even. He looked at his watch repeatedly, checked and then rechecked his cell phone and without wanting to be obvious, he turned his body to glance casually behind him as if he was expecting someone. He looked behind him so often that the barista eventually turned to stare out the windows to see if anyone was following the priest.

"Father, are you okay?" He had to repeat the question and when Stan finally responded to it, all he did was merely nod and then sneak yet another furtive glance behind him. The barista leaned across the counter and spoke in a low, confidential tone. "Father, do you need help with something?" Nearly everyone in the coffee shop would jump to their feet and help the priest if he just gave the word.

But no word was forthcoming. In fact Father Jefferies didn't even acknowledge the second question. He merely tugged a napkin out of the holder and promptly exited the store with his steaming cup of Joe. He had barely left the parking lot on foot when another man entered the shop and looked around quickly, assessing each of the employees and guests.

This man was the polar opposite of Father Jeffries. Where Father Jeffries was neat and tidy and nearly impeccably groomed, this man had a lazy, slouching appearance. His skinny jeans were faded and hung too low on his narrow hips. His diesel shoes were torn and stained and it was hard to tell if he had purchased them that way, or if he had fished them out of a dumpster somewhere. His five o'clock shadow spread down his neck and past his T-shirt collar, giving the impression that he desperately needed both a shower and a shave. He looked to be young, possibly early thirties and he had sharp, penetrating eyes that belied his casual, disinterested demeanor.

He was looking for someone and after waiting for several minutes without finding him he abruptly left without ordering any coffee. The barista's love of crime thrillers may have gotten the best of him, or he might have been a little spooked by Father Jeffries' odd behavior but one way or the other he was certain that something was wrong.

The priest was never flustered, seldom agitated and he seemed to possess an enormous well of courage. The barista remembered seeing Father Jeffries wade into the middle of a pending gang fight in the parking lot once to break things up before anyone got hurt. The gang members on both sides backed down and agreed to honor the request of the man of the cloth. When Father Jeffries had come in after the close call and ordered a refill of black coffee his hands were trembling slightly however, he hadn't been nearly as nervous or fidgety then as he was today. Yes, something was definitely wrong.

He wondered if he should call the cops to give them a heads up but quickly discarded the idea. What was he supposed to say? "Officers, one of my regular customers was a little preoccupied and jumpy this morning and then another guy came in, looked around and left without ordering any coffee. Something isn't right. Can you help me?" It sounded ridiculous and yet even as he pressed the coffee grounds and steamed the milk for the next customer's order he knew that it wasn't ridiculous. Father Jeffries was in trouble.

CHRIS JACKSON

Chapter Sixty Eight

"I want you to tell me everything."

Kevin Gunther leaned back in his leather chair and waited for Clay, the blood-spattered hit man, to explain why he had murdered the father. Ray was waiting as well, watching silently while also playing and re-playing worst-case scenarios in his mind. It was an unconscious habit he had picked up after so many years of practicing law.

The beat up young man seated beside him was a former Army Ranger, decorated for his skill as an expert sniper. There wasn't a lot of drama to his switch from a military career to a soldier-of-fortune (as he liked to refer to himself). It was all about the money for him.

He was young and disillusioned and he had the typical hedonistic appetites of a drifting youth who had seen and caused more than his share of death and destruction. He wanted to make a buck and spend it on his pleasures with no regrets and since a single "hit" paid more than he could make in an entire year with the military, he hadn't needed much coercing when Kevin Gunther's people offered him a job. It seemed like an easy enough case: shake up a Catholic priest without actually hurting him and because of its seeming simplicity, he had made a rookie mistake. He had underestimated his quarry.

As an Army sniper he used to do painstaking research on his assigned targets and he had even spent multiple days at a time buried on hillsides under camouflage, awaiting clear kill shots. He should have used that same patience and attention to detail before approaching Father Stan Jeffries but instead he had assumed that a measly, little priest would be a pushover. It was true that he had badly frightened the father but he hadn't counted on the courage that Father Jeffries' fear would awaken in him. Father Jeffries hadn't folded under the pressure. He had discovered a way to hit back.

That's what had caused Clay to escalate the level of force. As a Ranger he was trained to always increase the level of force against an opponent. If attacked by an unarmed man, use a knife or a club; if attacked by a knife-wielder, use a gun. So when Father Jeffries scheduled a meeting with Elliott Blythe instead of disappearing like he was supposed to, the ex-Ranger's default position was to increase his level of force.

True, Kevin Gunther had said not to harm him, but now Father Jeffries was trying to harm *Kevin* and that simply couldn't be allowed to happen. It was the Ranger way, loyalty forever and all that. At least that's what his justification had been when he explained to Kevin and Ray why Father Stan's mutilated body had been found in Santa Monica.

"I couldn't let him start talking. I had to shut him up for good." Clay looked Kevin in the eye as he said it. "He wasn't going to leave quietly. He was determined to bring you down."

Ray expected Kevin to go ballistic again but surprisingly he remained seated without responding or changing his expression.

After an awkward moment the ex-Ranger continued. "I followed him to his meeting with the attorney, Mr. Blythe and I got close enough to videotape their conversation."

At that revelation both Kevin and Ray interrupted him simultaneously, "You recorded their conversation? Where is the tape?" They looked at each other hopefully and for a brief moment optimism flared to life in their hearts. Now they wouldn't have to wonder what Stan knew and had revealed.

Their hopes were immediately dashed however, when the young man shook his head and said apologetically, "I did get close enough to videotape them and I even started to record their interaction but I got interrupted and I had to leave before I was able to capture much of what they said."

It was only partially true and even as he said it, both Kevin and Ray became aware of another patch of dried blood along his cheek that had blended in with his scruffy five o'clock shadow. Someone had clocked him cleanly on that side of his face too.

"So where were you and how much did you hear?"

Clay nodded at Ray's questions and replied, "They were meeting on a park bench overlooking the Santa Monica Pier. It was crowded and loud, which was how I was able to get close enough to film them. I was able to get them on my iPhone. The people around me probably thought I was simply texting someone."

Kevin interrupted him sharply, "Show us your iPhone."

The man hesitated but when Kevin's eyes took on a threatening glare he grudgingly conceded. He retrieved his cell phone, fumbled with its touch screen and then held it out for Kevin and Ray to view.

Sure enough they could see the back of Stan and Elliott's heads as they sat together on a bench near the Santa Monica Pier. Elliott was speaking in a subdued, strained voice and just as the phone steadied and they were able to make out his words, Father Jeffries' head cocked slightly to the right like he had been distracted by something. He then abruptly turned and stared directly into the phone's camera screen. His kind face was lined with fear and determination and almost as if it was a reflex, his right arm pulled back and fired a thunderous punch into the direction of the camera.

There was a loud thud and a guttural grunt and then the screen went blank.

Ray and Kevin both looked at the cut along Clay's cheekbone and he shrugged. "The priest had a good right hand."

"So you killed him?" Ray's question brought the conversation back on task.

"No, not then. That came later."

Chapter Sixty Nine

He ran. He never imagined that his priestly smock could make such a good track and field outfit. He hurdled the park bench he had been sitting on and dashed toward the nearest crosswalk, as his robes splayed out behind him like a superhero's cloak. He didn't feel like a superhero, however. His wrist felt broken; it was hurting him even as he ran and he had no idea how much of his conversation with Elliott had been recorded. He would have stopped to take the man's iPhone as a safety measure except that he had seen the handle of a nine-millimeter pistol tucked into the waistband of the man's faded skinny jeans and he knew that a lucky uppercut was no match for a semiautomatic pistol. As he ran, he hoped that Elliott would make a clean getaway too.

Luckily, the crosswalk favored him as he approached it and he was able to continue sprinting to the other side of the street where he ducked down an alley and ran to a parked taxicab that he had spotted one block away. He threw open the backseat of the taxi and yelled, "Drive!" It probably wouldn't have worked (the cab driver was off duty) except that the sight of a frantic Catholic priest with bloody knuckles was an interesting enough sight to compel the

bored driver to re-start his car and slip smoothly into the flow of
traffic.

"Where to, Padre?" the man asked amused.

Father Jeffries shook his head. "It doesn't matter. Just get me
out of here. Drive north toward Malibu." And then he sank into the
backseat, slid down low and risked a peek out the back window.
No one seemed to be pursuing him and he couldn't see Elliott
anywhere. He considered calling him but he knew that Elliott was
probably busy practicing his own hurdling and sprinting skills.

The man had staggered backwards under the weight of Stan's
punch but he hadn't fallen down and even as Stan raced by him he
was already shaking his head to clear his senses. For such a
scrawny looking kid, the young man was surprisingly tough and
Stan desperately hoped that his punch had given Elliott enough
time to get away too. He looked down at his bloody fist and flexed
his fingers gingerly. Pain shot across his wrist with the motion
causing him to grimace but then his grimace melted into a smile as
he remembered how solidly his punch had landed. It was a really
good shot.

As a man of the cloth devoted to peace and reconciliation, he
always had to take the high road and be forgiving and gracious
even in the face of personal insults or injustices. He usually didn't
mind, since he was, by nature, a kind and tenderhearted man
however, he had to admit that it had felt pretty great to throw a
heavy right hand, especially since he had been living in fear ever
since the man had visited him in confession.

Yes, he nodded to himself in the backseat of the cab that was
the guy. Even in their brief, violent encounter Stan could tell he
was the one and he also knew that the little headshake the man had
given him had indeed been a warning.

He suddenly felt a renewed sense of the danger he was in and
he began praying that Elliott had gotten away. The attorney
wouldn't have been able to run as fast as Stan in his expensive suit
and leather loafers. Besides, Elliott didn't have the look of a very

physically fit man. He was thin enough for a man his age but it was the thinness of genetics not of a disciplined, healthy lifestyle.

Father Jeffries, on the other hand was a fitness nut. At least that's what his constituents always said. He regularly lifted weights and played basketball in a local recreation league. He would have been a decent ball player if he hadn't been so short. His best vertical leap could only carry him halfway up the net, so he was usually relegated to either riding the bench or occasionally getting some playing time as a point guard but at least he played hard and maintained a strict lifestyle of healthy eating and exercise.

He shook his head suddenly, surprised at how random the human brain could be. He had just cold-cocked a man and then ran for his life and here he was thinking about his exercise routines. He chuckled grimly to himself and then felt his cell phone vibrate from within the folds of his robe. He fished it out and read Elliott's name across the screen. He answered with a quick, "Hello," and then waited for a response on the other end. He could hear someone breathing but no voice came through. He considered speaking again but then snapped his phone shut abruptly. Perhaps the man had taken Elliott's phone and was attempting to get a bearing on Stan's location.

Another thought cut across his thinking then. Perhaps Elliott was injured and wasn't able to speak. He sat in anguish for several agonizing seconds unsure of what to do. The cab driver was clearly intrigued and kept stealing thoughtful glances at the priest from his rear-view mirror.

"Still heading to Malibu?" the driver asked curiously.

Father Jeffries nodded, "Yes, just keep driving, please. I'm not worried about the meter."

Then he flipped open his phone and decided to call back. He waited tersely as the phone rang and when he heard a click and then the same sound of labored breathing, he offered a weak, "Elliott, is this you?" A few seconds later a cold reply sent terrified chills up and down his sweaty back. He would never forget that voice.

"Forgive me, Father, for I have sinned."

Chapter Seventy

Elliott finally decided that it was safe to leave. He had been hiding in a bookstore pretending to read while desperately watching the street outside. He had taken advantage of Father Jeffries' swift right hook and he had surprised himself with how fast he could still run. He slipped nimbly past a group of slow-moving cars on the crowded street and then sprinted two blocks before sneaking a peek behind him. Other than a few shoppers who found it odd to see a man in a business suit running full blast down the sidewalk, no one even seemed to notice him and he couldn't see anyone following him either. After surmising that he wasn't being watched, he slipped into the bookstore to get his bearings and think.

He didn't need to worry about being followed. Having been momentarily bested, Elliott's pursuer was regrouping as well. The young hit man wasn't one to react foolishly in a situation like this. He had already underestimated the priest and he wasn't going to make another mistake by running through the Santa Monica tourist district waving a pistol in the air. Once he saw that Elliott and the priest both had the jump on him, he simply assessed his face's damage from the little priest's punch and then slowly headed down toward the Santa Monica Pier. He had loved the pier ever since he was a little kid and he decided that he might as well have some fun while he was here.

He chuckled to himself as he made his way down the winding staircase and the suspended footbridge that spanned the Pacific Coast Highway. He was an Army Ranger who had been deployed on harrowing shoot-to-kill missions and he currently had a deadly handgun tucked casually into his waistband and yet he couldn't wait to get on the pier's ancient roller coaster and lift both of his hands up into the air during the scary sections. He was a deadly assassin and a playful, little kid all at the same time.

Boy, when he finally decided to see a therapist, they would have a field day with all of his issues.

He had done some pretty twisted things in the name of the U.S. Military and he had done even worse things in the name of cold, hard cash. As he approached the pier and began climbing the steps up to the rickety looking roller coaster, Clay decided that he would add one more twisted act to his resume. He really would kill the father.

He flipped open the cell phone that Elliott Blythe had dropped and began scrolling through the recent contacts. Sure enough, the priest's number was near the top, so he tapped the screen and sent him a call. The priest's frightened voice greeted him on the second ring but rather than immediately responding, he decided to have a little fun with the man. He deserved at least that much. His jaw was still throbbing from the guy's short right cross so he decided to breathe loudly into the phone like someone might breathe if they were seriously wounded and struggling for breath. The priest listened to his wheezing for several seconds before disconnecting the line.

Clay laughed cheerfully as he stood in line to purchase roller coaster tickets. He was just laying down a crisp twenty-dollar bill at the ticket counter when Elliott's phone rang in his pocket. He pulled it out and smiled as Father Stan Jeffries' name greeted him across the top of the screen. He accepted the call and resumed his labored breathing.

Stan's concerned voice reached out across the satellite signal, "Elliott, is this you?"

Clay paused for a moment contemplating how he wanted to respond and then it came to him. Brilliant. The father would get a kick out of this. He repeated the first words he had ever spoken to Father Stan Jeffries, intentionally keeping his voice quiet and low. "Forgive me, Father, for I have sinned."

He was still laughing to himself several minutes later as he settled into a front seat on the old Santa Monica roller coaster. After a slow, grinding start the coaster began picking up speed and he giggled with the rest of the kids on the ride. It was a clear, sunny day and he could see miles out into the Pacific Ocean. As the ride dipped and twisted around sudden drops and turns, he started to feel hungry. He had spied a soft pretzel stand near the entrance to the pier. A salted pretzel would definitely hit the spot he thought contentedly.

Meanwhile Elliott Blythe was inching slowly out of the bookstore doorway in an attempt to escape the 3rd Street Promenade undetected. Nothing seemed out of the ordinary and the man was nowhere in sight. He realized then that his cell phone was missing but he didn't dare head back to try and locate it. He decided to risk replacing it with a cheap Go Phone from a kiosk directly ahead of him. Despite his fear, he knew he couldn't be without a means of communication. He cut the sales clerk short when she asked about the terms and coverage of his current cell phone plan. He wasn't upgrading, he just needed a phone. Now!

A few minutes later, he was hailing a cab and giving its driver instructions on where to take him. He needed to be with his family and ensure that they were okay. If he had been followed to his covert meeting with Father Jeffries, there was no telling where else he had been followed to or from. He wished he could call the priest to make sure he too had gotten away but he couldn't recall what

Father Jeffries' number was. That information was safely stowed on his lost phone, his phone that was safely tucked in the hip pocket of a thirty-year old assassin's skinny jeans.

Chapter Seventy One

"Uncle Ray, it hurt so bad." Moriah was still crying as she said the words. She had been crying when he picked her up and she hadn't stopped crying the entire drive home. Ray's heart was in his throat and his guilt was cannibalizing him from the inside.

"I'm so sorry, honey," he said weakly.

"Please don't make me go back," she pleaded pitifully.

"Moriah, it's the only chance we have to cure your tumor. I know it hurts but we *need* you to go back." He couldn't believe what he said next. "Sweetie, we need you to go back to the doctor and remember that you absolutely cannot tell your mother."

She looked at him through her tears and asked the same question she had posed to her father earlier that morning, "But why can't I tell my mom? Why doesn't she know about these treatments?"

Although Ray and Kevin had rehearsed their response to this inevitable question, Ray could barely get the words out. "Your mother wouldn't approve of the treatments. She would never let you go through this much pain, even if it could help you in the long run. She loves you too much to watch you hurt like this. Your dad loves you just as much but he thinks that if you can endure the pain, it will save your life and then once you recover you'll have the rest of your life to enjoy with your mom and your friends and, someday, a husband and a family of your own. Moriah, I am so sorry, but you cannot talk to your mom. It has to be this way for now."

She nodded her understanding and then turned her face to the window and continued weeping softly. Ray was dying inside. He couldn't believe that he had leveraged his relational influence with his young goddaughter to get her to quietly undergo a brutal series of experimental drug treatments that would set her little nerve endings on fire to the point of making her wish she was dead.

Tears were pouring down both of their cheeks as he drove. He knew he couldn't take her home yet. There was no way Shelly could see her in this condition. Her pain needed to subside and the memory needed to fade a bit. "Moriah, is there anywhere you would like to go before I take you to see your mom and dad?"

She was quiet for a minute before answering and then she asked softly. "Can you take me to church?"

Ray was startled by her request but then nodded, "Of course, honey."

He would take her anywhere at that moment if it would help her process her deep trauma.

"Do you want to see Father Stan?"

She nodded without answering and Ray changed lanes and began making his way across town to Father Stan Jeffries' parish. He glanced at his watch. It was mid-afternoon. Father Jeffries would be available in confession right now.

By the time they reached the parish and made their way inside, Moriah's tears had subsided somewhat and Ray was beginning to breathe a little easier. He trusted Father Jeffries and believed that his church was one of the safest places he could find for Moriah to do her processing. Additionally, the priest's vows of confidentiality made Ray feel doubly safe in taking her to him. Ray knew very well that a priest's vow was iron clad, stronger than court subpoenas and injunctions. Yes, it would probably be okay to let her talk to Father Stan.

He offered to walk her in but she declined his help. After all, she knew exactly where she was going. Father Stan Jeffries had been the Gunther's priest for nearly a decade. His was the voice that had spoken numerous blessings over Moriah and she still remembered the proud little wink he had given her at her confirmation. He was like a second father to her and she knew she could talk to him about anything.

Ray knew that too but there was something else that he didn't know. Having chosen his career above meaningful, intimate relationships, he still didn't understand how strong the bonds of human love and devotion could be. Yes, Moriah was his goddaughter and even though he was crazy about her, he still lacked the ability to understand that some relational bonds were stronger than vows of confidentiality.

Stan had sworn to the Catholic Church that he would keep the confidences of people in confession but he had sworn an even deeper vow to God and he wasn't the kind of man to let a child be harmed on his watch, especially not a child like Moriah.

Stan's heart had been ripped to shreds with the horrifying revelations of the Catholic Church's rampant child abuse scandals and then its subsequent failure to adequately punish the offending priests. He would have left the priesthood over these crises and fulfilled his devotion to the Lord through another denominational expression, except that at his core he was a puritan and he still believed the church could be restored to the wonderful institution that God originally intended it to be.

However, even though he was deeply loyal to the church, his loyalty paled in comparison to his loyalty to God and God's children. He would chuck his vow of confidentiality before he would keep silent in the face of Moriah's shocking confession.

Ray Gibbs had never anticipated that reaction. Even as he sat slumped on the couch in Shelly Gunther's oceanfront office remembering all of these details, he was still shocked at how he could have so badly underestimated the little priest.

Father Jeffries had loved Moriah more than he loved the priesthood.

And as he thought those words, Ray Gibbs desperately wished that he had been the one to love Moriah enough to call a stop to the whole thing. Instead, he had betrayed her, leveraging his influence to convince her to continue with the Velorum treatments and then he had done it again when he pressured her to keep the experience a secret from her mother. He understood Kevin's rationale. Desperate fathers seldom think clearly when they're fighting for the lives of their children but what was *his own* excuse? He was Kevin's legal *counsel.* He should have slapped some sense into Kevin and told him he was committing both political and relational suicide by allowing his daughter to be experimented on. However, he hadn't. He had been too blinded by political ambition and by the allure of being the voice behind the man who would make history.

Shelly was right to hate them both. He had another brief thought of chugging the rest of the scotch whiskey and then filling his lungs with saltwater from the ocean and ending his guilt and grief right there. Then he shook his head no. He may have screwed up royally and he would probably never earn Shelly's forgiveness, or recapture his own self-respect but at least he could do the right thing now.

He could come clean to Kevin.

Kevin never knew that Ray was the one that had helped Moriah confess to Father Jeffries. Ray had let the blame for that fall on Elliott, another casualty of Ray's prodigious ego. Instead, Ray would try to make that right.

He punched a preprogrammed number on his cell phone and waited for his assistant to pick up. When he did, Ray spoke firmly, "Release Elliott Blythe and let him return home. We're done with him." Then, "Also call Kevin to let him know that I need to speak to him. Tell him that I'll be there within the hour."

He hung up and glanced outside at his driver who was still waiting patiently beside Ray's luxury car smoking a slow-burning cigar. What a boring job, Ray thought as he watched the man smoke but at least it was an honest one.

He considered returning Moriah's journal to her room but then decided to hold onto it. He gathered it along with Shelly's journals and safely stowed them all in his wide, leather briefcase. He stretched his back and took one last look at his reflection in the giant picture window. It was the last time he would see himself like this, a free man.

Life as he knew it was coming to an end.

Chapter Seventy Two

"Mr. Blythe, you are free to go."

Elliott looked up from his curled up position in the corner of the stark interrogation room. His body was trembling from the combination of cold air conditioning, exhaustion, pain and low blood sugar. He hadn't eaten anything all day and he was crashing badly, barely able to think clearly or even stay awake.

He glanced at a small clock in the corner of the room. It read 10:00 p.m. Only fourteen hours had passed since his meeting with the other lawyers in Kevin Gunther's conference room and yet that meeting felt like it occurred a year ago. He was so tired that he was on the verge of tears and he momentarily failed to understand the words that had just been spoken to him. He looked blankly at the messenger who repeated, "Mr. Gibbs just called and said that you're free to go."

"Where am I?" asked Elliott as he struggled up to his knees and then a standing position and began flexing his leg to work out a cramp. The man ignored his question and continued, "A car is waiting to take you wherever you would like to go."

"I want to see Kevin." Elliott's voice was hoarse and gravelly as he said it. "Can your driver take me to see the mayor?"

The man paused shortly as he considered the request. He hadn't expected that from Elliott. He was certain that Elliott would ask to be whisked to his comfortable tri-level home where his wife and twins were waiting for him. "I'll see what I can do." The man offered and then exited the room.

Elliott stumbled after him. The door had closed behind the man but when Elliott turned the handle and applied some pressure it slipped easily open. It appeared that he really was free to go.

He had no idea where he was, however. As he peeked out of his holding room, he saw a long, windowless corridor that was utterly devoid of décor. He tried shuffling down the hall but needed to pause to catch his breath after just a few steps. The effects of the fatigue and the torture were taking their toll on him and he couldn't walk on his own. Fortunately, his captor quickly returned and offered him an arm of support.

As they worked their way slowly down the hall, the man spoke to him. "Mr. Blythe, Mr. Gibbs said that you can certainly see the mayor but he won't be available for the rest of the night. You can see him tomorrow morning. However, in the meantime, he wants you to know that their plans have changed. He is terribly sorry for today's events and he will process all of this with you tomorrow."

Dual emotions went off inside Elliott at the words. The first was an incredulous mockery. "Ray, said he's 'sorry for today's events'? You mean the events of torture and the threats against my family?"

Elliott's blood began boiling and it released a surge of fresh vitality into his wooden limbs, but then the second emotion stepped forward and curbed his anger. He wondered aloud, "Why would the plan be changing? How and why would Ray and Kevin be having such an abrupt change of heart?" He suddenly grabbed the shoulder of the man beside him and demanded, "I need a phone."

The man looked at him curiously and then offered him his cell phone. Elliott's hands were trembling so badly that it took him several attempts to punch in a set of numbers and hit the send button. He waited anxiously while the call went through and finally a quick, "hello" greeted him on the other end.

"It's Elliott. Hold off on making the call. We need a little more time."

A shocked reply sounded, "Elliott? Are you okay? Where have you been? Your wife's been calling all evening." Elliott interrupted him, "I'm fine and I'll explain everything when I see you, but for now I need you to stop both the call and the delivery."

An awkward pause followed his demand and then, "Elliott, it's too late. The call has already been made like you ordered and the documents have been hand-delivered to the police."

CHRIS JACKSON

Chapter Seventy Three

"Stratton, there you are! I need to talk to you."

Detective Louis Stratton looked up from his borrowed laptop and his frantic reading of the documents on Elliott's computer disks. He was so engrossed in his reading that he had almost forgotten where he was. He blinked his eyes and glanced around at the machines in the dimly lit ICU room until his eyes focused on his young captain, Troy Majors.

The captain had an intense but deeply compassionate look on his face as he lowered himself into a chair beside Stratton and encircled his arm around the older man's broad shoulders. Stratton glanced at him guardedly, feeling a mixture of curiosity and annoyance. "What's up, captain?"

"First of all, I'm so sorry about Robyn."

Stratton bristled at the younger man's attempt to play the concerned, supportive leader. He was the one that had ordered Louis and Robyn to stand down from their investigation into Kevin Gunther's administration. The captain noticed Stratton's reluctance and quickly removed his arm.

"Stratton, I was wrong about the mayor."

Louis looked at him wordlessly so the captain continued. "We just received a call and a delivery from Elliott Blythe's office and they've given us a boatload of information about Kevin Gunther and something called 'the Velorum operation.' Is this what you were looking into?" He glanced at the open laptop questioningly.

Stratton remained silent, absorbing his captain's words. He had no reason to suspect Elliott. This was undoubtedly part of his whistle blower's insurance policy but he didn't know if he could trust his captain. Captain Majors was a good man and an excellent cop but his loyalty to the mayor was legendary and Stratton had a difficult time believing that a file from Elliott Blythe's office could so quickly shake those loyalties.

"What did Blythe's office say?" Stratton asked cautiously.

The captain didn't seem troubled by Stratton's evasive answer. He plunged ahead, "We have multiple files of evidence that are being reviewed even as we speak but in the summary document it accused Kevin Gunther and a team of pioneering doctors and scientists of experimenting with an illegal drug called Velorum. Apparently, the drug has some amazing abilities that allow its user to self-diagnose even severe medical ailments and traumas. According to the document it's a wonder drug that actually works and will someday change the face of modern medicine.

"The problem is that during its developmental stages, Kevin's team has experimented on living patients despite some known heinous side effects." He paused to read Stratton's reaction. The older man couldn't hold back his recognition of these assertions so the younger captain nodded and continued.

"Okay. So that is what you and Robyn have been investigating." It was a statement and Stratton had no choice now but to hope that his captain was more loyal to the law than to the mayor.

"So, how much trouble is the mayor in?" Stratton asked quietly.

His captain pursed his lips thoughtfully. "I'm not sure. Pushing the envelope like this is typical of Kevin Gunther and ultimately his goal was to help humanity. Depending on the types of disclosures and consents his team received from their patients, he could get anything from a slap on the wrist to several years in prison. If he gets linked to Father Jeffries' murder however, all bets are off. At the very least, his public life will definitely be over for a while, which will be a tragedy. There haven't been many men in office like Kevin Gunther."

Stratton tensed inwardly at the words and braced himself for his captain's order to bury the evidence and forget it was ever brought to their attention. Fortunately, that order never came.

"It will take several hours to study and categorize all of the file contents and then a little longer to obtain additional search warrants but I can tell you one thing, Mr. Blythe's office was incredibly efficient. The case is so iron clad that I'm not even sure if Ray Gibbs will be able to get Kevin out of this hot water."

Stratton realized that he had been holding his breath so he exhaled deeply and then leaned back in his chair. "So am I back on the investigation?" He asked with a grin.

His captain grinned back. "No, I need you right here waiting for your partner to wake up."

"Yes sir." Stratton said softly as a grateful tear slipped quickly down his graying, stubbly cheek.

Chapter Seventy Four

"I'm going to kill the father."

The words kept sounding in Father Stan Jeffries' ears as he lay restlessly in his bed attempting to sleep. He was exhausted and in desperate need of some rest but was beginning to think he would never drift off. He considered taking a strong sleep aid, when his doorbell rang several times followed by several strong knocks on the front door. His heart lurched into his throat and his pulse began pounding frantically. He lay stiffly in his bed forcibly slowing down his breathing and craning his ear to listen.

There was another loud knock on the door followed by another series of quick doorbell rings. Whoever it was, they weren't leaving anytime soon. He considered waiting them out, but then he decided that he needed to know for certain who it was. A fear that it was the man from the park bench, the man he had decked, gripped him and he flexed his sore hand and slid out of bed as quietly as he could.

His floors were all hardwood and fortunately he knew every squeaky board by heart. He was able to move noiselessly out of his bedroom and down the hallway to the front door. All of his lights were turned off but patches of light from the street lamps still drifted in through the windows. He wished he had a weapon. Even a baseball bat would do but he had nothing so he simply moved cautiously to the peephole and peered outside.

A face was staring back at him and then another loud knock caused him to jump back and audibly cry out.

"Father Jeffries, I know you're in there. I'm so sorry to bother you but I really need to talk to you."

Stan knew that face and he recognized its voice. It was one of his parishioners, a young man named Robert who had recently been released from a stint in the local jail. He had a string of petty offenses but he was headed down a path toward more deviant crimes when Stan was brought in to help reform him. Stan had liked him immediately even though he was overly talkative and wasn't yet self-aware enough to realize that everyone cringed when he jumped into their conversations. Stan had to pace the frequency of their meetings simply because he didn't have enough time for the young man's persistent ramblings.

Tonight, however, he felt relieved to see him. He couldn't sleep anyway. He was jumping at shadows and it might help to take his mind off of things. He slowly opened the door and said a shaky but pleasant, "Hello, Robert."

There was no reciprocal greeting, just a frantic, "Father, I need to talk to you. I'm sorry to come to your house but something bad has happened and I really need your advice."

He continued with his stream-of-consciousness way of speaking while Stan gently ushered him off the doorstep and into his home. He peered both directions down the street expecting to see a sinister figure watching him from a parked car but everything looked pretty normal.

When he re-entered his house and locked the door behind him he noticed for the first time how large his young visitor was. He hadn't seemed that big sitting across from Stan's desk at the church but here in the dimly lit living room in the middle of the night he was frighteningly large and he was very agitated.

He hadn't sat down like Stan suggested but rather began pacing back and forth in front of the couch. He was talking the whole time and the more he paced and talked the more emotional he became. Stan tried calming him down. "Son, sit down and take a deep breath. Let me get you something to drink and then you can tell me all about it."

The young man nodded and then dropped his bulky frame onto Father Jeffries' simple couch. "Okay. Thanks Father."

Stan slipped around the corner to the kitchen and flipped on his coffee maker and waited for the water to heat up.

The timing of this visit was peculiar. Stan certainly wasn't afraid of this young man and this wasn't the first time that a distraught parishioner had knocked on his door after hours but something didn't feel right. He peeked around the corner and saw Robert's big head drooped forward into his hands. He appeared to be crying. His shoulders were shaking and he was sniffing quietly. Stan's heart softened when he saw it and he thought that perhaps this wasn't anything for him to be alarmed about after all.

When the coffee was finally ready and Stan re-emerged from the kitchen with two steaming mugs, the younger man had composed himself a bit and his face had a grim resolve to it. Father Jeffries handed him the cup and then sat across from him. "Tell me everything," he said with a gentle smile.

"Father, my mother is dying of cancer." His voice broke as he said it and then his next words came out in a rush, "They found out too late to be able to help her. If they had caught it a few months earlier they could have helped her but they said it was too late and there is nothing they can do now except make her comfortable and wait for her to die."

Stan's heart melted with compassion for this lost and hurting young man and he began to offer some words of comfort when the young man interrupted him, "Father?" He asked questioningly. "Have you ever heard of something called *Velorum*?"

Chapter Seventy Five

"Velorum?" Clay, the eavesdropper, repeated the word softly to himself as he hunched over the sound system in his common, non-descript van. He had been parked down the street from Father Stan Jeffries' house for most of the evening, waiting for the perfect time to pay the little priest a final visit when an angry-looking, hulk of a young man shuffled down the sidewalk and began banging on Father Jeffries' front door.

After several minutes of persistent knocking, Father Jeffries had opened the door and invited the large man inside. He then looked nervously up and down the street but didn't seem to pay any attention to the van. As soon as Father Jeffries shut the door, Clay turned on his high tech surveillance equipment, a parting present that he took for himself from the U.S. Military and positioned a pair of headphones firmly against his ears.

He had inserted the recording bug in Father Jeffries' living room several days earlier, immediately after Kevin Gunther gave him the green light to contact the priest. Although he had underestimated the priest's courage, at least he had still been thorough with his wire-tapping. His multiple nights of eavesdropping had been fruitless at first but now he was pleased with himself for being willing to do the boring, mundane part of the job. Now they were getting somewhere.

"Velorum? Where did you hear about Velorum?" Father Jeffries' voice was trembling noticeably.

"At the hospital, or actually in the hospital parking lot when I was leaving. After they told my sister and me that there was nothing they could do for our mom, we decided to go home to get some of her favorite things so she could have them with her at the end. On our way out one of the doctors followed us and asked me if he could talk to me in private. He said he had a proposition for me. He said that in addition to his work for the hospital he also worked for a research team that was in the final stages of developing a drug called Velorum and that it could possibly save my mom."

Inside the house, Father Jeffries' heart was pounding so loudly that he wondered if it could be heard outside of his chest. He was also getting scared. What were the odds of one of his *parishioners* being approached about Velorum? He knew something was off with this midnight visit. He suddenly wondered if somehow Kevin had gotten to this young man and was using him to get to himself. He noticed again how large his younger friend was and he began to feel cramped and trapped in his little house.

"Father, are you okay?"

Clay's eavesdropping ears perked up at the question and he made a mental note of it. Something about this "Velorum" thing must have hit a nerve with the priest.

"Yes, please continue." Father Jeffries replied in a small voice. Since he didn't have many options in front of him but to listen, he might as well hear where all of this was going.

"Okay. So this doctor tells me that he works for a team of scientists and doctors who have developed a drug that could possibly help them discover some alternate ways of treating my mom, ways that might have been overlooked with their standard testing. I asked him why they hadn't already tried Velorum if it was so wonderful and he said it was because it hadn't been approved for distribution. However, he said it was close. In fact he said it was so close that they just needed to try it with a few more patients and then it would get the final FDA approval they were working toward. He promised me that it was a real thing and that it would probably save my mom's life. Still, he said I would have to move fast. It was crucial to give the Velorum to her as quickly as possible so my mom and the doctors could work together to figure out how to treat her.

"I didn't understand what he meant by my mom and the doctors working together. My mom is practically in a coma and I'm not sure how she could help them but he seemed to be legit. He gave me this form to sign and I told him I needed to think about it. Then I dropped my sister off at our house and came straight here to see what you think I should do."

Robert handed Father Jeffries a folded-up piece of paper and Stan's skin tingled as he looked at in the young man's massive hand.

There were several seconds of silence and the eavesdropper in the car wished desperately that he had been able to plant video surveillance equipment in the house. He knew instinctively that the paper was important and he started getting fidgety and agitated wishing he could see Father Jeffries' reaction to whatever the document contained.

Father Jeffries was hoping that the dim light in his living room was concealing some of his emotions as he reached out a shaky hand and accepted the offered piece of paper. It was letterhead. He could feel the quality weight of the paper as his fingers touched it. He was reluctant to read whatever it was that the letter contained so he took a slow sip of his cooling coffee, before opening the paper.

It was on Elliott Blythe's corporate letterhead and it was a disclaimer and a waiver of patients' rights. "I, the undersigned, agree to participate in the Velorum trial and I waive all rights of counter-action in the event that the trial is unsuccessful." He noticed darkly that the list of possible side effects included some "mild to moderate discomfort or pain."

Anger began building inside him as he wondered how often Kevin's experimenters preyed on hopeless family members who felt that they had nothing to lose but to allow their dying loved ones to be experimented on. He scanned the rest of the document and then asked abruptly, "Did this doctor happen to mention my name?"

Clay sat up straight in his van at the question. Yes, he wanted an answer to that question too. Had Kevin contracted more than one person to silence this little priest? The young man shook his head no but of course the eavesdropper couldn't hear a headshake inside his van.

His curiosity began to grow.

Chapter Seventy Six

The euphoria was unbelievable. I was in absolutely no pain and my thinking was unusually precise and clear. Despite the many knuckle-headed choices of my youth, I was fortunate to have been spared from any drug experimentation however, if I had to guess, I was certain that this is what banned drugs would have felt like. My body seemed light and surreal, like I was floating in a buoyant salt sea. A cheerful glow surrounded me like an aura or an angelic halo and I was happy and carefree, enveloped by the warm arms of peace.

I had the same biological awareness that had overwhelmed me earlier but now it served me instead of burying me. I was still aware of endless medical minutiae but now it was neatly categorized and filed in my brain instead of crashing over me like an indecipherable wave. At my own pace I could calmly and analytically study every detail of my broken body.

Yes, I was still broken. Not even Velorum's prodigious powers could save me at this point. However, there was no fear or dread in that knowledge. It was almost like the Velorum had blocked any negative emotions while cradling me in a cloud of joy. With a little smile on my lips, I calmly surveyed the data about my body:

shattered spine, torn aortic artery and multiple puncture wounds that had left my internal organs a limp and failing heap. Yes, that was pretty much the assessment. I was a goner and I was actually surprised that my heart was still beating as strongly as it was. It must have been the result of this mysterious wonder drug.

There was also one other thing that had captured my attention. In addition to my newfound peace and calm, my memories had completely returned. I knew who I was, where I was and why my captors had taken me here. I knew what they were after and why they were so intent on getting me talking. A parade of faces marched past me, Rachel, Shelly, Moriah, Elliott Blythe, Ray Gibbs and Kevin Gunther and I realized with crisp clarity that I possessed critical information about each of them.

Kevin was right to believe that I was the key.

"I think we've done it! We've hit the sweet spot." I was distantly aware of the doctor's voice as he declared the great news. A chorus of cheers, applause and affirmations answered him from the roomful of doctors and scientists that were gathered around me. Kevin Gunther was standing just a few feet away from me and as he received the great news, a triumphant smile spread across his handsome features. "How long can we keep him here?" he asked. Typical Kevin.

"Unless something else breaks down in his body and alters the chemical balance, we should be able to keep him in this state for close to an hour." The doctor was smiling at Kevin as he said it. "This is it right here. This is Velorum at its world-changing best. If we can dial in on this spot at will, then we will have succeeded in changing modern medicine. The drug will serve as its own painkiller while it heightens the patient's internal awareness. Gentlemen," he said grandiosely to the assembled team, "We've just packaged a miracle and the world as we know it is about to change. Kevin, after you get your information out of him, a glass of champagne would be well within order."

Even though I was the human guinea pig in the room I couldn't help but being moved by both the impromptu speech and what it represented. I knew from my enhanced sensory capacity that if they had found Velorum's "sweet spot" for me just a little bit sooner, I wouldn't have had to die. I would have been able to tell the doctors exactly what my body needed to make a full recovery. I could have told them which organs were the most critically injured and which ones would repair on their own. I could have told them exactly how much blood I had lost and which meds would most rapidly start the healing process. Velorum would have saved my life and even though my life was beyond saving now, I still marveled at what I was both witnessing and experiencing. Even on my deathbed I was overwhelmed with how huge this breakthrough would be for the human race and how much needless sorrow and suffering would be alleviated as a result of it.

I found myself cheering for Kevin Gunther. The world needed Velorum and I suddenly understood why he had done the things he had done. Even if his immediate circle of acquaintances came to view him as a monster, the world would remember him as a saint. We needed Velorum and I understood what had driven him to do the things he had done.

Kevin was smiling warmly at the doctor and shaking hands with everyone in the room. It wasn't long however, before he shooed everyone out of the room and wheeled a short stool beside my hospital bed and leaned in close to me. Even in my happy, Velorum-soaked state he was a little too far into my personal space and I started to feel uncomfortable again. He still frightened me and I tried inching away to the other side of my bed, reluctant to look him in the eye. He noticed my discomfort and grinned at me, a harsh, exultant smile. He leaned even closer and stared at me, a clear understanding connecting us now. When he spoke it was obvious that he knew my memories had fully returned.

"Your sister is here to see you."

As he said it, his cell phone rang loudly in his suit jacket pocket, startling both of us. He muted it immediately and frowned at the screen before answering with a curt "Hello?"

He was still sitting so close to me that I could hear a distressed voice on the other end of the line say, "Mr. Mayor, we have a major problem. Elliott Blythe's office just called and said, 'As a courtesy to Mr. Gunther, Mr. Blythe wanted you to know that he's gone public with his knowledge. Tell the mayor that the authorities will no doubt be contacting you within twenty-four hours.'"

Kevin was silent as he absorbed the words. After a prolonged pause, the voice on the other end spoke up nervously, "Sir? Do you think they're bluffing, or is this actually something to be concerned about?"

Kevin never answered. He disconnected the call and was about to speed-dial Ray when his phone rang again. It was Ray. He smiled grimly as he shook his head and answered, "Your response time is always impeccable." He stopped abruptly as Ray interrupted him in a muffled tone that I couldn't quite decipher. Kevin's back stiffened at one point and then he dropped his head in a gesture of bewilderment. Then he walked briskly to the door and left my room without a backwards glance in my direction. As the door closed behind him I heard him mumble a greeting to someone and I immediately recognized the voice that shouted angrily at him in response.

It was my sister's voice.

Chapter Seventy Seven

Rachel Parker was standing in the doorway of my hospital room and even though her features were concealed in shadows I could tell that she knew.

I had betrayed her and there was no way around it, no viable justifications and no way to take it back. I watched conflicting emotions move rapidly across her delicate features while a cold ache of futility swelled through me. Although Velorum's warm glow still surrounded me, my overwhelming feelings of self-loathing and regret started growing so intense that my brain could feel the pressure. My head felt like it was going to split in half.

While her emotions shifted from shock to hurt to anger and back to shock again, mine held steady at guilt-ridden regret. I hated that I had wounded her so deeply, especially since I had devoted so much of my life to *protecting* her from pain. I had loved her, served her, and done my best to lay my life down for her but now it was all in jeopardy. It could take her years to recover from this betrayal.

I hadn't set out to wound her. God knows I would never intentionally deceive or damage her. I thought I was doing the right thing and I was still convinced that I *had* done the right thing.

It was for her safety and protection that I had spoken out. I had to. To do otherwise would have been inhuman.

Yet, there she sat with teary, red-rimmed eyes that reminded me of the little picture toys that change scenes when you shift the picture in the light. One moment her face bore anguish and sorrow, and the next it took on a frightening anger that turned the blood cold in my veins.

I certainly understood her outrage. She was mortified and my decision to breach her trust had left her feeling completely humiliated and alone. Ideally, she would have spoken up on her own. She wouldn't have needed me to reveal what she knew. However, I knew she never would.

People who have suffered abuse seldom do.

So I told. I had delivered her confession to the authorities and even though it hadn't gone public yet, in a very short time she would be forever marked as a whistle blower against the Velorum campaign. It would probably end her career and I doubted that she would ever be able to forgive me.

After all it wasn't the first time I had used her confession against her.

I had done it once before when we were children. I used her secrets to get the police to take our stepfather away. I knew I had done the right thing and that she would thank me in time. Years later she did, but now she was sitting in front of me with the same painful look of horror that she had worn as a little girl when I had reported our stepfather for assaulting her and her anger was just as frightening now as it had been then.

"How could you?" Those three little words can pack a pretty stout punch.

"Rachel, I didn't have a choice."

Rachel looked at me with such a frantic expression that I started fearing for her emotional stability. "How could you have quoted me without talking to me first? I went to you for advice!" Her voice was raised and bordering on hysteria.

I desperately wanted to de-escalate the situation, but I couldn't think of a thing to say that would help her understand. She was right of course. I shouldn't have surprised her with my decision. I should have spoken to her first. However, in my defense, I hadn't known how deeply involved she was with Kevin Gunther. I didn't know she was in love with him.

"Rachel, I didn't know…"

"But you knew enough!" She cut me off and I knew this conversation would be more about me listening to her than it would be about me explaining myself to her. I knew it was useless to argue. We had been having these types of discussions since we were kids.

She was my sister.

I hadn't remembered it when I woke up attached to life support machines and I hadn't remembered it when I studied her features in the stack of pictures they gave me to try to jog my memory. When I saw her pretty face smiling up at me from her portrait, I knew that I loved her but I couldn't place who she was. I certainly remembered her now.

She was my sister, my kid sister and my love for her was the love of a big brother that had been her biggest cheerleader and protector since our father died and our mother quickly remarried and replaced him with an angry, violent drunk.

In mom's defense, he didn't start out that way. He was actually pretty great at first. He never tried to replace our dad and he was kind and understanding and gave us plenty of space to grieve and sort out our tangled emotions.

Rachel warmed up to him right away but I was a little more reserved, not wanting to betray dad's memory by giving my heart away to another father. He probably would have won me over in time if he hadn't started drinking.

It began with a drink or two after work, and then quickly turned into an alcoholic cliché that culminated with him metamorphosing into something entirely other than he was while sober. The couple of after-work drinks turned into drunken binges that more often than not got nasty and ugly.

The gentle, understanding guy disappeared as soon as the alcohol did its thing and we were left with an angry, violent monster. Fortunately or unfortunately based on how one looks at it, we didn't have to live with him in this state for long. His was not a gradual descent into hell. It was a rapid one that culminated with him beating Rachel black-and-blue around her arms, back and midsection.

Of course, he was apologetic the next day and in her heart-broken innocence Rachel was willing to forgive him and pretend it never happened.

But I wasn't.

Though only a few years older than Rachel, I was determined to do what my father would have done. If I had been bigger and stronger, I would have handed the man a beating that would have made my dad proud but since I was just a kid myself, I lied to Rachel to get her to visit a police station with me. I fabricated some story about this really cool police officer that had visited our classroom and offered to give any of us students a personal tour of the police station if we ever came by to visit him.

She didn't want to do it and she was afraid of getting in trouble because a walk from the school to the police station after school would mean that we would be AWOL when our mother came to pick us up. Rachel cried and begged me to just go home with our mom, but I convinced her to go to the station with me and take the tour. When we got there, I humiliated her.

I asked the dispatcher behind the bulletproof glass if we could speak with an officer, any officer was fine. I said it was in regard to a highly confidential matter. I said we were afraid to go home and that was when Rachel realized what I was doing.

Tears immediately began pouring down her cheeks and she stared at me with a pleading, horrified look. "Please don't tell," she whispered.

It was too late. An officer was already ushering us into a private room to talk and before I lost my nerve, I pulled up the sleeves of Rachel's shirt and exposed the nasty, purple bruises.

That was the beginning of the end. Our stepfather was arrested and taken away. Mom's heart broke into a million pieces and Rachel promised that she would never forgive me.

"How could you?" She had said those words all those years ago when she was grieving the loss of our father and trying not to disappoint our mother and she was saying them again now that I had once again pulled the rug out from under her.

"Rachel," I said slowly, measuring my words. "I told you that Kevin Gunther is not who you think he is." I looked nervously at the doorway aware that Kevin could walk in on us at any moment.

"Rachel, you need to get away from him. You're innocent in this whole thing and you need to distance yourself while you still can."

Her face had lost all of its color and she swayed dangerously on her long legs.

"I don't know what to do. An hour ago I thought you were dead and then I heard you were alive but about to die and then I received a 'courteous heads up' from Elliott Blythe's office letting me know that I was being formally listed as a whistle blower against Kevin Gunther."

Her voice broke off into a sob and then she suddenly lunged toward me and buried her face in my chest as the wells of sorrow became uncorked in her broken heart. I was distantly aware that she had torn out several stitches in my abdomen but I was far more concerned about my sister than my already destroyed body.

I cradled her the best I could and then I forced her to look at me. "Rachel, you need to get out of here. This won't be easy and for a while you will feel like your life is over but I promise you that you will get through this and," I added, "your conscience will be intact when you do. Time will prove that you were right and Hollywood will eventually forgive you."

I gave her a grin with that statement. She and I had always joked about how quick Hollywood was to forgive its fallen heroes.

"You aren't complicit in the Velorum operation and you'll eventually be seen as the good guy but you need to hurry. This is bigger than you realize and you need to distance yourself from Kevin as quickly as you can."

I realized then that several monitors were beeping loudly around me. She must have disconnected some leads from the monitors when she fell on me and I could already hear footsteps approaching the door. "Please Rachel, go. You need to trust me. Don't contact Kevin again."

She looked at me with a pleading expression.

"I love you," I said softly.

There were tears in her eyes but then I realized they were in my eyes too and I could hardly see her as they streamed down my face.

The door opened and two doctors entered in a concerned rush. They nodded gruffly to Rachel and then leaned over me to adjust the leads and check my fragile vital signs.

As they fussed over my condition, Rachel slipped quietly out the door.

Forever.

I knew that when she got herself composed and then returned to check on me and continue our conversation, it would be too late. I would be gone.

Chapter Seventy Eight

Father Stan Jeffries knew that his life was most likely over. It was just a matter of time before they killed him. He was not a spy or an action hero. He was a Catholic priest and he didn't know how to change his identity or blend into a foreign culture. He didn't have a lot of spare cash and he didn't have any friends in high places that could call in a favor to rescue him. His friends were probably gathering their yard sale items for their upcoming "community mall" day.

He smiled in spite of himself as he thought of that. He really had loved being their priest and if these were his final hours, he was grateful that he didn't have a lot of regrets to haunt him. Certainly, he regretted the damage his betrayal would cause Rachel and he knew that it would most likely destroy their relationship when she found out that he was the one that had revealed her as a source in his deposition with Elliott Blythe's attorneys. They assured him that she was innocent and that there was no fear of any charges being brought against her. She was an uninformed believer in Kevin Gunther's humanitarian aims. She had no first-hand knowledge of the Velorum operation.

It was true that during their brief relationship, Kevin had made a colossal error in judgment and had confided in her about his anguish over Moriah's treatments with an experimental wonder drug that he said was her best shot at surviving her brain tumor. However, that was all she knew. She hadn't personally witnessed anyone receiving the drug and she didn't know how dangerous it was. When she told the priest about Kevin's admission, it wasn't to expose him or bring him down. It was for her own benefit.

She had been torn up with guilt over her relationship with the married, White House-bound mayor and she needed to find some solace for her soul. As she always did when she didn't know what to do, she turned to Father Stan Jeffries but this time she was shocked by his response. She had always known him to be the picture of gentleness and forgiveness but when she told him this particular news, he went ballistic.

He wasn't trying to condemn or wound her, he was simply heart-broken for her and he was outraged that Kevin Gunther would take advantage of her vulnerability. Shortly after storming out of the room and slamming the door behind him however, he returned and gathered Rachel into his strong, fatherly arms. She cried like she used to do as a little girl when she was grieving both the physical loss of her father and then the subsequent emotional loss of her mother. Stan's compassion got the best of him after a moment and he too shed some tears as he held her against his chest.

When their emotions had subsided a bit, he pleaded with her to call off her relationship with Kevin and create as much distance from the Gunther family as she possibly could. It couldn't possibly end well for her. If word leaked, Shelly would be devastated and Rachel's reputation would be crushed along the way. The celebrity side dish never fared well in these high profile scandals.

She assured him that she would break off her affair with the mayor, but even as she said the words, she knew in her heart that they were hollow. She didn't know if she had it in her to do it.

Despite her beauty and her talent, she was still a broken, little girl who terribly missed her dad. It wasn't that she was consciously trying to fill a father-wound with a fling with an older man. It was just that her heart ached and Kevin somehow assuaged its pain.

At least in the moment he did. Whenever he left her to return home to Shelly, her grief and depression escalated into an overbearing wave. She nodded at the priest with a stronger resolve. "Yes, I'm finished with Kevin and I'm so sorry." Her eyes had a little girl vulnerability in them and his heart melted as he stared into them.

"Thank you for trusting me," he whispered. She nodded. "Please don't tell anyone about Moriah. I'm not even sure he was thinking clearly when he told me about her."

Stan's back stiffened a bit and he recoiled from her before responding. Finally, he said to her, "Rachel, Kevin *was* thinking clearly when he spoke to you. Moriah confessed to me."

Rachel covered her mouth in horror, a desperate look spreading across her delicate features. Stan nodded to confirm her unspoken question and then added, "And Shelly knows too."

Rachel shrieked at that. "Shelly knows? She told you?" Stan nodded again silently as she continued, "Does Kevin know that she knows? Did she tell you what she plans to do?"

"Rachel, Kevin Gunther has to go down for the whole Velorum debacle. Too many people have been hurt." Then he hesitated before adding, "Rachel, I need your permission to quote you as an innocent source. I need to do it for your protection before the investigation gets underway and accusations start flying."

She shook her head adamantly, "No way. You can't bring me into this. Please don't say anything yet. I'm so confused. Don't say anything until I can talk to Kevin."

His voice rose angrily in response, "Absolutely not! You are not speaking to Kevin Gunther about this, Rachel. You need to stay clear from him until this whole thing goes down."

She nodded meekly, all of her remaining strength draining out of her. "Can you please wait just a little bit longer before you tell? Please give me a little time to process."

Her eyes looked so forlorn and overwhelmed that he had nodded in agreement. "Okay, I promise you that I'll let you know before I go public with the information."

She thanked him, kissed his cheek and then left on trembling legs.

He never called her first.

Chapter Seventy Nine

Father Stan Jeffries and Robert, his midnight visitor, finished their conversation abruptly with the priest urging the young man to think long and hard before subjecting his mother to any Velorum experimentations. Yes, Velorum was a real thing. No, it wasn't a hoax. Yes, there was a remote chance that they could get some additional insight into her condition, but no, it wasn't likely that they would be able to save her and the "mild to moderate" pain side effects would actually be excruciating.

It wasn't easy to tell the young man, no. A part of him wanted to tell him to take the risk. After all, the miracle drug might actually work. None-the-less, in his gut he knew that the young man's mother was already too far gone. Kevin Gunther's medical team was simply looking for more data to collect.

It made him seethe with anger to think that Kevin's people would prey upon hurting families and exploit them in their grief. He understood the need to test the drug and he certainly believed in the future of the drug. That's what made the whole situation a moral dilemma but he could not with a clear conscience encourage anyone to subject a family member to that level of excruciating pain.

"Son, I know you're hurting and I know you would do anything in your power to help your mom, but I really don't think that Velorum is your answer. Go get her special things, take them to the hospital, and spend the remaining time you have loving her and thanking her for never giving up on you."

The younger man was crying freely now and when Stan ushered him out the front door, Robert turned and scooped the little priest up in an enormous bear hug that nearly cracked the priest's ribs. After a moment, he let him go and quickly headed down the street.

From inside his van former Army Ranger Clay continued his eavesdropping and snapped several photos of the departing man and then glanced at the string of photos he had recently developed. They were pictures he had taken several nights earlier of Stan and Shelly Gunther in the front seat of a dark sedan. They had been so engrossed in their conversation, and each other's arms, that they hadn't even noticed when he drove by and took a rapid-fire series of photos.

When Clay first followed them and snapped their pictures from a distance, he thought they were having an affair and he guessed that their covert meeting was an attempt to conceal their relationship from the public eye. He assumed that her husband, Kevin, knew about the relationship and had thus contracted him to shake up the priest.

Father Jeffries and Shelly were so caught up in their little moment in the car that they didn't even notice how close he veered toward them while snapping a sequence of photographs. He had planned on having a little fun and possibly leaking his find to the Internet. Word would get out anyway and it might be nice to be the source of such a scandal but when he developed the pictures in his apartment's darkroom, he discovered that it wasn't an affair after all. He wouldn't be able to shock the world with the revelation of a fling between a celebrity wife and a man of the cloth.

Shelly had been crying and the priest looked like he was about to cry too. Either they were breaking up or they were privy to some painful information. Why else would they be meeting so secretly? Clay's curiosity had been mounting throughout this entire job and he still couldn't figure out why Kevin Gunther was so concerned about a simple Catholic priest. Now that he had overheard this conversation about some drug called Velorum, he believed that he had possibly stumbled upon his answer.

Kevin was somehow connected to the development of a supposed wonder drug but the drug was not quite ready for commercial release. Consequently, they were secretly testing their drug on desperate patients who had nothing else to lose. On the surface, it didn't seem like a monstrous thing to do. The drug would eventually change the world and provide hope to millions of people and the people on whom it was being tested were going to die anyway. If Velorum worked, they would get a second chance at life and if it didn't work, they would at least die having provided a little more information that would hasten the day when the drug *would* work. The eavesdropping hit man certainly understood that logic.

Additionally, he also understood why some people would be morally revolted by the idea. Human beings were not guinea pigs on which to be experimented and then it clicked in his thinking. Elliott Blythe must have been in on it and his conscience must have gotten the best of him. Kevin didn't know anything about Father Jeffries and Shelly. Kevin wanted to know what Elliott had told the priest.

He was smiling broadly in his darkened van as all of the various pieces began falling into place. Perhaps each of the central players had confided in Father Jeffries and he was now the key to Velorum's success or unraveling. If he kept silent, the project could go on and would eventually be a phenomenal success but if he broke his vows of confidentiality, Kevin Gunther would be exposed and his political, medical and personal ambitions would grind to a very public halt.

Wow, this was one intense situation! Clay smiled again pleased with his sleuthing ability and then he realized what his next move had to be. He needed to discover what Father Jeffries knew. Suddenly he felt a twinge of compassion for the little priest. The man had no idea how many people were out to discover his secrets.

Chapter Eighty

So this is what it feels like to be moments away from death.
The thought kept cycling through my thinking as I lay in what would shortly become my deathbed. I took a small amount of comfort from the knowledge that at least I wouldn't die alone. The parade of doctors and technicians who were monitoring me would certainly be with me at the end to watch how Velorum affected my death. They kept interrupting my conversation with Kevin Gunther to check and adjust my leads and monitors. It's not that they were overly concerned with keeping me comfortable. They wanted to collect as much Velorum-induced data from me as possible.

Kevin kept sending them out of the room so we could speak in private but they kept returning before we could finish. He would shake his head in annoyance but keep his attention focused on me. He was irritated by their intrusions but he was too defeated now to protest. I was still hoping he would tell me what Ray had said on the phone. The result of that brief conversation had broken him and I desperately wondered what he was thinking. I also kept thinking my original thought: *So this is what it feels like to be moments away from death.*

Kevin had returned shortly after Rachel left and he appeared to have aged before my very eyes. He suddenly looked tired and washed up, like a man who had gambled with his soul and lost.

My amnesia must have driven him crazy. I could understand why he was so desperate to get me to talk. I knew far too many of his secrets.

"Is amnesia frightening?"

He had an uncanny way of asking me about the very thing I was thinking. I shook my head. "It's not as scary as recovering your memory and discovering that your memories have made you a dead man."

Kevin nodded in understanding. "What happened in the garage?" He asked.

The scruffy looking hit man stretched out in his van determined to get a few hours of sleep. After Father Jeffries' midnight visitor left, the priest had gone back inside, re-locked his front door, poured himself a glass of ice water, swallowed a handful of ibuprofen and one half-tablet of Valium. Since he would be sleeping peacefully through the night, the Army Ranger-turned-hit man decided to follow suit. He would trail the priest in the morning and wait for the perfect spot to finish the job.

Of course, the objectives of the job had changed. Originally, Kevin Gunther had merely wanted to shake him up a bit, get him to forego any thought of going public with the lies that had been confessed to him. However, now that he had learned about the Velorum research, he would extract the confessions from the little priest and then decide how he might be able to use the information to his advantage. Kevin didn't seem to have any shortage of cash and if Clay played his cards right perhaps this could be the job that would put him into early retirement. A thirty-year old retired multi-millionaire in France could have a lot of fun.

Clay smiled happily to himself as he kicked off his dingy shoes and wiggled his toes under a thin fleece blanket. Tomorrow would probably not be Father Jeffries' best day but it would be a great one for him. He smiled again, double-checked his recording devices and fell almost instantly to sleep.

Inside the house, sleep was eluding Father Stan. After staring at his darkened ceiling for forty-five minutes, he considered finishing off the other half of the Valium pill but then he decided to do something proactive instead. He decided to write down everything he could remember about Moriah's confession. He flipped on the lamp beside his bed and reached for a crisp yellow legal pad. Although typing would undoubtedly be quicker, he preferred to write long hand so he could truly feel the emotion as it flowed from his heart onto the paper and for the next several hours until daybreak, he wrote down vivid details of Moriah's heart-wrenching confession.

His hand ached when he was finished and as the sun began to cast a warm glow around the edges of his closed curtains, he was finally cured of his insomnia. He decided to snooze for just one hour and then he would regroup and strategize about his day.

Several hours later Stan was still snoring, the sound echoing rhythmically across the van's speakers. Clay looked even scruffier than ever and he desperately wished he could break away for a shower and a shave. He actually hated facial hair. He was only wearing his little beard now because of his cover. He would have had time to shower and change clothes several times over by now but he didn't want to risk missing Father Jeffries. With each passing minute and Stan's continued snoring, his annoyance was growing. He wasn't in the military anymore and he could certainly live without these miserable stakeouts.

As a Ranger sniper, he had spent countless hours on stakeouts, sometimes waiting for days until his target moved into an acceptable range for a kill shot. The range had to be just right, close enough to kill but not so close that he couldn't escape. If he hadn't been so curious to learn what Father Jeffries knew about Kevin, he might have considered pulling the plug on the operation and moving on with his life. Kevin had already paid him and he could easily disappear like he always did after a job. However, what he really wanted was to be done with these kinds of jobs altogether. He wanted to make a boatload of money and then sail away somewhere to retire and forget all about his horrible life as a Ranger sniper.

No, he couldn't leave. Kevin Gunther was his target now and he was also his ticket to a new life. Clay would patiently wait for the little priest to finish his beauty sleep and then he would wring all of the Velorum confessions out of him and then blackmail the mayor for all he was worth, or at least for a cool ten million. Yes, ten million would probably be enough.

Chapter Eighty One

The priest was moving fast. He was obviously planning on skipping town for a while, probably going into hiding until criminal charges were leveled against Kevin Gunther. Through an opened window curtain, Clay had watched with bleary eyes as Father Jeffries packed an overnight bag and carefully withdrew two thick files from a shelf. He stuffed the files into a worn, leather briefcase, slung the overnight bag bandolier-style across his chest and then headed outside. He locked the door and looked furtively down the street, pausing as he saw that the van from the night before was now parked directly across the street from his living-room window. The van windows were darkly tinted though, so there was no concern of Father Jeffries seeing the hit man inside. He couldn't tell that high-powered, surveillance cameras were photographing him.

The cameras kept snapping away as Father Jeffries shuffled down his front steps and around the corner to a modest sedan. Father Jeffries' hands were noticeably shaking as he unlocked the trunk and tossed in his bags. He adjusted his priestly robes and then slipped into the front seat and started the car in one fluid motion. He backed the car out onto the street and began driving quickly away.

After an appropriate amount of space had been created, the van's engine started and Clay navigated it down the same streets that Father Jeffries had taken. He wasn't overly concerned about being seen. He just wanted to know where Father Jeffries was going. He would confront Father Jeffries personally very soon.

Clay followed the little priest to a nearby ATM where he watched him withdraw a handful of bills and stuff them inside one of the pockets of his black robe. Then the priest drove another half-mile before yanking his car into park and jumping out to use an ancient looking pay phone. The follower was impressed. The little priest was sure using some cloak-and-dagger tactics.

It didn't matter that he couldn't hear who was on the phone. There were only two people Stan might be calling right now: Shelly Gunther, or Elliott Blythe and the hit man didn't care what he said to either of them. He was either saying goodbye, or setting up a location for them to meet in person. It didn't matter because he would be intercepting the priest soon to get him to talk. Clay thought about taking him right here but there were too many people milling around, which was probably why the priest had chosen this spot and it was probably also why he had worn his long, ceremonial, black robes instead of his more efficient suit and collar. People were more apt to notice that he was a priest and it would draw more attention, making it tougher for someone to accost him. Clay laughed and shook his head. This priest was pretty clever.

The phone call ended and Father Jeffries hung the phone up and darted back to his car and then he was back on the road heading in the direction of Santa Monica.

Father Jeffries drove carefully through residential neighborhoods, stopping dutifully where directed and slowing significantly through unmarked intersections. He wanted to make good speed without getting stopped. After a little while, it became apparent that he was heading toward the famous 3rd Street Promenade, a fun shopping district near the Santa Monica Pier. It was the same area where he and Elliott had met for their interrupted conversation when he had slugged their eavesdropper in the jaw. His hand was still sore but he was secretly pleased that he had been able to pack such a strong punch.

In the trailing van, Clay was thinking the same thing. His jaw ached horribly from the hit. Being punched in the face by a grown man was far more traumatic than it looked in the movies. As Clay gingerly rubbed his jaw, he was intrigued that the priest would be heading back to the Pier area and he wondered if he was trying to reconnect with Elliott for another covert conversation.

A dog growled from the back seat behind him, a Rottweiller, and he patted her head lovingly. "Easy, girl. We're getting close. You'll get a chance to run soon."

The hit man's plan was simple. Since he needed to frighten the priest without doing any serious long-term damage, he decided to let his attack dog have a little fun with him, frighten him and maybe nip him a bit, before he called her off and ran to the priest's rescue. If anyone was watching, they would be furious about the loose dog but they wouldn't suspect any foul play. With the priest hurting and off balance he would either walk with him or force him into his car, where he would then extract all of the dirt that he had on Kevin Gunther. Clay hoped the priest would volunteer the information but he was also willing to use force if necessary. His beloved attack dog was extremely well-trained and knew the difference between a nip and a tear and if Father Jeffries refused to cooperate, he would consider letting the dog's wild side out.

Father Jeffries pulled his nondescript car into a public, underground parking lot and after waiting several seconds, the van did the same.

In his intense focus on the priest's destination, the van's driver failed to notice that *he* had been tailed as well and several seconds after the van entered the garage a third car did too.

CHRIS JACKSON

Chapter Eighty Two

Father Jefferies exited his car, aware of the van that had been following closely behind him ever since he left his home. He probably should have skipped this prearranged meeting with Elliott but since Elliott didn't have his cell phone and he wasn't returning Father Jefferies' numerous calls to his office, he figured he at least needed to show up in case Elliott did. Elliott had the information that would bring everything to a stop. If he could help Elliott find the courage to step forward with the information from the deposition, the authorities could take over from there and all of this freaky surveillance stuff could be put to rest.

He just hoped he could get to Elliott before his follower stopped him. He didn't own any weapons and he was terribly vulnerable in his constricting priest attire but he didn't have any other choice but to proceed. Elliott was supposed to be waiting for him in a rental car on the bottom level of the parking garage and they would leave together to formulate their next move.

He heard the van moving slowly around a corner one floor above him and he started to jog. He should have driven all the way to Elliott instead of carefully parking his car. The long jog across the packed parking area left him open and exposed.

The van pulled around another corner and came into view one aisle away from him so he began running as fast as his robes would allow. He probably had about fifty meters to go, when another car peeled around the corner closely behind the van. Father Jeffries saw the van stop abruptly, allowing the other car to zoom past it and fly directly toward him.

Father Jeffries leaped in between two parked cars, as the speeding car screeched to a stop, effectively pinning him between the cars and the concrete wall of the garage. Before he could decide how to react, the car door flew open and a large, intimidating man stepped out. It was Robert, his parishioner who had knocked on his door in the middle of the preceding night.

At first, Father Jeffries was terrified and he assumed that his negative premonition about him was correct. Somehow Kevin had gotten to his young parishioner and was using him to take Father Jeffries out. That fear went out the window however, when the Robert spoke, "Father Stan, are you okay? I came by to talk to you again and I saw this creepy guy in a van start following you." He shifted his bulky frame and glared at the van that had stopped at the far side of the parking garage.

Father Jeffries nodded wordlessly, not sure what to make of this story. The younger man spoke again, "Father, wait here. I'm going to see what this is all about."

Father Jeffries watched Robert turn on his heel and swagger toward the parked van that was waiting behind them. The van's headlights clicked on and as the young man raised one hand to shield his eyes from the glare, Father Jeffries saw something shiny in his other hand. It was a long, wicked looking knife.

The van door opened and a slouching, shadowy figure emerged. "I would stop right there if I were you," a flat, hollow voice spoke from the shadowed figure. Father Jeffries wondered if he would ever forget that voice. It was his assailant from the Pier, the young man who had threatened him in confession.

CONSCIENCE

Father Jeffries was too alarmed to cry out. He stood helplessly, trapped in between the wall and three cars as his young friend stopped several paces in front of the waiting van and its mysterious driver.

"What do you want with Father Stan?" Robert asked in a menacing voice. He was an intimidating figure with his muscular girth and angry eyes and Stan wondered how the much thinner hit man would fare against him.

The sharp click of a .44 automatic chambering a round answered the question for him. "I said stop right there."

Stan's friend stopped, his knife still gleaming in the glare of the headlights. "And while you're at it drop your knife."

He shifted the knife in his big palm but hesitated before dropping it and that's when the first bullet ripped into his thigh dropping him to his knees.

The shooter moved one step closer to the fallen man and pointed the gun and its silencer directly at the man's chest. "I'm not here to talk to you. I'm here to talk to him." He jerked his head in Father Jeffries' direction and saw that Father Jeffries was trying to climb over one of the parked cars that had trapped him in place.

He sent a silenced bullet whizzing into the wall beside Father Jeffries head forcing him to drop back inside his makeshift prison.

"Not so fast, Padre," and then to the fallen young man in front of him he said, "Besides you have better things to do. You need to sign those Velorum disclosures so the doctors can save your mother's life." There was a hint of amusement in his voice and it served to awaken a swell of pent up emotion in the larger young man.

With a snarl he used his good leg to launch himself up and propel him into an attack. His knife was raised for a vicious thrust until the pop and hiss of the pistol's silencer sounded and brought him up short. He reeled backward several steps and then another muted shot ripped through the air sending the large man down with a crash. In a fluid series of movements the shooter rushed to his

339

side, pried the knife from a meaty, clenched fist and proceeded to stab the man repeatedly in the chest and midsection.

Father Jeffries was both horrified and mesmerized. He couldn't look away but the sight of what was happening was making him physically ill. He had only known the young man for a short time but to see anyone, let alone someone who was acting out of protectiveness for him, shot repeatedly and then slashed and mangled with a knife was more than he could handle. He coughed and choked and vomited on the car beside him and then he saw the scruffy looking hit man start moving toward him.

Father Jeffries looked frantically around the parking structure for Elliott but there was no sign of the attorney. He was alone with his attacker. "Father, this is not what you're thinking." The shooter said as he moved within a few feet of the priest's location. "I'm not trying to hurt you at all. I just need to talk to you about Kevin Gunther and the Velorum project."

Father Jeffries still couldn't take his eyes off the crumpled figure of his friend. He tried to talk but his voice came out like a hoarse croak. "Is he dead?"

The other man nodded. "But that doesn't have to be your fate, at least not today. I just want to talk to you about why Kevin Gunther would hire me to shake you up a bit."

"'Shake me up a bit'?" Father Jeffries was incredulous and his fear was beginning to give way to a building fury. "Shake me up a bit? You stalked me at confession, you eavesdropped my conversations, you spied on my home and you just shot and stabbed my friend. Is that what you call 'shaking someone up'?"

Father Jeffries recognized how incredibly vulnerable his situation was, and he needed to do something to try and turn the tables. "Okay, let's talk," he said. "Let's talk about Kevin Gunther and the Velorum operation. What do you want to know?"

The man shook his head. "Not here. Get in the van."

Father Jeffries knew that a ride in that van would be a one-way trip to the morgue. He shook his head resolutely. "No, we talk here or not at all."

That aggravated the other man who looked nervously around the parking garage. Other drivers would intrude on this crime scene at any moment. He squeezed into Father Jeffries little prison and pointed his pistol at the priest's midsection. "Come with me now, or I will shoot you through your little priestly robe."

CHRIS JACKSON

Chapter Eighty Three

"I can't believe you shot him." Kevin Gunther was livid. "You were supposed to frighten him, get him to talk. You were never supposed to lay a hand on him." Clay remained slouched in silence in the face of Kevin's scolding. Ray Gibbs also sat silently off to the side, evaluating potential courses of action.

"Did he talk to you before you shot him?" Kevin's glare was so intense that for the first time the indifferent young shooter began to feel uncomfortable. Clay had been around lots of leaders in the military but there was a determination about Kevin Gunther that warned him to carefully plan his words.

"He did talk." Clay paused after he said it and then he added, "And he told me about Velorum." Both Kevin and Ray reacted in surprise. *Bingo!*

"He told you about Velorum?" There was some suspicion in Kevin's voice as he wondered aloud why Father Jeffries would start talking about Velorum to a would-be assassin. "What did he tell you about Velorum?"

Clay stalled again. He was bluffing. Father Jeffries hadn't actually said anything about Velorum and he hoped he hadn't made a tragic blunder in suggesting that he did. He was very quick on his feet however, so he spun what little he had overheard into an accusation, "He told me about how your doctors try to recruit people that are desperate enough to participate in the Velorum research." Clay paused and held his breath hoping that his guess was close enough to the mark to throw Kevin momentarily off balance.

It was. Kevin sat back in his chair again and looked at Ray before asking. "What else did Father Jeffries say?"

Clay smirked, his arrogance returning as he felt the upper hand in the conversation shifting back to him. "He said there was a plan in motion to bring you down." Another reaction as Kevin nodded.

"So we were right." Kevin's statement was directed at Ray who nodded thoughtfully in response. "Should we cancel the meeting today?" Kevin asked.

Ray shook his head. "No, I think we should keep it. Let's see how Elliott reacts or if he even has the nerve to show up. We might still be able to contain things and if we can, we'll still need some of those lawyers to help us. I say we hold steady."

Kevin nodded in agreement and then to the young man across from him, "Did Father Jeffries say how he was going to bring me down?"

"He said he was going public with all of it." And then Clay added, "He also said that Elliott is in on it as well." He was still bluffing but his bluffs were based on enough hearsay and strategic guesswork to be convincing.

Kevin didn't seem suspicious anymore. He believed the story and his mind was now racing as he considered his next move. The young hit man decided to capitalize on Kevin's vulnerability. "Mr. Gunther, I took care of him for you. I kept him from going public and I can take care of Elliott for you too." There was an insinuation in his voice and Kevin eyed him narrowly before responding. "What are you suggesting?"

"I'm suggesting that you triple my fee and throw in a few million extra for good measure." As Kevin's face flushed angrily,

Clay added quickly, "Kevin, I think a few million for the priest's silence is a bargain and I'll do Elliott for free. It's a great deal for you and besides, you wouldn't want *me* to ever let the information slip would you?"

That last statement was a mistake and he realized it as soon as he said it. Kevin reached across the desk and grabbed his sagging T-shirt collar with a quickness that surprised the former Army Ranger.

"Are you attempting to blackmail me, son? You have no idea who you're up against."

For the first time in all of their interactions the Ranger started to feel some fear. Perhaps he had underestimated Kevin Gunther. His history of deadly assassinations had filled him with such confidence that he never stopped to think that maybe he wouldn't be able to defend himself against a forty-something, desk-bound, city mayor.

Kevin's next words hit him like a hammer to his chest. "You didn't kill him. He survived. We're the ones who picked him up and very soon he's going to talk to us and when he does he'll have evidence on you too."

Clay couldn't hide his surprise at the revelation that Father Jeffries was still alive and he saw how wrong he had been to try and threaten the mayor.

"Mr. Gunther, I'm so sorry," he began but Kevin cut him off. "So you think you know about Velorum, huh? Would you like to experience it first-hand?" There was a sinister look on Kevin's handsome face and the young man knew he had made the biggest mistake of his life. He momentarily considered fighting Kevin and Ray but then the door to the office opened and some burly security agents entered with drawn weapons.

"Ray, can you handle this for me?" Kevin asked as he stepped away from his desk and calmly exited the office.

As he was pistol whipped across the face and roughly handcuffed, the young hit man still couldn't believe that Father Stan Jeffries had lived.

Chapter Eighty Four

Father Stan stared into the silenced muzzle of the .44 automatic and wondered when his life would start passing before his eyes. He heard a groan from the heap of what had been his young parishioner and he gasped. "He's still alive."

The gunman's eyes flickered toward the fallen man just long enough for the priest to launch his compact, little body in a violent assault. If he felt good about the right hand he had thrown by the park bench in Santa Monica, he knew this one was even prettier. It was a soaring right hook thrown with all of the torque of his hips and midsection behind it and when it connected with the assassin's jaw it sent him sprawling backwards into the nearest parked car. The gun flew from the man's hand and he crashed unceremoniously on to the concrete floor of the parking garage where he lay unconscious on his face.

Before Father Jeffries could congratulate himself however, an agonizing pain started throbbing along his right wrist. It was broken, the price of his newfound talent for fist-a-cuffs. He cradled his damaged arm against his chest and scrambled across the hood of a car and over to his fallen young friend who was still groaning slightly. He used his good arm to raise the young man's head and he spoke to him reassuringly. "You're going to be okay, son," even though he knew he wasn't. The man was a bloody mess and his life was leaking away like the drainage from his many wounds.

He heard his attacker stirring and Father Jeffries quickly looked for the long, sharp knife that had fallen a few feet away from where his friend lay dying. He had to lower his friend's head to the ground and then use his good arm to reach for the knife. His right hand was too fractured to be of any help. In the time it took to locate and secure the knife, his attacker was on top of him. Father Jeffries felt the heavy thud of a kick crash into his ribs and then the sharp edge of a pistol's butt ram into the back of his head. He was knocked cold instantly.

The young assassin was sweating profusely. The whole ordeal had taken only a matter of seconds but in a crowded city like Santa Monica, it was inevitable that someone would drive up and see them at any moment. He was fortunate that the parking garage was packed and all of the would-be-parkers were being directed to the upper levels instead of this lowest one however, it was still just a matter of time before they were discovered.

He still had an ulterior plan though and he didn't want to merely escape. He could easily have gotten away if that was his goal. His van was still idling across the parking garage and he could have simply re-joined his anxious Rotweiller who was starting to bark loudly from the backseat and driven out of the story forever.

Instead, he still wanted his millions from Kevin Gunther and he needed the priest to help him. He knew that he had become involved in a scandal that was much larger than he had imagined and he knew that other people were undoubtedly looking for the priest as well. It wasn't likely that he was the only person that Kevin had assigned to shadow the priest's every move. He glanced fearfully around the parking garage and knew what he needed to do.

A shrill ringing in his ears greeted Father Jeffries as he groggily regained consciousness. He had only been out for a few seconds but he was disoriented and fuzzy and it took him a moment to remember what had happened. When he finally remembered, he became aware of a very peculiar sensation. His robe was missing and someone was pulling a baggy shirt over his head.

They had already taken off his pants.

He turned his head to the side and saw the young man from his congregation, the young man who had been shot and stabbed for trying to defend him and saw that his grotesque wounds had been covered by Father Jeffries' own robes and he was dressed to resemble a priest. Even Father Jeffries' clerical collar had been stretched around the other man's meaty neck and was quickly turning red from the flow of his multiple gunshot and puncture wounds.

When the shirt was pulled securely down over Father Jeffries' shoulders, his attacker saw that the priest was awake and again smashed the butt of his gun into his bloody face. Father Jeffries fell back roughly to the pavement but as he fell his fingers touched the handle of the discarded knife and he instinctively gripped it tightly and flung his arm upward in a vicious arc. He felt the sharp edge connect with flesh, heard a strangled cry and then he momentarily blacked out again.

This time when he came to everything was different. He wasn't afraid and he couldn't feel any pain. He quickly realized that he must have gone into shock, because despite the lack of pain he was bleeding profusely. He was barefooted and naked except for his boxer shorts and a baggy T-shirt that was quickly becoming slick with a covering of thick red blood.

Blood had snaked up and down Father Jeffries' forearms like ornate, crimson tattoos and he also noticed that a wicked looking knife was gripped tightly in his left fist. That's when he noticed another man that lay in his own pool of blood several feet away from him. Father Jeffries crawled over to the man and saw that he was a priest, a dying one.

The dying man's clerical collar was stained a bright scarlet and blood was flowing freely from multiple puncture wounds along the man's midsection and thigh. Father Jeffries didn't recognize the man and he briefly thought how tragic it was to see a priest come to such an untimely end and then a panic hit him when he remembered his own wounds and the knife that he still clutched in an iron grip. Surely, he hadn't been the one to murder this fallen priest?

A shout from behind him brought him around and then the priest groaned drawing Father Jeffries' attention back to him. The man's eyes fluttered open and a flicker of recognition crossed his dull, smoky gaze. Father Jeffries panicked, "He knows me and he knows what I've done to him."

The dying man lunged up to grab Father Jeffries' shoulder but his chest was spasming and Father Jeffries pushed him roughly back to the concrete floor and clamped a hand tightly against his gasping mouth. He couldn't bear to hear the man confirm what he was beginning to fear.

That's when the shouting began again and then another sound was added to the mix. Barking. Father Jeffries saw a limping man open the side door of a parked van to release the leaping form of a huge Rotweiller. The dog stood bristling and barking as it looked in Father Jeffries' direction. Father Jeffries didn't wait to see what it would do. He leapt to his bare feet and began running toward the nearest exit sign.

Everything was a blur as he ran. He couldn't remember who he was, or why he was running. He started to feel a searing pain in his abdomen and realized that he must have been shot. Suddenly another gunshot sounded and he tripped over his own feet and fell down hard. He staggered back to his feet and felt a surge of fear-induced adrenaline propel him up a flight of steps and onto the street level of the parking garage.

Brilliant daylight was in front of him and as he staggered toward it with the last of his strength reserves. He prayed that he could get there before the barking dog tore into him from behind. He sprinted the few final steps toward the exit expecting to feel the dog's fangs in his shoulders any moment but it never happened. He made it.

The daylight blinded him as he lurched onto the sidewalk to a chorus of terrified screams from passing tourists. He barely had time to notice these things before an unmarked van peeled up the street beside him. Its side door opened and strong hands jerked him inside and then the van pulled back into traffic and rushed him away from Santa Monica and the 3rd Street Promenade.

CHRIS JACKSON

Chapter Eighty Five

"Hello, this is Shelly Gunther."

I remembered her voice so clearly, instantly peaceful and disarming. "Uh, hello. Mrs. Gunther. You gave me your card earlier today and asked me to call you."

"Oh yes, thank you so much for calling so quickly. I really need to speak with you but I can't do it over the phone. Can you meet me later tonight?"

I could still recall my conflicted emotions as she made her unusual request. I didn't even know this woman and although I could understand why she might feel safe with me after I had saved her daughter from a near car accident, the request to meet privately at night with such a well-known public figure unnerved me.

She obviously sensed my hesitation. "It won't take long and I promise I'm not a psycho. I just need a safe place to talk."

I laughed in spite of myself and despite my misgivings agreed to a time and place before hanging up the phone.

As the memory of those emotions washed over me in what would undoubtedly be the last room I would ever see, I wondered how different things might have been if I had skipped our rendezvous. I could have just gone on with my life and avoided this whole mess. I hadn't helped change anything anyway. I hadn't helped save Moriah and the comfort I provided for Shelly certainly wasn't worth the terrible repercussions.

That meeting with her had cost me everything. It set the stage for all of the crazy events that would follow over the years and it ultimately drew me inextricably into the Velorum nightmare and now, with Velorum coursing freely through my veins, I knew that it had also cost me my life. It wouldn't be long now.

I had never been afraid of death. Indeed I had often welcomed it. Not in a morbid, suicidal way mind you but in an excited anticipation of the after-life. I was prepared to die. My personal affairs were in order and I was at peace with God. I shook my head at the thought. At least, I *hoped* I was still at peace with God.

The door to my hospital room opened then, and Shelly's husband, Kevin, entered. He looked exhausted and drained, his earlier confidence replaced with a defeated, haunted expression. Ray must have told him something on the phone that had changed everything.

He slumped into a chair beside me and smiled at me wearily. "How are you holding up? How are those stitches of yours?"

He seemed to be reading my mind because I was thinking about my gunshot wound as well. Even as I replayed my initial encounter with Shelly and the subsequent conversations that had taken my life down so many terrible turns, I couldn't get the memory of my shooting out of my head.

I glanced down at my hospital gown and saw that it was stained red from a fresh flow of blood that was oozing from between the loosely sewn stitches. "Not the best." I smiled back at him.

"What did it feel like?" He still spoke softly with a hint of genuine empathy in his eyes.

At first, his words increased a cold, dull ache inside me and I thought he was baiting me like he had tried to do earlier in the day but when I looked up at him I realized that he was genuinely asking and I could tell he was unraveling.

I didn't hate him. Although he inevitably became my enemy along the way, I actually felt tremendous compassion for him. None of us on the outside could know the grief that he and Shelly had experienced. He wasn't evil. He was hurting and I realized that if I could help him find some peace, I would, especially now that it was over for me. There was no hope of escape and if in my final minutes on this earth, Kevin Gunther opened a door for me to his humanity, I would walk through it.

I closed my eyes and re-entered the memory before responding. The pain of the gunshot wound was unlike what I would ever have imagined it being. It felt like a hammer blow that knocked the wind out of my chest but it didn't hurt in the way I would have anticipated. I must have gone instantly into shock.

"It hurt more than you could imagine but not as much as recovering my memories."

Kevin nodded thoughtfully at that and then asked, "So all of your memories are still intact? They haven't left again?"

I nodded. "Which ones do you want to talk about?"

He leaned back in his chair and ran his fingers through his gelled, black hair. Exhaling deeply he said, "I want to know everything that Moriah told you."

I nodded. Yes, that was the obvious direction. It was a strange, sudden turn of events to be sitting so close to him without fearing him like I did earlier in the day. His fierce intensity seemed to have drained out of him and he appeared like a man who was coming to terms with the fact that the end was near.

"Father Stan, tell me about my daughter."

CHRIS JACKSON

Chapter Eighty Six

My name was Stan Jeffries and I had been the Gunther's priest for nearly a decade. It started after I saved Moriah's life in the middle of the street near the 3rd Street Promenade in Santa Monica. Unknown to me, the Gunthers were in the market for a priest. It was always funny to me how people would shop for a church or a minister as if they were dispensable commodities and when Shelly saw a man of the cloth save her daughter from an oncoming wave of traffic, she took that as a sign that I was the man for her family.

When I responded to her request for a meeting, she sheepishly confessed that she and her husband, the newly elected mayor of Los Angeles, had been absent from church for most of their adult lives. "However, we have Moriah now," she explained, "and we can see that we're going to need help dealing with the incredible toll that a high profile, political life can take on a family. Do you think you would be willing to be our priest?"

She giggled nervously as she said it and, as would always be the case when I was in her presence, I was smitten.

It wasn't an impure thing. I never loved her in an inappropriate way. There was just something about Shelly Gunther that drew people in. She was one of the most genuinely kind, authentic

357

people I had ever known. "Of course I would be happy to be your family's priest."

They joined my parish and although Kevin never regularly attended, he was very supportive of Shelly and Moriah's participation. He beamed with pride at Moriah's confirmation and seemed genuinely pleased with her spiritual growth through the church.

We had some rousing conversations over the years and I frequently chided him for his lack of church attendance. His reply was swift and severe. When people in church start caring for the things that really matter in the world (and then he would launch into a political stump speech), I'll consider the possibility that they have something I need in my life.

"What about Shelly?" I would counter. "Do you see anything in her that you don't have, but need?" That was always my reply when he started criticizing church people for not caring enough for the needs of the world around him and as usual, it silenced him.

"Shelly is an exception." I always laughed good-naturedly at this point and conceded that yes, she was a special exception.

"And so is Moriah."

Then we were both in agreement again.

I looked up at him from my hospital bed. "Yes, I'll tell you what Moriah said to me but first I have a question for you." He nodded at me to continue. "Why did you save my life in Santa Monica? Why didn't you let your man finish the job and shut me up for good? Were you looking for another subject for your Velorum experiments?"

Kevin shook his head firmly at each question. "No. I never wanted to hurt you. I never wanted to hurt anyone. This whole project was supposed to be about *saving* human life. That man was never supposed to put a finger on you. He was simply supposed to verbally bully you into keeping quiet about Velorum!"

"But how did you know that I knew?"

"Elliott. We could tell that he was having second thoughts and we were afraid that he was considering blowing the whole thing open so we started following him. Did you know he drove around your church three days in a row before going in and talking to you in confession?"

I shook my head. I didn't know that.

"We figured he was planning on spilling his guts to you since you were a safe place. Your vows of confidentiality would allow him to come clean while still keeping all of our secrets. When he finally went into see you on the fourth day, we needed to find out what he had told you and we needed to make sure that you never talked."

I absorbed the words thoughtfully for a moment and then asked, "So back to the parking garage in Santa Monica, how did you know I was in trouble?"

"Our guy went rogue on us and we were afraid he was going to kill you so we started following *him*. Once we picked you up we were actually trying to save your life. I didn't want you to die. You're my family's priest for God's sake but I also needed to know what you knew and I needed to know what you had done with the information. There was too much at stake." He hung his head in defeat and shame before looking at me with a desperate intensity and saying, "Stan, I hired him to frighten you. I brought him into the mix. It's my fault that you're dying." He paused again and then said softly, "Father Stan, I killed you."

It was true. Kevin Gunther had not only wrecked his career, fractured his marriage and damaged his dying daughter but he had also introduced me to my killer. I considered my response and decided to move in a different direction.

"Kevin, why didn't you ever come to confession?"

Kevin laughed at the question, a flicker of his haughty self returning. "Stan, there are some doors you just don't open. I'm a good person. Or I was a good person and I had better things to do than feel guilty about the mistakes I've made along the way."

"Kevin, I'm not talking about feeling guilty. I'm talking about getting free from guilt. We're *all* guilty. Confession doesn't make us guilty. It takes away the weight of our guilt."

Kevin laughed again, "Now you're getting all preachy on me. You know I never liked that. Tell me about Moriah." Our moment of familiarity seemed to be fading and Kevin was again resuming his adversarial role.

I carefully considered my response, knowing that my remaining time was brief and needed to count. Finally I knew which part of her confession to reveal. "Kevin, she said she loved you and she told me that she forgave you." The words hit him like a thunderbolt and he sat upright in his chair and stared at me with saucer-wide eyes.

"She understood that you were acting out of her best interests and she wanted you to know that it was okay."

He couldn't stand it anymore so he doubled over in his chair as a geyser of emotion erupted from the depths of his soul. The proud politician melted away and he sobbed like a baby for nearly a minute before looking at me through his watery eyes. "Stan, did she really say that?" I nodded and his weeping continued.

After a moment, I said a little more. "Kevin, I had to expose you. What you have done with Velorum is corrupt and needs to stop. But I've never doubted your love for your little girl and Moriah never doubted it either."

He snorted then, a scoffing sound. "But Shelly will never believe that. I've lost her forever. I can live without Velorum or the White House. Ray just informed me that those dreams are probably history but I don't know if I can live without Shelly."

I didn't answer immediately. I had my own emotions to work through where the whole Kevin-Rachel-Shelly thing was concerned. He seemed to notice, so he spoke to me in a softer tone. "Stan, I'm also very sorry for hurting your sister. I'm sorry for using her to assuage my own pain. It was unthinkable to get involved with her and it was unthinkable that I did that to Shelly." A strangled cry burst from his throat and he was crying again.

After a few moments of weeping, I placed my hand gently on his head and asked, "Kevin, do you want to try that confession now?"

Chapter Eighty Seven

Across town, Shelly Gunther intentionally missed her flight. She was still sitting in the boarding area as her plane took off and then shrunk into a speck in the sky. A few people recognized her and gave her casual glances as they walked by but for the most part, she was left alone.

Her latte had cooled in her hand and she sat so still that she seemed practically frozen in place. Internally, however, her mind was working overtime.

By now, Ray would have found all of the pertinent information in her journals and Kevin would know that she knew. He would be devastated and despite her rage at him, the thought of his pain tugged at her emotions too.

She was furious over his affair with Rachel and a part of her had already written him off for good. Nevertheless, another part of her heart knew that he was merely human and not a super hero like he was often portrayed in the media.

"Shelly, you married a sinner." That's what Father Stan had once said to her several years earlier when she and Kevin had hit a rough patch in what had generally been a fantastic marriage. The pressures of high profile political life had begun taking a toll on

CHRIS JACKSON

their relationship and when she went to the priest looking for some sympathy, he had turned the tables on her.

"Shelly, you married a sinner and so did Kevin and the only remedy for sin is forgiveness. If the two of you have it in you to forgive one another and re-prioritize your relationship, you'll be able to heal and move on."

At the time that was exactly what she needed to hear. Stan's words released the grace in her to not only forgive but also forget the things that were bothering her. She and Kevin reconnected, moved through the tough time and entered a season of marriage that was better than anything they had experienced up to that point.

However after Moriah became ill and died everything changed. She and Kevin died too, it was just that their hearts were still beating and their limbs were still functioning. They were both so lost on the inside and their grief was so absolute that she wasn't surprised that he acted out with Rachel. She could easily have been tempted too. Yes, he was a sinner and sinners do sinful things. She could possibly forgive him for Rachel.

But she could never forgive him for Moriah.

Also, she could never forgive herself. How could she have lived with her daughter in her final days and not notice that something else was going on? The question was unrelenting and haunted her like a splinter in her mind.

She suddenly felt an urge to talk to Stan. She had tried calling him the day before but he hadn't taken the call so she had left him a voice message and was still waiting for him to call her back.

No. She shook her head. She didn't need Stan right now. Confession used to help but not anymore.

And then a strange thing happened. In the middle of her cold anger and self-loathing a different emotion emerged. Hope. It was a distant feeling at first but then it grew stronger until she could hear a voice inside her head whispering that perhaps there was hope that she and Kevin could rebuild. Other couples had lived through furious storms and emerged stronger on the other side. Maybe they could too.

She did understand why he had tried the Velorum on Moriah. When she was able to set aside her rage and think objectively, she knew that he had her best interests in mind. He honestly believed he could save her and that he would have an entire lifetime to pay her back for the pain she had been forced to endure. He never would have tortured their daughter needlessly.

Also, he had been the one to call off the affair with Rachel.

Rachel Parker was the perfect storm for Kevin. Shelly had known for years how vulnerable the young actress was and how deeply her father-wound had affected her. Both she and Stan were still deeply wounded from their childhoods and they had each chosen unique ways to deal with their pain. Stan took his wounding into the ministry where he buried his own sorrow in the sorrows of humanity, while Rachel had taken hers to the immaterial world of Hollywood and quickly discovered that no amount of money or fame can heal the human soul. It can medicate it and numb it but it cannot heal it.

Yes, there were plenty of elements that made up the perfect storm: Moriah's death, Kevin's grief, Rachel's insecurity and a pride that somehow believed they were all impervious to shipwreck.

"No one is immune to a shipwreck." She said the words softly to herself as she considered all of this. She kept staring out the window at the departing flights and then she spoke again. "Yes, I could see how forgiveness might be possible."

Chapter Eighty Eight

Detective Robyn Macomber was awake. As she squinted against the ICU lights and her vision came into focus she immediately laughed and then winced in pain as the cut from her knife wound flared to life. When the wave of pain subsided, she smiled to herself and whispered softly, "Hey, old man, wake up."

Detective Louis Stratton had crashed into a deep sleep in the chair beside her bed. His head was tipped back and the deep snores that issued from his open mouth were nearly as loud as the humming of the monitors connected to Robyn's battered body.

She spoke again, "Louis, wake up."

The big man stirred and then sat up quickly when he saw that she was awake. A broad grin spread across his exhausted, concerned features as he greeted her. "You okay?"

She nodded an affirmative. "But why are you here? You should be helping Elliott."

Another grateful tear slid down his scruffy cheek and he leaned forward and kissed her forehead before repositioning himself in the chair and responding, "Well, there's been a slight change of plans."

She looked at him quizzically. "Tell me everything."

For his part, Elliott Blythe had spent nearly an hour talking non-stop to his wife, spilling his guts about everything he had gotten involved in within the Gunther administration. He told her about Velorum, He told her about Moriah and he told her about the freakish events of the last fourteen hours. They had cried and held each other and he eventually leaned back on the couch and said, "It's been an unbelievably long day."

When his phone rang and he recognized Ray Gibb's number he answered immediately. "This is Elliott."

"Elliott, can you talk?"

All of Elliott's guards went up but he was ready to hear why and how Ray's plans had changed. "Sure."

Ray sounded old on the other end of the phone. His usual composure was replaced with a humbled resignation. To his credit, he was gracious in defeat. "Elliott, I am so sorry for what we did to you."

Elliott's anger blazed at the words but he was too exhausted to reply. He let Ray continue. "You were our contingency plan." He paused to let Elliott absorb the words and then continued apologetically. "But we never expected to use it and if we had been forced to let the blame fall on you, we had a contingency plan for that as well."

Elliott scoffed at the words. "Oh nice. You had a follow-up plan after destroying my life. What might that have been?"

"A slap on the wrist sentence at a minimum security facility and the book rights to the Velorum project."

Elliott immediately saw the deeper layers to that plan. "Wow, Ray," he said. "You never stop. It's pretty admirable actually. You help me rebuild my finances, set me up as a celebrity author and then gain free advertising and campaigning for the Velorum project. You cleanse your conscience and still come out ahead. Not a bad plan at all. It's too bad you can't run with it. It's over for Kevin now. You know that right?"

Ray's silence was an acknowledgment so Elliott spoke again. "Shelly will leave Kevin and he'll be done for. He'll never be able to carry on without her."

Ray was silent on the other end of the phone. Elliott was right and that was why Ray was so willing to concede defeat and begin working on damage control. "You're right, Elliott. It's over. Kevin understands that."

"Where is Kevin?" Elliott asked suddenly.

Ray hesitated. "He's with Stan. Stan was not killed like I originally told you however he was badly wounded. A routine surveillance turned ugly. He's not going to make it."

Elliott absorbed the news quietly and then asked, "Is he on Velorum?"

Ray sighed, "Yes. But only because we thought it could save him." Then Ray caught himself and cut the thought off in mid-sentence. It was that kind of thinking that justified subjecting Moriah and dozens of others to their horrifying wonder drug.

"Elliott, I just called to tell you that I am so very sorry. I'm sorry for using you, for hurting you and for threatening your family. I'm sorry for everything. You've been one of my truest friends and I'm sorry that I lost myself along the way."

When Elliott didn't respond, Ray said in parting, "I would change so many things if I could." Then he disconnected the call.

He needed to get busy. The cops would be contacting them soon and he needed to have all of their disclaimers in order and he also needed to get on television and leak the information before the press was allowed to interpret things on their own.

He would reveal Velorum as the miracle drug that it was, but then point out the damaging side effects. He would humbly apologize and announce the withdrawal of the Velorum campaign and their commitment to compensate the families that had been hurt along the way. Scientists would go back to the drawing board until they could figure out how to curb the drug's challenges. By the time Kevin Gunther's name was dragged into the controversy, people would know two things: first, Velorum was a real hope that would someday be available to save their loved ones and second, drastic steps were being taken to ensure that it was safe for everyone.

He knew it was a long shot.

Today's media-frenzied world moved so fast that he wasn't sure how far his spin would carry the story before other voices rose up condemning him, Kevin and the entire operation. As he weighed all possible outcomes, he realized that there was only one person who could possibly minimize the fallout from this whole nightmare.

Shelly Gunther.

If anyone could convey a truly empathetic voice it was she. She was the only one who could communicate enough genuine remorse and empathy to provide a measure of healing for the families that had been manipulated and abused in the name of medical science. She would be his first phone call.

Even though Ray believed that Shelly was their best hope, he wasn't going to call her to try and solicit her help. She would probably offer that on her own. She wouldn't want anyone to feel hurt or betrayed by her husband or his research teams. He was going to call her to plead with her for forgiveness. Everything had crashed so quickly for him and Kevin and he was still trying to assimilate the events of the day but in the middle of his shock, there was one overriding emotion that gripped him, a need to be forgiven.

He would try to make things right with Shelly and he would ask her to forgive him and after that he might even follow Elliott's lead and find another priest to talk to.

Chapter Eighty Nine

"Forgive me, Father, for I have sinned."

Kevin Gunther's head was pressed so firmly against my hospital mattress and bed sheets that I could barely decipher his words. I placed my hand on his head and gently stroked his slicked back black hair as he cried like a heart-broken, little boy.

"Please forgive me. Shelly, I'm so sorry. Moriah..." his voice broke as more sobs wracked his chest and shoulders. "I'm so sorry."

I let him cry it out for several minutes before responding. "You're forgiven, Kevin, for everything."

He shook his head in refusal, unable to believe that forgiveness could be that simple. I continued, "Kevin, it wasn't your fault that Moriah contracted her tumor. She would have died with or without Velorum. Despite the horror of what she experienced during the Velorum trials, I know that you were, ultimately, pursuing her best interests."

His shoulders had stopped shaking and I knew that he was listening to me. "Additionally, I don't think it's irreparable with Shelly. Oh, I'm sure it will take a long time for her to ever trust you again, maybe even a lifetime. However, I think she will forgive you in time and I think she's worth the pursuit."

Kevin looked up at me then, his handsome features contorted from his internal agony. "I even told Rachel that you were dead." He whispered. "I let her think she had lost you before I told her the truth. I've broken trust with everyone. I don't deserve to be forgiven."

I absorbed his words for a moment and then responded. "You're right, Kevin and nor do I, but forgiveness is never something that is earned. It is a gift freely given by the giver. Shelly loves you and she may yet offer you that most precious of gifts. Moriah forgave you, as you know. She told me as much. Even more important than either of them, God forgives you, Kevin and He doesn't forgive you because you deserve it. He forgives you because He loves you and because He Himself bore your punishment on a wooden cross nearly two thousand years ago on an Israeli hill called Calvary."

Kevin didn't know how to respond to the God talk. He had heard Stan say similar things many times over the years but this time it felt different. An emotion flickered in his soul. Hope? Yes, that's what it was. Hope. "Do you really think I can be forgiven?"

I laughed. "You already are. You can keep asking for it and if it makes you feel better you can keep crying and mourning until you feel you've sufficiently groveled but that won't increase how much you're already forgiven. You're forgiven, Kevin. You're clean and if I were you, I would be on the next flight out of Los Angeles so you can recapture Shelly's heart before any more time goes by and after you start repairing things with her, you can start doing what you can to make things right with the families you hurt along the way."

Kevin looked at me with the faintest glimmer of hope in his eyes. "Do you think my career is over?"

I shrugged. "That's probably up to you. Rock bottom is a funny place. If you handle it right, it can be a springboard to a whole new future. The rest of your life depends largely on how you respond in this moment right now."

A coughing fit hit me then and I was distantly aware that some alarms had sounded around me. My heart rate had dropped dangerously low and I thought the end might have come. It rose again after a few seconds though and the alarm quieted. I had a few more minutes to live.

Kevin wiped his runny nose and rubbed his shirtsleeve roughly across his face. "What about Ray?" He asked me. "He's probably calling a press conference as we speak to try and spin the whole thing to our advantage. What should I say to Ray?"

"Ray will be on the same page."

He looked at me skeptically, so I added a little more. "Kevin, I shouldn't tell you this considering my vow of confidentiality and all but Ray came to see me too."

He shook his head and smiled in disbelief. "Has everyone in my life gone to see you?"

I gave him a weak grin in reply. "Everyone but you."

He smiled again and asked, "What did he say?"

"Well, suffice it to say that he too needed, and still needs, the very forgiveness that you are asking for right now." Another coughing fit hit me then and I knew I wouldn't recoup from this one. Kevin looked at me with compassion and said, "I'm so sorry. I should be more concerned about you than me right now."

I shook my head. "No, it's okay. I need this too. This is my closure. I'm ready to face my maker." I chuckled weakly. "And I hope He's ready to meet me." The coughing continued and, if the Velorum was correct, I was just about at the end.

When it passed I looked deeply into his handsome, hazel eyes and said, "Kevin, go get her back. Face your consequences like a man. Begin again. You're still young. You'll regroup. I'm convinced that the world has yet to see the best of Kevin Gunther."

He was nodding silently while the tears streamed freely down his face. I cupped his face in my trembling hand and directed his gaze to mine. "Oh and Kevin, one more thing." I said. I took a breath knowing even as I did that my next few words would be my last.

"I forgive you, too."

ABOUT THE AUTHOR

Chris Jackson is an author and pastor living in Southern California. He and his wife Jessica have two daughters, Amber Hope and Madelyn Joy.

To see Chris' other books and publications please visit www.chrisjacksononline.net

www.ingramcontent.com/pod-product-compliance
Lightning Source LLC
Chambersburg PA
CBHW071648260626
47170CB00001B/281